# OLD GIRLS GO GREEK

## MADDIE PLEASE

Boldwood

First published in Great Britain in 2025 by Boldwood Books Ltd.

Copyright © Maddie Please, 2025

Cover Design by Head Design Ltd

Cover Images: Shutterstock

The moral right of Maddie Please to be identified as the author of this work has been asserted in accordance with the Copyright, Designs and Patents Act 1988.

Every effort has been made to obtain the necessary permissions with reference to copyright material, both illustrative and quoted. We apologise for any omissions in this respect and will be pleased to make the appropriate acknowledgements in any future edition.

A CIP catalogue record for this book is available from the British Library.

Paperback ISBN 978-1-83656-026-5

Large Print ISBN 978-1-83656-027-2

Hardback ISBN 978-1-83656-025-8

Trade Paperback ISBN 978-1-80656-048-6

Ebook ISBN 978-1-83656-028-9

Kindle ISBN 978-1-83656-029-6

Audio CD ISBN 978-1-83656-020-3

MP3 CD ISBN 978-1-83656-021-0

Digital audio download ISBN 978-1-83656-022-7

This book is printed on certified sustainable paper. Boldwood Books is dedicated to putting sustainability at the heart of our business. For more information please visit https://www.boldwoodbooks.com/about-us/sustainability/

Boldwood Books Ltd, 23 Bowerdean Street, London, SW6 3TN

www.boldwoodbooks.com

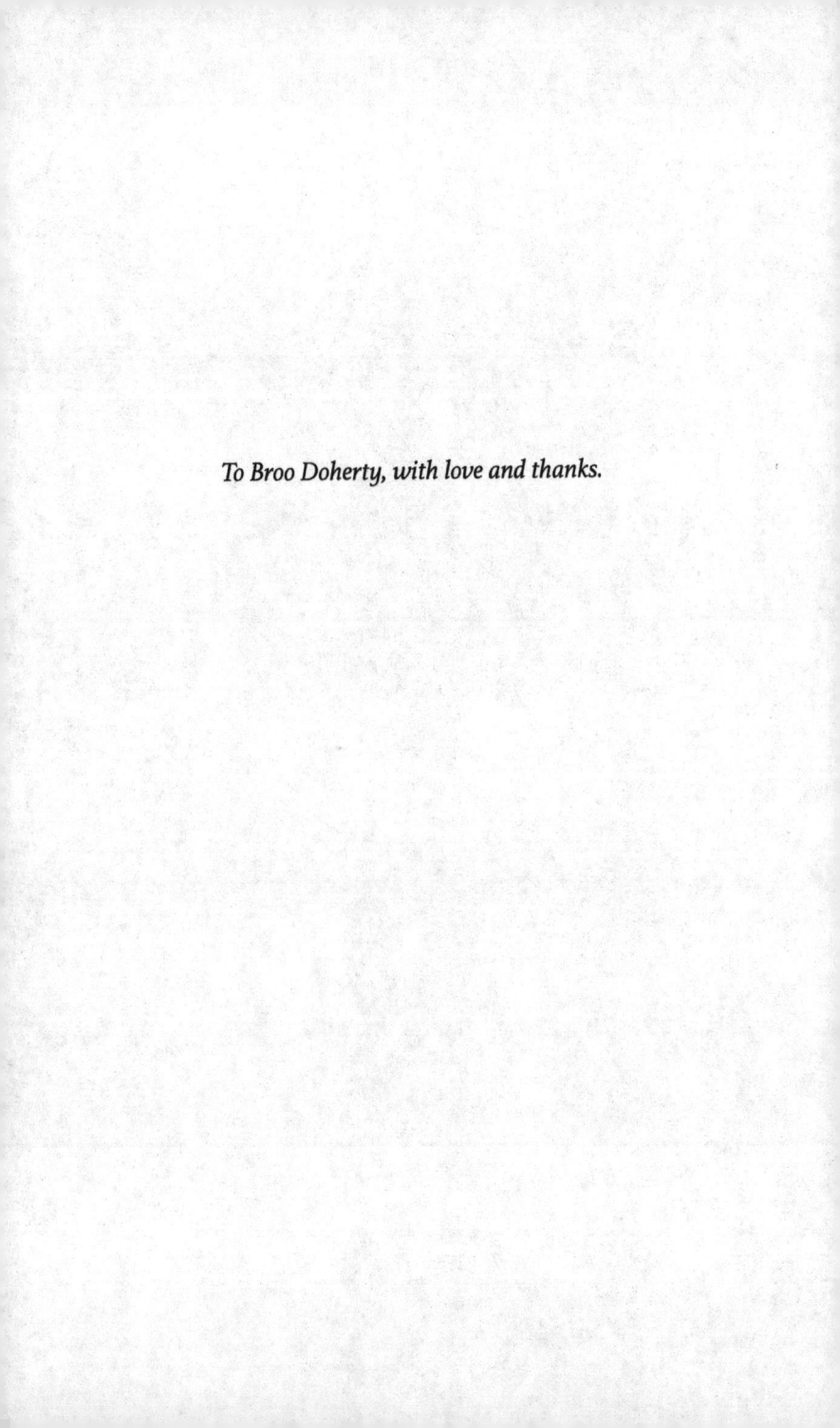

*To Broo Doherty, with love and thanks.*

# 1

Being older could be so quiet.

I don't mean I was deaf, although I know I was lucky in that respect. A lot of my contemporaries were. Several of them were sporting complicated and by all accounts very expensive hearing aids by the time they passed sixty. One of them, who had been a keen attender of punk concerts and festivals back in the day, put this down to 'speaker damage'. He had liked to stand right next to them, head banging in time to the pounding beat. Another had worked as a builder, a place where a lot of noisy equipment comes into play on a daily basis, and that was in the days before ear defenders.

No, what I meant was since I had moved to Lower Begley, my average day was very quiet. Sometimes I didn't actually talk to anyone, apart from my black cat, Ivan the Terrible, and he wasn't a great conversationalist unless I was rattling a bag of cat treats. Then he had a lot to say for himself.

When I was a baby, there was always noise, mostly from me if my mother was to be believed. Then with the arrival of my sister, the decibels increased. There was always someone shouting from their bedroom, arguing about school, who had left the lights on upstairs, why had someone put an empty milk bottle back in the fridge door.

After that there was university, and the aforementioned discos and what are now called gigs. We couldn't text or email each other because the technology hadn't been invented; instead, we just left our doors open and shouted to each other. Then with marriage to Malcolm, and the arrival of our own daughter, the cycle began again.

But suddenly at sixty-four, everything went quiet. Well, it did for me, because I had moved, on my own into a house on a no-through road in the middle of the countryside. Beautiful but relatively silent.

My daughter had grown up and gone out into the world, my husband ditto. Well, at least Malcolm had gone, running off into the uncritical embrace of his secretary. Whether he had grown up was debatable. And that left me, moving out of the marital home where I had expected to end my days, suddenly living quite happily, for the most part, on my own. And after about three weeks, it struck me how noiseless, how utterly soundless, a house could be. It was a fairly modern place too, so there wasn't even the friendly creaking of old beams, the tiny scurry of mice in the attic. There was just me.

Occasionally I would hear the slam of my neighbour's car door or the hum of her husband's lawnmower on sunny afternoons. Or there might be the rumble of a tractor going past my house to the fields beyond it.

Tranquillity suited some people, but I didn't like it much. I was used to the bustle of work and family life. I liked it when my daughter brought home her friends for unexpected visits and raids on the fridge. I'd always like company, friends dropping in for coffee and perhaps a grumble about how it was impossible to buy comfortable shoes that looked more attractive than the boxes they came in. Within a few weeks of moving, I knew I needed to do something. Well, no one else was going to do it for me. That's another thing I had realised. I might still have family, friends and relations, but in the end, after the divorce, the buck for everything – bills, utilities, repairs, gardening, decorating – stopped with me. It took some getting used to.

I tried a few different activities. I was fortunate in that there was a village hall within walking distance of my house, where a lot of people like me (grey haired, retired) congregated for classes. There was yoga, slimming, knitting, pottery painting, badminton, jewellery making, that sort of thing.

After a few failed attempts to find something that would keep my attention, I decided to try the art class which was restarting for a new term and had been much publicised in the local village WhatsApp group. Well, I did get a grade four at O level all those years ago, and although my mother had rolled her eyes at this, at least I had passed.

### The New Brush Art Class

Spring term starting this week. 10 a.m. – 1 p.m., beginners welcome, no special materials needed, just bring your enthusiasm.

It was held on Tuesday mornings. I went for the first time on an unusually beautiful day in February when the sun was shining, the sky was the pure, cloudless blue of an Enid Blyton illustration, and birds were twittering in the hedges as I passed. The small car park of the village hall was already filling up, and I could see ladies of my vintage, some of whom I sort of recognised, a couple of them lugging art folders and impressive boxes filled presumably with paints and pencils and maybe crayons for all I knew.

I meanwhile had dug out the battered tin of Rowney water-colours that had been Nicky's when she was at school, and every pencil I could find, plus a new eraser, and I had stashed them all in an old canvas holdall and slung it over my shoulder. I felt quite bohemian.

As I reached the door, I took a deep breath and strode in.

'Hello there, I didn't know you were coming too. I would have given you a lift if I'd known. It's me, Anita.'

I turned to see a cheerful-looking woman of about my age who I recognised as my nearest neighbour. We had waved at each other from our cars a couple of times, and once she had dropped off some post which had been put through her door by mistake. Like me, she was looking around at the bustle of other people, most of whom seemed to know what they were doing.

'Meg Foster, lovely to meet you properly. Well, I thought I'd give it a go,' I said, pleased to see a familiar face. 'I can't spend my life hoovering, I'll have no pile left on the living room carpet if I carry on.'

Anita pulled a sympathetic expression. 'Me too, and now the spring is here, Rick wants us to be out in the garden from dawn till dusk. He's so fussy.'

'Yes, but your garden is beautiful, I've seen bits of it over the fence. Not like mine. I like to describe it as a wildlife haven. Heaven knows what is living in the woodpile.'

'Don't look,' she said with a grin as she lifted two chairs from the stack. 'Are you any good at this painting lark?'

'I doubt it, I haven't picked up a paintbrush in ages for over forty years, unless it was to finish off my daughter's homework.'

'Great. Come and grab this chair and one of those easel things and sit by me,' she said. 'I started last year. I'm completely hopeless but I do enjoy it, and after the terrible weather we've had, if I stayed inside any longer I would lose the plot completely. And they are a nice group, and it is quite fun, although some of them take it very seriously.'

The sound of several elderly people getting themselves sorted out was deafening that morning. A tall rather stout man in a baggy Arran sweater had taken charge and was shouting over the hubbub, trying to organise everyone, and happily all the women were largely ignoring him. It took a good twenty minutes before we had settled into a circle, easels propped impressively in front of us.

It turned out Arran-sweater man wasn't actually in charge at all, and the class was being led by a young, blonde woman in fuchsia dungarees and a batik headscarf who had turned up ten minutes late, much to Arran-sweater man's annoyance.

Completely unabashed by his hard stare, she went to stand in the middle of our circle and clapped her hands to shut us all up. The noise subsided quite suddenly, so that only Arran sweater man could be heard muttering.

'...paid good money to come here. Ten o'clock means ten o'clock.'

Our tutor ignored him. 'Good morning, everyone. And welcome. For those of you who are new today, my name is Cassandra—'

'In which case, I don't believe a word she says,' I murmured, and next to me, Anita giggled.

'—and I run this group and also one in Begley Mortimer and one in Begley Moor. If you have any friends over this side of the river who want to join us, we're a bit down on numbers at the moment which is why some of the other Begleys have joined us for the time being – and I know you want to get started unleashing all those lovely, flowing, creative juices—'

'Don't worry, I've got some tissues in my bag if things get messy,' Anita muttered back, and I stifled a snort of laughter.

'—so I thought we would start by very quickly introducing ourselves so that the new people know who is who. Would someone like to start us off?'

'I'm Dennis Kitteridge from Lower Begley Farmhouse,' Arran-sweater man said, taking the initiative, 'and I'm delighted to see I'm still the only rooster in this henhouse of lovely ladies—'

'I think he means cock,' Anita whispered, and this time I did laugh and had to pretend I was sneezing.

'I used to paint a lot as a child; that was before I went into finance. I got a Blue Peter badge for a painting I did of John Noakes and Shep. My wife says my paintings are as good as anything you see on that BBC programme. In fact, I've applied three times, but I never seem to get asked – not even as a wild-card entry.'

Cassandra gave a wide-eyed slightly mad smile. 'Marvellous, welcome back Dennis, and who's next?'

Cassandra went quickly round the circle, introducing Maureen, who used to be a nurse, Irene, who was a retired dentist, Beryl, who had worked for the government *but if I told you more I'd have to kill you*, Gwen, who seemed very flustered by the question and didn't quite know what she had done, Polly, who had worked on the delicatessen counter in the local super-market *doing cheese*, and Janet, who had been a hairdresser. Anita had been an accountant and I had been a school secretary.

'Excellent, now we are all friends, let's get started. There is tea and coffee and biscuits in the kitchen for anyone of course, and I have some vegan rice cakes if anyone wants one.'

'Pass,' I murmured.

'Won't fight you for those,' Anita agreed. 'Give me a Tunnocks Tea Cake any time.'

Cassandra had brought along a bunch of sunflowers from the local supermarket, which she unwrapped, dumped in a milk jug and put in the middle of our circle on a table.

'And remember, there is no such thing as bad painting,' Cassandra added confidently. 'Just remember to think about those marvellous elements. Shape, Form, Texture, Space, Value, Colour, and Line. Those are the magic ingredients. The shape of these flowers. The space they occupy. The vibrant colours of nature.'

After a bit more chatter and Gwen fretting in case anyone wanted tea already or should we wait, we finally got down to some painting.

I stared at the blank paper in front of me and wondered where to start. Eventually I did a few hesitant pencil strokes and then rubbed them out again. I looked around, worried in case anyone had seen the depth of my inability.

Next to me I could see Anita was already splashing water-colours onto her paper with some abandon.

'Last term I tried Realism; this time I've decided to be an Impressionist,' she said in answer to my enquiring look. 'I'm doing my impression of those flowers, focusing on – what did she say? – colour and shape.'

'Those flowers are yellow,' I said, a bit confused.

'They are blue and red to me; I refuse to be hidebound by convention. I think I'll put my new dog in there too. You must have heard him barking at the squirrels in your oak tree? Bonzo's only a pup. He loves a squirrel.'

The morning passed quite peacefully and Cassandra wandered around behind us murmuring comments and encouragement.

'Lovely shape, Irene. Gwen, you could use a bit more of the space, don't you think? Rather than squeeze everything up into a corner? You don't have to be afraid of the paper. It's your friend. Yes, Dennis, I can see where you are going with this, and daring use of – shall I say – an almost architectural approach. Anita, very bold use of form. Beryl, excellent as always. Meg, let your brush lead you onwards. Those flowers are happy, aren't they? Paint them with joy. Daphne, splendid execution of the jug.'

I did my best and halfway through when we were allowed a ten-minute break for coffee, we sneaked glances at our class-mates' paintings. They were all very different, and sitting on the other side of me, Beryl's was by far the most accomplished.

I stopped to admire it.

'Gosh, this is absolutely brilliant,' I said.

Beryl, who looked about my age and was swathed in a jumble of brightly coloured scarves and sweaters, smiled modestly.

'I haven't painted for ages. I'm enjoying this. I wish I'd started up again years ago. My last husband used to say I should stick to walls and skirting boards. But what did he know? He couldn't sign a Christmas card without expecting a Nobel prize for literature.'

'Do you ever sell them?' I asked. 'That's really gorgeous.'

Beryl tilted her head at her painting and smiled. 'Actually, when I was short of cash I used to work as a life model in Paris back in the seventies. Now, if times get hard, I'm thinking of selling off my old nudes. Ten quid to get one, twenty quid not to get one.'

'I think my dog should be bigger,' Anita said, flicking her paintbrush carelessly at the canvas. 'Perhaps I will give him a ball too. And Bonzo is growing a sort of doggy moustache. I'll add that.'

'You're crackers.' I laughed, loading up my brush with more yellow paint.

'I've spent more than enough of my life being told what to do,' she said, wiping a smear of blue paint off the floor. 'Now I'm retired I can do what I like as long as I don't break any laws. Anyway, this is an impression of Bonzo's ball, because the real thing is punctured and rather flat. I'm quite proud of him actually. There's not a dog toy out there that he can't destroy.'

On the other side of the circle there was a small commotion as Gwen knocked her water over, and she did a strange little tiptoe dance, trying not to get her canvas shoes wet while Polly laughed and shouted, 'Clear up on aisle three.'

'You're new to the village, aren't you?' Polly called across from the other side of me. 'Haven't you just moved into High Winds?'

I agreed I had.

'Nice house, we went for a look round when it first came on the market. We didn't want to buy it; we were just being nosey. Anyway, Bruce said there wasn't room for his model railway. It just about fills our attic. Sometimes he goes up there in the middle of the night to change the points when the new timetables come into operation. Still, he's not hurting anyone and I never have a problem wondering what to buy him for his birthday. Are you all settled? Boxes all unpacked?'

'I did them all in the first week,' I said proudly.

'Marvellous, well done you. Bruce and I still have some packing cases we haven't looked at, and we moved into The Briars thirty-one years ago next week.'

'Got any cardboard left over?' Anita said. 'Rick's always looking for some to flatten and put down over bits of the garden. Cheaper than weed-proof membrane and more ecological.'

'The trouble is, I find myself agonising over cardboard boxes these days,' Beryl said. 'Some of them are really good boxes, and I hate to get rid of them because they look so useful.'

'And are they?' Anita said.

Beryl shrugged. 'No, not very often. But it's no worse than

men keeping random bits of wood in the shed because they might come in handy one day.'

We chattered happily about life in the village for a few minutes, and I began to relax. I was enjoying the company of new people too. I began to think this could be the activity and the group for which I had been looking.

All of a sudden, I stopped applying paint with an uncertain hand and a small brush and started being a bit braver with my brush strokes. Perhaps Anita was right; I shouldn't be hidebound by convention either. I swiped a rather bold brushful of pale lavender paint under the edge of a leaf to create a shadow and leaned back to admire it. I was rather proud of it actually. Maybe a bit more colour in my life was what I needed. That and the occasional bit of excitement.

'There you are. Such a happy little flower, isn't it?' Cassandra said, coming up behind me and clapping her hands unexpectedly.

My paintbrush flew up into the air and landed on Anita's lap, splattering her jeans with purple paint.

She gave me a look. 'These jeans are my favourite; they are Versace, I'll have you know.'

I gave a gasp of horror. 'Really?'

Anita rolled her eyes. 'No, of course they aren't. They were from the market about ten years ago. Stop looking so tragic!'

* * *

When Cassandra called that it was time to start clearing up, I was amazed. The hours had passed so quickly. And for the first time in ages, I had really enjoyed myself.

Everyone seemed very jolly and encouraging, and there was a fair bit of local gossip floating around too. Details of the couple who had taken over the shop, whether or not the produce fair in September was going to take place, how someone called Elspeth had a gentleman caller who used to be married to Judith, the woman from Scotland. What the Young Farmers were doing in the pub on Saturday nights and who everyone suspected of breaking the window in the bar (someone called Short Kev). It was fascinating and a great insight into village life.

Dennis began barging about, organising the chairs back into the storage room, while Gwen collected the mugs on a battered tin tray decorated with the Queen's Silver Jubilee and started washing up. Beryl, meanwhile, was standing admiring her painting until Dennis took her easel away.

'Typical man,' she said, giving him a hard stare. 'He was just as bad last term, trying to organise us all the time. I hate it when people do that. We're not at school. How did you both get on?'

'Good fun,' I said, 'as long as no one looks at the painting.'

Beryl flapped a hand at me. 'It's fine. We are all a bit anxious at first. You'll get the hang of it. Nice brushwork with those leaves. And Anita, I'm loving that dog, he looks a real character.'

'What dog?' Dennis blustered, overhearing. 'There wasn't a dog.'

'He's my spirit animal,' Anita said. 'Couldn't you see him?'

Dennis stomped off, muttering, to fold up some more easels, and Anita and I grinned at each other.

'So how have you settled in? You've been there for a few weeks, haven't you? I kept meaning to come round and say hello properly, and then it was Hogmanay and Rick and I went off to Scotland with our dance group for two weeks and I came back with the lurgy that's been going round. Now the spring is coming I won't see anything of him. He will be out birdwatching with his mates or mowing and fussing and doing all sorts of manly things in the garden. He's planning a bonfire too, so apologies for that when it happens.'

'I like the smell of a bonfire,' I said, 'as long as you're not planning on burning car tyres.'

'I shouldn't think so, although we do have one. He's got some idea he might paint it white and turn it into a planter.' Anita looked at her watch. 'I must get back and make some lunch, but why don't you come round to my house tomorrow about three for a cup of tea and a Jammie Dodger? Rick's planning to spend a few hours in his greenhouse, and if you are there, he can't expect me to come and help. He was washing the glass panes the other day and even after all these years he still thinks I will find it as exciting as he does. What do you say? You'd be doing me a massive favour? And I have a hidden agenda. And I can make up for my lack of hospitality at the same time.'

'I'd love to,' I said.

'Excellent, you can tell me everything about yourself. Word is in the village you are a rich widow looking for a new husband, one of the new brand of London escapees who any day now is going to complain about the smell of the farm up the lane.'

'Totally wrong on every point,' I said. 'I'm a divorcee from Bristol. I've moved up here to be closer to my daughter and her husband who live in Cheltenham.'

'Lower Begley is a nice village,' Beryl said. 'You'll like it as long as you don't get involved in local politics. I've lived here most of my life. I watched the new estate by the old post office being built, and your house too. I remember when all this was green fields. That's the sort of thing old people say, isn't it? Still, I suppose people have to live somewhere.'

Gwen came out of the cupboard with a triangular floor brush that was taller than she was and started sweeping up some debris, fretting about the paint water spillage and wondering if she needed to do anything more about it.

'Stop making such a fuss. It's just a splash, Gwen,' Dennis boomed across the hall. 'The new girl made more of a mess than you did. There's a splodge of her purple paint by the window, and by the way, you've missed a bit. I sharpened my pencil over there.'

'I'll blooming sharpen his pencil for him,' Gwen muttered through gritted teeth.

'He did call me a girl though,' I said.

## 2

The following afternoon, I cleared away my rather unsatisfactory sandwich lunch (cheese and pickle) and fed the cat for the second time as evidently the first offering wasn't acceptable.

'Is that better, my booosiful boy?' I said in the squeaky voice I sometimes used when speaking to Ivan.

My cat returned a baleful stare and looked pointedly at the cupboard where I kept the Dreamies.

'Does he want a treat?' I said, trying to annoy him. 'Does he? *Does he?*'

Ivan almost sighed with impatience and if he could, I think he would have tapped his claws on the floor.

He rewarded me with a couple of meows, and heaven help me, I meowed back.

I'd read somewhere that people meow more to their cats than their cats do to them, and it looked as though I was slowly sliding into cat owner senility. I would be buying him seasonal-themed collars next. And little hats. It really was time I got out more.

I slung a few random treats into Ivan's bowl, the one decorated with a smiling cat, which was so far from Ivan's nature as to be ridiculous, and having told him where I was going and assuring him that I wouldn't be long, I walked down the lane to Anita's house. It really was the most beautiful part of the country, with broad fields, distant views of the Black Mountains and wildflowers just beginning to emerge from the hedgerows.

It was certainly a lot different from where I used to live, a house that Malcolm and I had bought together forty-something years ago, just after we had married and where we had raised our daughter Nicky. Originally we had been on the edge of a small town, but over the years new housing developments had gradually eroded the fields and enclosed our garden, and Malcolm had become increasingly tetchy as a result.

Then six years ago, his branch of the bank had closed down and he had been offered early retirement. And shortly afterwards it had all come out about the affair he had been having with his secretary, his dissatisfaction with life and with me. How he needed to 'find himself'. Possibly under some rock, I had suggested.

Once things had been put in motion, everything had changed, not just my marital status. In fact, it had almost been a relief when he agreed we should sell up as part of our divorce, and I had left the noise and muddle of the new ring road and moved to the countryside where traffic disruption usually involved two tractors or some cattle being moved up the lane to a new pasture.

When I went through the front gate that afternoon, I saw Anita hanging out some washing while a small brown and white dog leapt and barked encouragement at her feet.

'Ah, there you are,' she said with a wide smile. 'Come on in. Don't take any notice of Bonzo, he's just excited to see you. Although he gets excited at everything. I'll give him some peanut butter, that will shut him up.'

I followed her through the back door into a large kitchen where wooden cabinets and cupboards surrounded a scrubbed pine table and chairs. There were bits of shredded dog toy and a tumbleweed of dog hair under the table. Bonzo pounced on the remains of a dismembered toy dinosaur and raced outside into the garden. Anita closed the door behind him with a sigh of relief.

'Excuse the mess,' she said, picking up a pile of paperwork and unopened letters and dumping them at the other end of the table. 'Now then, tea or coffee?'

'Either,' I said.

'Express a preference,' Anita said, holding up her hands, 'otherwise I would have to decide and I'm no good at that.'

'Tea,' I said.

She flicked the kettle on and took some mugs out of a cupboard.

'Yorkshire tea or compost? I've got some rooibos somewhere. Rick wanted to try it. We had one cup because he'd read it was health-giving. I told him it that might be true, but it would also cause me to lose 94 per cent of whatever joy I had left in life.'

'Ordinary, and I've brought you some biscuits,' I said, pulling them out of my bag.

'Perfect, Rick's just eaten the last of the Jammie Dodgers I promised you. Either that or Bonzo has got at the tin. Like master like dog. Both of them are so greedy. Now then, what did you think of our little gathering yesterday? I must warn you, take no notice of Dennis. He behaves like Michelangelo in a tweed jacket half the time. Beryl is far more of a leader and a much better artist too.'

'She certainly is, and she seems very interesting,' I said.

'We all think she used to be a spy, but we have no actual proof of it. Not that you would expect to see her with a secret camera going round Tesco. Or lurking in the library waiting for her Russian handler to walk in with a copy of *Woman's Own* under his arm.'

'Page ten,' I said in a Russian accent. 'The microchip is underneath the article about cholesterol.'

Anita spluttered with laughter and passed me a mug of tea.

'So, you'll keep coming to the art class? I do hope so. We could do with some fresh blood, and you seem very jolly. The tutor used to be Maud, who ran the village shop, but when that was sold she went to the Cotswolds to live with her daughter in Lower Slaughter.'

I agreed I would and we chattered pleasantly for a while, drinking tea and eating biscuits until Anita's husband Rick appeared at the back door holding out his hands in front of him like a surgeon.

'Boots!' Anita shouted, and he kicked off his wellingtons.

'You must be Meg,' he said with a smile as he padded over to the sink. 'I won't shake hands, and don't come too close. I've been up to my elbows in Blood Fish and Bone. Have you asked her?'

Anita fixed him with a glare. 'Rick, mind your own business. I'm just softening her up with her own biscuits.'

'Asked me what?' I said.

Anita gave a dramatic sigh.

'The painting holiday, hasn't she mentioned it yet?' Rick said, drying his hands on a tea towel. 'You'd better agree otherwise Dennis will monopolise her. Did you know he's got the hots for my wife? And no one wants to watch that all week, do they? Can you imagine him, telling everyone where to go and what to do all the time? Trying to corral everyone onto the bus and insisting everyone stays together?'

'Well, I'm not having that, I'd rather not go at all,' Anita said. 'Look, if you'll just let me get a word in, I'll tell Meg the details.

There is a painting group trip to Greece in May. So in three months' time, Beryl, Gwen and I were planning to go with Beryl's sister Effie, who wasn't there yesterday because she's walking the Pilgrim Way in Spain, probably with a cockle shell in her hat. And then she is off to America to stay with some friends, so we probably won't see much of her at all before we go. Now Gwen has told me she doesn't think she can come on the trip at all. She's having her garden wall repointed and she feels she needs to be around to supervise things. And if he finds out, Dennis's ears will prick up like Bonzo's do when he hears the postman's van coming down the lane, and I don't think we could bear it if Dennis brought his brother Ronald in Gwen's place. So please say you'll come? Everything is arranged. Cassandra's sister Jillian lives out there, and she's going to be our tour leader.'

I did what I always did and tried to think of a reason why I couldn't go. I played for time.

'Wow,' I said, 'that's a bit of a shock. I wasn't expecting that.'

'It's his fault,' Anita said, giving Rick a hard look, 'I was hoping to ease it into the conversation more gradually. He's going to be away birdwatching in Scotland that week with an old friend, so it was his idea that I should have a break too. You do seem good fun and it would be such a great opportunity. And Gwen is already fretting about what might happen to her wall if she isn't there to watch. I don't think she is planning to actually wield a trowel, but she was captain of the Girl Guides back in the day, and you never know what they've picked up. She is already starting to witter on about losing her holiday deposit, so you'd be doing her a favour too. It's May seventh for eight days, flying out from Birmingham to Santorini, which is such a lovely Greek island. Nice hotel near the seafront in an adorable town, and a minibus to drive us to various locations.'

'It does sound tempting,' I said thoughtfully, 'and I haven't had a proper holiday for years.'

'I'll send you an email with all the details,' Anita said. 'Beryl went a few years ago with her sister Effie, and she says it's lovely, and even if you don't do any proper painting, it will be nice to get some sunshine, won't it? In fact, I've got a printout somewhere. Maybe in this basket.'

She started rifling through the stack of paperwork, eventually pulling out some sheets of paper held together with a giant paperclip that looked like a fish.

'Take a look. Don't hang about. And then I'll make you a copy and then some more tea.'

'And me?' Rick said, pulling up a chair. 'By the way, I saw Steve this morning. He's been riddling out his shed and he gave me some really great bits of wood he's been keeping.'

'And what are you planning to do with those?' Anita asked, giving me a knowing look.

'Oh, I don't know, but they are too good to throw away. I'm sure they will come in handy.'

* * *

I got home to find my cat had left a dead mouse in the middle of the kitchen floor, which he obviously wished to exchange for something more palatable. Perhaps my daughter, who only lived twenty minutes away, would watch the house for me and feed Ivan if I went on holiday? Yes, the more I thought about it the more the prospect of a trip to somewhere different did sound really appealing. I felt a little shiver of excitement at the prospect.

The last holiday I'd had was to Spain with Malcolm, where he had made friends with a group of car dealers who were on a works jolly, and largely left me to my own devices. Except for mealtimes when he had complained about everything from the cutlery to the service. Being on my own and yet with some friends would solve the problem of being a solo traveller, and I would have my own room and bathroom, possibly one with a sea view, and the opportunity to do something a bit different for once.

I browsed through the paperwork Anita had copied for me. The hotel looked clean but basic. The views were simply wonderful. All the locals seemed to be happy and smiling. There was a little internal courtyard where breakfast was served, lemon trees in the gardens and olive groves on the hillside outside the town. And actually, the more I thought about it, I couldn't think of any reason why I couldn't go.

No, that wasn't the way I needed to think. I should go for a positive reason. Because it sounded like fun, and I *wanted* to. And travelling to Santorini, a bit of painting, seeing the blue of the Mediterranean glittering in the sunshine. New food to try, new friendships to consolidate, a bit of – dare I say it – excitement. Yes, they were good reasons to accept the opportunity. The alternative was nowhere near as interesting.

Ivan barged in through the cat flap as he always did, his progress impeded by either his thick black fur or his increasing gut from too many treats, and he stopped with something like outrage to see me in my own kitchen and fixed me with a look.

I tried meowing at him a couple of times to no effect and then went to check my emails. Then I watched a delightful reel on Facebook of adorable cats nuzzling up to their owners.

Ivan jumped up onto the other end of the kitchen table and watched me, so I turned the laptop around to show him.

'That's what you should be doing,' I said. 'Look at that nice cat, being cuddly and grateful. He's not sneering at that rather hunky fireman who has just rescued him from under the floorboards as though he is useless. I bet that cat won't hawk up furballs in the middle of the night right where the fireman puts his feet down in the morning.'

Ivan reached out a casual paw and knocked a tin of pencils onto the floor.

'Right, that settles it. I'm going on holiday,' I said. 'I'll get Nicky to come in and feed you while I'm away. If you're lucky.'

Ivan sat down neatly, curling his tail around his front paws.

'If you don't like the idea, I'll put you in the cattery for a week.'

Ivan ignored me, stretched hugely as though he had just finished a hard day's work, and jumped down and started sniffing around the kitchen obviously looking for his mouse.

\* \* \*

Three months later, after a horribly early start, we arrived in Santorini on a bright, sunny morning and found the transfer bus waiting outside exactly where it should have been. Then there was an hour's journey from the airport to the village where we were staying until at last we stood outside our hotel. *Hotel Costas* was painted in curly script on the wall.

The building was charmingly rustic, with faded blue shutters at every window, canvas sun canopies over the balconies, and there to welcome us at the front door, a tabby cat with her three kittens. Almost immediately, the mother cat started meowing and practically pointing at her empty feed bowl.

A feisty-looking woman with an impressive bosom underneath her flowery overall came out and shooed them away, and they scattered, the mother cat leaping up the bougainvillea that covered the front of the hotel, reaching almost to the roof.

She threw her arms up. '*Kalós ílthate se ólous sas* – welcome everybody!'

We did what any party of older English tourists would do – we nodded and smiled and said how happy we were to be there.

Beryl leaned forward. '*Boroúme na boúme?* Can we come in? It's very warm out here.'

We looked at her in amazement.

'I didn't know you spoke Greek,' I murmured.

Beryl gave a modest smile. 'I picked it up when I worked in Athens in the late seventies. The wonderful scent of all the citrus trees, red carnations all over the ground. I remember it like it was yesterday. There was a lot going on then and I had to blend in.'

'Welcome to Hotel Costas! I am Nina,' our hostess said with a wide smile, and she ushered us into the cool of the marble floored hallway where we saw a woman I assumed was our leader Jillian pacing around on her mobile phone and looking rather stressed and annoyed.

Her face lit up when she saw us and she ended her call.

'Come on in, ladies, I'm Cassandra's sister Jillian. So sorry not to be at the door to greet you. I've been having a few last-minute problems. There's always something. Never mind, let's get you settled into your rooms.'

She picked up a wicker basket of keys and started to hand them out.

'Costas and Nina are the owners; they are here to answer all your queries. There isn't a lift but Costas will take your bags to your room for you, so please don't struggle. Now then, Anita and Meg, here are your keys, rooms four and five. You are in the front of the building on the first floor. Beryl – I know you and your sister wanted ground-floor rooms, so you are in room one. Effie is next to you in room two. She came on an earlier flight from Paris. I think she's up on the roof terrace at the moment.'

'I know what that means,' Beryl said. 'She's sneaking a cigarette. I've been telling her to quit for years.'

'All the others will be arriving soon. They chose the later flight and I think it was delayed,' Jillian said, stabbing at the buttons on her mobile again.

'What others? I thought it was just Dennis who hadn't arrived,' Anita said.

Jillian looked surprised. 'Didn't Cassie tell you? Honestly, she's so scatterbrained sometimes. But it's always nice to meet new people, isn't it? Such a treat. And I couldn't possibly do this for just four people; think about it. And Dennis of course, so that makes five. I'm surprised he didn't come with you. But then he and the others said the early flight and a four o'clock start would be too much for them. Anyway, let's get settled in and then at three o'clock prompt we can all assemble back down here, and I will take you for a special introductory walk around the town. I've lived and worked here as a tour guide for years and I know a great deal about the area. So, synchronise your watches.'

Our rooms were small but spotlessly clean, each with white-washed walls, a tiny shower room and pale blue curtains and shutters which were closed against the rising heat of the day. Pushing them open, I stepped out onto the little balcony which was shaded from the sun by a white canvas awning. I could see that it was also the kitten's daybed, and three furry faces peered down at me. Heaven knows how they had got up there.

Looking across, I saw Anita on her balcony.

She called across at me. 'Isn't this great? Quick, get unpacked and we can go and find Effie. She's quite a card, you'll love her. Then we can get a drink and a late lunch somewhere. I'll be round in ten minutes.'

'What about the guided walk?' I called back.

Anita pulled a face. 'Not likely. I'm not waiting. Are you?'

'Cooeee,' someone shouted from the street below us, and we leaned over the balcony railings to see Beryl and another grey-haired lady sitting on the bench outside the front door.

'Hurry up,' Beryl called up to us. 'We're ready to go exploring. See you in a bit.'

I absolutely loved the thought that I was about to go out exploring the little town, and with some new friends too. It sounded far better than being taken on a guided walk, as though we were a school party who couldn't be trusted not to get lost. I couldn't wait.

I heaved my case on to the bed and unpacked it, wondering why I had brought two thick sweaters and even a scarf with me. Had I brought enough t-shirts? And should I have brought more than one sundress?

I hung everything up in the little white wardrobe, which threatened to topple forwards unless I spaced everything evenly along the rail, and then put all my toiletries into the bathroom.

Instead of the usual supermarket own brand, I had made some impulsive holiday purchases of expensive shampoo and conditioner, and I put them on the shelf inside the shower with considerable satisfaction. I was filled with the wonderful sense of being at the start of an adventure. I was somewhere different, sunny and undeniably picturesque. Outside there was a delightful view of white houses, the occasional blue cupola and the tantalising backdrop of the sea shimmering in the sunshine. And Anita, Beryl and Effie were waiting for me to join them. Yes, I could have done this trip alone, but I had the feeling it was going to be a lot of fun with them there too.

'Come on, there's no time to waste,' Anita said as she came in after a perfunctory knock on my door. 'Oh, do hurry up, I'm dying to get out there and look around, and I'm so hungry, it's ages since we had anything decent to eat. Beryl and Effie are still waiting for us by the front door.'

'So we definitely aren't doing the guided walk?' I said.

She shook her head and flapped a hand in dismissal.

'I am not being herded around like a party of school kids. And Beryl and Effie have been here before so they won't want to be shown where the chemist is or the supermarket. It's much more enjoyable to explore on our own, don't you think? And it's an island; remember, the worst that can happen is we go round in a big circle. I always used to think that when *Bergerac* was on television back in the 1980s. There was nearly always a car chase, and what was the point when there was nowhere to go?'

'Still worth watching for John Nettles though,' I said as we went downstairs. 'He was so handsome. I had such a crush on him. And in *Midsomer Murders too*.'

'There can't be anyone living in Midsomer these days, what with the abnormally high death rate. You would think the Met would want to investigate,' Anita said, and I laughed and agreed.

Outside, the afternoon was warm and pleasant, and incredibly quiet. Just the occasional sound of a voice, or music playing from someone's open window. I was introduced to Effie, who was dazzling in a swirling green maxi dress and a yellow sunhat patterned with cartoon ducks. She looked a slightly younger and fluffier version of Beryl.

'Effie,' she said with a sweet smile, 'short for Euphemia before you ask. Thanks, Dad. Now let's get going before Jillian spots us escaping and drags us back for roll call.'

There didn't seem to be much traffic at all, just once or twice a delivery van passed the four of us as we made our way down the road towards the sea.

At last, we stood, transfixed by the prospect of the shining Mediterranean in front of us.

'Isn't it marvellous?' Anita said. 'I remember when I went to Rhodes with a group of friends. We couldn't believe how blue and clean it was. And they had a great time in Mallorca. I wish I could have gone. There was a bit about the Mediterranean in my friend's guidebook. She went down quite a rabbit hole with that one. Apparently there is lots of light and carbon dioxide in the Med, but not much ammonia or nitrates and not much mixing of the deep water either, which means the sea doesn't get full of algae.'

'You're a mine of information,' Beryl said, sitting down on a stone bench and taking a stone out of her shoe.

'Should you have worn those?' Effie said. 'They don't look very comfortable.'

'*Il faut souffrir pour être belle*, as Mother used to say. One must suffer to be beautiful,' Beryl replied.

Effie sniffed. 'It's going to take a lot more than a pair of Clark's sandals, dear. Even if they are red.'

'Do you two go on holiday together a lot?' I asked.

Effie nodded. 'We've shared lots of trips. We're both on our own now and both of us are outraged by the single supplements one has to pay. It's far cheaper to go together and for me to invest in some decent earplugs.'

Beryl snorted. 'I'm the one needing earplugs.'

'I think not. Sharing with you is how I imagine it would be to bunk up with a capybara. Anyway, it's more fun. Not to have to think about what the menfolk are doing or wanting these days. Not having to watch sport on the television.'

'We're Old Ducks,' Anita added, pulling on a bright yellow canvas hat identical to the ones Beryl and Effie were wearing. 'Our friend Juliette started it. We are all over sixty but definitely not past it.'

'I'm pushing seventy,' Beryl said, 'and Effie is sixty-eight.'

'Oh, thanks for telling everyone. And not in my head I'm not,' Effie said. 'I always thought getting to be this old would take much longer. I prefer to think I'm thirty-five plus post and packing charges. In fact, I'm a thirty-five-year-old trapped in a sixty-eight-year-old's body.'

'In which case perhaps you should get someone to put a couple of darts in,' Beryl snorted, earning herself a light slap on the shoulder from her sister.

'I'm nearly sixty-five,' I said, feeling perhaps for the first time that it wasn't something to be embarrassed about.

'Then you qualify too,' Anita said kindly. 'I will put your application forward to the president. Juliette's on holiday at the moment, in Ibiza.'

'Her husband wanted to go to Scotland, didn't he?' Beryl said.

'And yet – there they are in Ibiza,' Anita replied with a knowing look.

Beryl pulled her shoes back on and stood up.

'Right, now then, I thought we were going to get a late lunch and a drink?'

'You're the one holding us up. We could all die of thirst waiting for you,' Effie said.

Anita and I exchanged a look as we followed the sisters along the road.

'Are they always like this?' I whispered.

Anita nodded. 'Sometimes worse. It's marvellous.'

We started walking along the dusty track beside the sea, passing a couple of wine bars and cafés, all of which looked perfectly splendid to me. Eventually after much discussion, we went into a place decorated with white plastic pillars and garlands of artificial flowers, where we were welcomed by several very handsome waiters with such enthusiasm that it almost seemed their lives had been meaningless up to that point. This in itself made a lovely change from the service I had come to expect, where the sight of four older women was usually met with eye rolling, sighing and a table next to the toilets.

'Lovely ladies, I am Yanni. I will lead to you the best table. A view of the sea, plenty of shade, and wonderful food. But first a drink? I have beautiful white wine from my brother's vineyard. Nectar of the gods.'

'You're my type of guy,' Beryl said, rewarding him with a brilliant smile.

'Down, tiger,' Effie murmured, 'we talked about this. Remember Dubrovnik? And Padua?'

'Do you really have to remember everything?' Beryl said.

Effie snorted. 'Well, one of us has to.'

Yanni brought us a carafe of white wine and four green recycled glasses which were filled while we juggled with the massive, laminated menus.

'A toast to us,' Anita said, and we clinked our glasses over the table.

Well, this was fun. I felt more excited and happier than I had for months. Perhaps it was the warmth of the Greek sunshine, the blue of the Mediterranean shimmering in front of me, or maybe it was the company of my three new friends. The wonderful realisation that I had no pressing problems or tedious chores to attend to.

My life recently had been filled with those sorts of things. Finding someone to go up a ladder and clean out the gutters, rewriting my will, trying to sort out the broadband, washing out the recycling bin where apparently a new life form had developed. It turned out to be the remains of a lasagne which my daughter had put in there by mistake.

'I'm going to have something properly Greek,' Effie said. 'Calamari or moussaka. That sort of thing.'

'I want a real Greek salad,' I said. 'I bet it's nothing like we get at home.'

'A rare steak, which is what Maria Callas liked,' Beryl said, 'although she never finished one. Just used to cut it up and push it around her plate.'

'You met her?' Anita said.

Beryl shrugged. 'Once or twice. She had absolutely beautiful eyes. I went with David Frost to interview her in the seventies. Now then, shall we order?'

'Good heavens, David Frost? What was he like?'

Beryl looked wistful for a moment and then she gave a little smile.

'He was utterly charming and terrifically handsome in the flesh.'

The food was as good as the occasion as far as I was concerned. And the four of us sat there for a long time, chatting, marvelling over the beauty of the day and occasionally wondering when we would actually do some painting.

The island seemed to hold a lot of promise for inspiration, with rocky crags plunging down into the sea, white houses strewn along the coastline and a few fishing boats moored alongside the harbour. There was a strand of beach too, where people were sunbathing, reading under the shade of parasols or, in the case of a group of girls, giggling over their phones. Customers came and went, the ever-attentive waiters happy to bring us chilled water, more wine and offer desserts.

Beryl took a deep breath and breathed out slowly.

'Isn't sea air simply marvellous? It really does make one feel better, don't you think? My second husband said it was the ozone. I was thinking about that recently. How amazing the world is. And lots of different things are made up of the same elements. Carbon, hydrogen and oxygen. Which makes water, sugars, carbon dioxide, gas and of course alcohol. Isn't nature miraculous?'

'I've no idea what goes on in your head,' Effie said. 'If I can't find something here to inspire me to paint, I never will, although I'm hopeless. Beryl is the talent. I didn't actually come along for the art, I just fancied the holiday.'

'I don't think I have any particular ability,' I admitted. 'I enjoy it though.'

'Nonsense, I thought your painting of the wall outside the village hall was excellent,' Anita said.

'Yes, but it was more of – what would Cassandra call it? – an architectural approach. Dennis said I should have put in a snail or something to liven it up a bit.'

'Pooh, what does Dennis know about anything?' Beryl said. 'Have you noticed he is very free with his criticism but rejects everyone's opinion? What is it he always says? It's—'

She held out her hands so that we could finish the sentence.

'A work in progress,' Anita and I said together, and we both laughed.

'He was very annoyed when he found out you had taken Gwen's place. I know he wanted to bring his brother along. But he was too late and Cassandra said she had filled all the places for our group allocation and Ronald would have to go on the cancellation list. A near miss I think.'

'But I was allowed to come because I got in early even though I don't come to the group very often, and I gave a raffle prize for the Christmas party,' Effie confided.

'Dennis would call that corruption,' Beryl said, 'and let's be honest, you're hardly ever in Lower Begley despite leaving all that stuff in my spare room. Now, are we going to have anything else or should we carry on exploring? I remember from my last visit, there are some little shops further up. I quite fancy looking for a bad taste fridge magnet.'

We paid the bill, splitting it equally between us, and left with the kind wishes of Yanni and his staff echoing down the road behind us. A most satisfactory start to our holiday, we all agreed.

'Quick, hide, there's Jillian with the others,' Anita hissed a few minutes later, and startled, we all followed her into a shop where she peered out theatrically from behind a wire rack of postcards.

We even crouched down a little and watched as Jillian walked past holding a completely unnecessary little red flag, followed by a small group of our fellow artists. Two of them were women of about our age. There was a man who no one recognised, tall, quite distinguished with his Panama hat pulled low over his fore-head, and the last one, dressed in a striped shirt buttoned up to the neck, some disreputable khaki shorts, white socks and sandals, was of course Dennis. He was briskly surveying his surroundings and looking very pleased with himself.

'Why are we hiding?' Effie whispered.

'I don't know.' I giggled.

Beryl hissed, 'Who is that gorgeous man with them? Just think, he's carbon, hydrogen, oxygen too, and a lot more besides. He's not one of ours, is he? I know I'd remember him.'

We came out into the open and stopped lurking, much to the relief of the shop owner, and watched as the group walked on, Dennis ostentatiously holding up his thumbs and forefingers to frame the view.

'This could work,' he said loudly, 'if it wasn't for all the people getting in my way.'

## 3

We waited for a few minutes until they had gone and then wandered along the side of the sea, finding a tourist information kiosk where we picked up a lot of leaflets about the island, most of which were in Greek or German and probably of no use to any of us except Beryl.

'Wine tasting,' Beryl said, pointing at one that was smothered with enticing-looking photos of happy people laughing and holding up their full wine glasses. 'We are supposed to be doing that, aren't we?'

'And a trip to the ruins of some ancient town further along the coast,' Anita added. 'Minoans, weren't they? I like that sort of thing. What could be finer than the distant echoes and cries of a long-lost civilisation, the ceaseless sound of cicadas vibrating in the heat of a magical Greek day *and* an ice cream shop by the entrance? Life doesn't get much better than that.'

'Ice cream is a funny thing, isn't it?' Effie mused. 'For decades there was just vanilla, now there are over a thousand different sorts apparently. And there are dozens of crisp flavours too. Is this really the best way that civilisation can spend its time and money? So people can try haggis and asparagus crisps with their dirty martinis?'

'It's progress,' I said, laughing. 'I read somewhere that there are over three hundred sorts of KitKat in Japan.'

'Nonsense! That can't be true,' Anita said firmly.

'Oh yes, it's true,' Beryl said. 'I was in Japan in the eighties, when Hirohito died, and I still have friends there. Last time I visited I tried red bean flavour. The Japanese think KitKats are lucky because "Kitto Katso" in Japanese means "you will surely win".'

'What did it taste like?' I asked.

Beryl pulled a face and shrugged. 'Red bean.'

'Have you travelled everywhere? You seem to know so many different countries and languages,' I said.

'Universal tourist, that's me. Actually, Effie is just as bad – once you get the travel bug, I warn you there's no cure,' Beryl said. She looked up and down the water's edge. 'Now then, there was supposed to be a short boat trip to some deserted little beach around here. I can't remember where it goes from.'

The heat of the afternoon gradually cooled as the sun began to dip down towards the horizon.

Walking alongside the Mediterranean, we came across a large group of people, laughing and chattering away to each other, all of them about our vintage. Smartly dressed and cheerful.

We slowed down to negotiate them because they were blocking the road and then we stopped and a very nice-looking man offered us glasses of champagne in elegant flutes.

'*As giortásoume!*' another man said, throwing one arm around Effie's shoulder.

'He said, let's celebrate,' Beryl said, taking a glass and raising it in his direction.

'Yes, let's!' Effie shouted.

The man threw back his head and laughed, showing excellent teeth, and then he clinked his glass with ours.

'*Mia tóso charoúmeni méram,*' he said.

'What a happy day,' Beryl agreed, and we all raised our glasses and chinked them together again.

A young waitress came towards us with a platter full of delicious-looking treats and we cheerfully accepted some.

'Well, isn't everyone friendly,' Anita said approvingly. 'I didn't expect this.'

'The Greeks are famous for it,' Beryl said, taking a tiny blini and eating it in one mouthful.

The man with the excellent teeth topped up our glasses and we all shouted 'Yamas' at each other, and then another man with a beard and glasses came towards us, doing a restrained little jig before he offered us a plate of some miniature cakes, which really were works of art.

'Isn't this marvellous,' I said. 'I'm loving this.'

We stood around knocking back the champagne and smiling, and every few minutes we were presented with a platter of dainty morsels to eat. Tiny pastries, little tomatoes stuffed with feta cheese, beautiful little segments of fruit on cocktail sticks and bite-sized bruschetta. Some minute *pasta flora*, which were like much improved jam tarts.

After a while, a man with an accordion came along and started playing and, fired up with excitement and champagne, we all joined in the dancing. We linked arms and did a bit of uncoordinated Zorba, the Greek-style prancing and kicking. An elegant grey-haired woman with flowers in her hair seemed to be taking the lead alongside the man with the beard, who then had a matching flower between his teeth.

The dance finished with a loud *Hey!* from a man who had shed his jacket and rolled up his sleeves, and we all turned and hugged our new friends. My word, this was a splendid way to spend the afternoon. Who knew Greek people could be so welcoming?

Everyone stopped, laughing and gasping for breath, and the champagne glasses were refilled.

'Is anyone going to smash a few plates?' Effie panted. 'I love doing that.'

'Better not,' Beryl puffed back, 'those plates look very expensive.'

Meanwhile, the little waitress was wandering around with a clipboard and a puzzled expression, ticking things off and nodding. She got to us.

'*Ta onómatá sas parakaló.*'

'She wants our names,' Beryl said. She turned the clipboard to look at it and frowned. 'It's a seating plan.'

'Why does she need our names?' I asked.

Beryl emptied her glass, put it down on one of the tables and pulled an agonised face.

'We'd better just quietly go,' she said. 'I've realised we've gate-crashed a wedding reception.'

'Ah,' Effie said. She widened her eyes and then looked down at the ground. 'And let's be honest, it's not the first time.'

I was speechless with a mixture of embarrassment and bewilderment, and I didn't even have the language skills to apologise to someone. At the same time, I wanted to laugh. I hadn't had so much fun or felt so naughty in years.

I hesitated for a moment and then turned to see the other three scuttling off down the road without me. I gave a cheerful wave, blew a kiss to what I then realised was the bride and groom and hurried after my friends.

\* \* \*

After rushing away to a safe distance and making sure no one was coming after us, we slowed down, stopped giggling and began to enjoy the view. Out at sea were a few small fishing boats, and further out still, a speedboat towing someone behind it. A water skier, something I had always wanted to try when I was younger but never had. I wasn't sure I had the upper-body strength any longer. It looked fun though, whoever it was dipping and swooping behind the boat and even competent enough to wave at one point. If I tried that I would undoubtedly fall over and end up spitting out seawater.

'I wish I could do that,' Effie said.

'Me too, I was just thinking the same thing,' I said. 'It looks so much fun. But I doubt I could hang on for long enough to stand upright. Not with my dodgy knee.'

Effie looked sympathetic. 'I tried on one of those banana boats years ago. I think it was when Vladimir and I went to Tunisia. The four of us were on one banana. I fell off, of course I did.'

'Vladimir?' I asked.

'A Russian diplomat. So handsome, such marvellous cheek-bones. I was just asked along as the second fiddle. He was very well connected. I was trying to soften him up for Beryl.'

'You tried so hard,' Beryl commiserated, patting her hand.

'Until I found out he had a wife who was well connected too,' Effie said mournfully. 'That put the *kot sredi golubey* – the cat among the pigeons. I backed off pdq. I do have some standards.'

I looked at the others as we laughed together and Effie told another story about Vladimir and an incident with a trombone and some melted chocolate. Perhaps I had been living a life that was far too careful. Too sensible and predictable. Maybe it was time to think about having some adventures of my own?

* * *

We carried on exploring for a while, looking in cute little shops full of incredibly inexpensive 'designer' sunglasses, floppy tiered sundresses and glittering jewellery and then we made our way back to the hotel. We took the wrong turn on a couple of occasions, finding ourselves in the back streets where feral cats slept in the flowerpots and a man in a Bon Jovi t-shirt was apparently disembowelling his moped all over the pavement. How we could have got lost when the hotel was so close was anyone's guess. We then had a discussion about who had the worst sense of direction, which Effie won when she told us about the time she had forgotten where she had left her car. Having clicked her key fob at just about every car in the seven storeys, she then realised she was actually in the wrong car park.

Anyway, at last we saw the familiar blue shutters and white walls of Hotel Costas and went gratefully into the cool of the hallway.

'I suppose I could have a little rest before dinner,' Beryl said, pulling off her sunhat, 'and then we could meet up later.'

'In which case I think the rest of us should go up on the roof terrace and ask Effie for some more juicy gossip about you,' Anita said.

'I'm not having that; she would just make stuff up and probably get all the details wrong. I'm coming too,' Beryl said, 'just to make sure you have all your facts right. And I want to take a look at the pool.'

'It's not very big, and it's not heated,' Effie said, 'so don't get your hopes too high.'

'I'd better change into a clean t-shirt,' I said. 'I've got jam down the front of this one.'

Back in my room there were two kittens in my bathroom,

asleep on my bathmat. They scarpered pretty quickly when I came in and hurried up the bougainvillea to join their mother on the canvas sunshade. Perhaps I should close the doors to the balcony when I went out in future.

I found my adaptors and put my phone on charge so that I could send a couple of photos to Nicky. I added a brief summary of what I had been doing and, reading it back, I had to admit it sounded fun. Spending time with some new people, seeing new sights, gatecrashing a wedding and eating different foods was all great. Why hadn't I thought of doing this before? Perhaps I needed to be a bit braver in future.

Nicky replied to my message almost immediately. Allowing for the time difference, I guessed she had just got home from her work at the library.

> **NICKY**
>
> Sounds like you're enjoying it. Lovely pics. I've had a rubbish day; someone said our library might be in line to close at the end of the year. So unfair. We are always busy. We are going to start a protest. Ivan is fine, I took him some left over chicken and he snarfed it up as though he was starving. Don't you ever feed him? And then he sat on my lap while I was having a cup of tea. I've never known a cat with such a loud purr. What are you doing tomorrow? Are they organising you all?

I gave a rueful smile, remembering how the four of us had hidden in the gift shop from the official guided walk that afternoon. But also, in those last few hours, how much fun we had shared. I typed out a reply.

MUM

We were supposed to be going on a group tour but instead the four of us (me, Anita, Beryl and her sister Effie) sneaked off and had a lovely walk by the sea (that's when we mistakenly joined a stranger's wedding reception), had lunch in a restaurant (I had a fantastic proper Greek salad) then back to the hotel. There are kittens here!! And Ivan purred and sat on your lap? He's never once done that to me. And yes I do feed him, that cat is a liar. He usually looks at the food I give him and walks away from it. I bought him some new stuff, beef in gravy, he might like that? Sorry to hear about the library. Perhaps you need to write to your MP or get a celebrity to endorse you? Do you know any? Off to the pool on the roof terrace now. Jealous?

\* \* \*

I pulled on a clean blue shirt and made my way upstairs to the roof terrace, where in one corner there was a small pool, an even smaller jacuzzi and, most unexpectedly on the other side of the roof, a bar where Costas was sitting looking gloomy reading a newspaper. Beryl, Anita and Effie were already settled at one of the tables in the shade of an oversized white parasol. It looked idyllic.

I'd been on the mailing list of some Italian garden furniture company, and their catalogue was filled with photographs of wonderfully attractive people on massive lounging beds and lavishly cushioned chairs. I'd spent quite a long time indulging in a fantasy where I had the Sorrento dining experience, with seats for twelve, a cantilevered parasol and matching fire pit. Or perhaps the Ischia daybed, with floating white curtains and the same sublime view over the Bay of Naples which I too would be sharing with a companion who looked like a young Franco Nero. Instead of that I'd made do with some chairs from a discount outlet store and Malcolm's mother's picnic table. Although there had been more than a bit of Nero in Malcolm's character as he aged.

How lovely to have the space and the money for those things, but of course back home in Herefordshire there would have been a continual to-ing and fro-ing with the seat cushions, the elegant, cantilevered parasol would be blown down the end of the garden in minutes and Ivan the Terrible would have made short shrift of the billowing voile drapes.

I went over and swished my hand in the water. It was a bit too cold for my liking.

'Isn't this lovely?' Anita called. 'Just glorious. I wish I had something like this at home. But then the view wouldn't be the same. Or the climate. I tried to get Rick to put in a hot tub after we got back from Rhodes, but we argued about where to put it so much that in the end we didn't get one.'

'I don't think a hot tub would be much fun on one's own,' Beryl said, and she winked. 'Far better to have company and the ensuing entertainment.'

'Beryl! Really!' Anita spluttered.

'Depends on the company,' I said.

'The others aren't back yet then?' Effie said, leaning back in her chair with a happy sigh. 'I wonder what they will be like.'

'Well, we know there's Dennis,' I said, 'and didn't that other man with them look familiar to you?'

'Not particularly,' Beryl said. 'I asked Nina about him. She said he booked a place here ages ago. She doesn't know much about him. She told me she believes he's a history buff. Very keen on the Minoans. Nina and I had such a nice chat. I know all about her bunions and how she wants her son to get married and have a family. He's working as a DJ on Mykonos. Now then, shall we have a coffee? Costas has one of those clever machines behind the bar, and my caffeine levels are running low.'

Anita went off to order some and Effie pushed her chair back a little way, took a cigarette out of a silver case and lit it with a pleased sigh.

'I've cut down a lot,' she said as she saw Anita coming back. 'I tried nicotine patches once and then I had a cigarette as well because I forgot I was wearing them. I didn't half have a headache.'

'That shows you how bad for you they are,' Beryl said, 'although back in the sixties nearly everyone did. We both used to smoke Sobranie cocktail cigarettes which had gold filter tips. Do you remember? And I had an amber cigarette holder just like Princess Margaret's. I don't think I actually inhaled, just waved them around a bit.'

We could suddenly hear the sound of chattering voices from out in the street and the unmistakeable boom of Dennis laughing and shouting at the others.

'Now, come along, ladies, there will be plenty of opportunity to find blister plasters later. Will wants a drink and I for one agree. So, everyone upstairs to the terrace.'

The four of us grinned at each other.

'Incoming,' Beryl murmured.

\* \* \*

A few minutes later, Dennis appeared in the doorway onto the terrace and stopped theatrically when he saw us, causing his companion to bump against the staircase behind him.

'Ah, there you are. Did you not read Jillian's notes? About

the guided walk? Susan printed them out. You missed an absolute treat. This is a fascinating little place. You can ask me anything.'

'Why are you so incredibly noisy all the time?' Beryl whispered under her breath, and I giggled.

Dennis's gaze swivelled on to me.

'Ah! There she is. The new girl. Maggie, isn't it?'

'I don't think I count as new any longer, and I'm Meg,' I said.

'That's what I said. We have had a grand old time, I must say. I'm glad I am as fit as I am. That's what comes of being practically but not exclusively vegetarian and not smoking,' he said, fixing Effie with a stern look.

'I'm so pleased for you,' Effie drawled with a sweet smile, blowing a plume of smoke into the air. 'You look a fine figure of a man.'

Dennis looked confused for a moment and then gave a modest smile.

'Anyone got any blister plasters? Susan here had the wrong shoes on.'

A small white-haired woman went to sit down at the next table with a sigh of relief.

'Please don't fuss, Dennis,' she said. 'I'm fine.'

'Blisters need looking after. I remember a chap in the ATC when I was at school. Blister went septic, almost lost his leg. Now then, let's move these tables together and shift around a few chairs.'

The next few minutes were taken up with introducing everyone to Susan, rearranging the terrace furniture and pulling chairs from other tables while from behind the bar, Costas fixed us with a brooding gaze and rustled his newspaper to convey his disapproval.

'We had a grand old time too,' Anita said, 'and a lovely lunch.'

'I should have come with you,' Dennis said, favouring her with a roguish twinkle.

'Where did you go?' Susan asked. 'We went to a place by the little quayside after our walk. Really nice if you like fish. Which luckily I do. I had the freshest sardines I've ever had.'

'I had a bulgar wheat salad, which is a nutritional power-house,' Dennis said, thumping his broad chest. 'I'm up for anything. Now, where are the other two? I thought they were just behind us. And Will? Where's he got to? I wanted to talk to him about the Minoans.'

Susan gave a shrug.

'Jillian was just sorting out my shower and she needed an aspirin. She's prone to headaches.'

'I have a few plasters in my first aid kit,' I said, leaning towards her. 'Dennis is right, you don't want to leave that blister.'

'Anyone got any ideas for a painting yet?' Anita asked. 'The view from my balcony alone would be ideal.'

'Isn't this place nice?' Susan agreed. 'Not too fussy. I wouldn't have dared come on my own, not abroad or anything, but June said it would be fun. She'll be here in a minute. She's my neighbour. We go to the Begley Moor painting group on a Friday.'

'Ah, here come the stragglers,' Dennis said, turning round in his chair. 'Come along, everyone. We've started without you.'

Another woman in a flowing sundress and cardigan came out onto the roof terrace followed by the tall man. He was quite handsome in a rugged, Mark Harmon sort of way (I'd watched a lot of *NCIS* at this point) and he came to sit down opposite me and gave me a quick look with wonderful blue eyes before he put his sunglasses on.

'Here we are, so now you have met, this is Susan, and this is Will who has come here independent of us all, poor fellow,' Dennis said, 'but we're old friends now, aren't we chaps, so we need to make him welcome. The gang's all here so let the battle of the brushes commence. Shame you missed out on the group walk earlier. I know Jillian was disappointed not to see you there.'

'We just needed a little stroll and some fresh air,' Beryl said.

Dennis shook his head in sorrow. 'Valuable connecting time.'

'I'm not much of a connector, more of a rheostat,' Effie said and gave him a mischievous smile. 'We have plenty of time to connect.'

'Painting, that's what we should be doing,' Susan said. 'I can't wait to get my paints out. Those views are just catnip, aren't they?'

'We've got catnip in our garden,' June said eagerly. 'It's powerful stuff. Sometimes when I go out there, it's like some sort of feline drug den. A lot of yowling and writhing, and that's just me.'

I snorted with laughter and started to giggle, and then everyone joined in.

Will looked over the top of his sunglasses at me and grinned. He was very attractive when he smiled, there was no doubt about it. But why was he so familiar?

4
_____

We sat there for about an hour while the chat flowed between us. Jillian appeared once or twice, looking harassed and slightly panicky. Apparently there were problems with the showers in two bedrooms, and breakfast had been rescheduled for eight o'clock in the morning instead of seven thirty, because Costas had a darts match that evening and was evidently anticipating a late night.

'I don't care either way about the shower dribbling,' Susan said. 'I can always use June's, and if I start to pong, just sit down-wind of me.'

'But it's a basic human right,' Dennis blustered, 'and we were promised proper facilities, it says so in the brochure.'

'Life, liberty and the pursuit of happiness,' June said, finishing her coffee. 'Nothing about water pressure.'

'Well, I wish I had brought my tool bag,' Dennis said. 'I'd have it sorted out in no time.'

'Perhaps it needs a good whack with a mole wrench?' Beryl said. 'You know, I've always thought that sounded a bit cruel. Why would anyone want to wrench a mole?'

'Rick would,' Anita said. 'We had terrible troubles with moles across the lawn last year. He used to go out at night and sit for hours in a deckchair with a torch and a giant pepper mill as a weapon. He never saw a single one.'

'I don't think they were an anti-mole implement, I think they were invented by a Mr Mole,' Will said.

It was unexpected and rather nice to hear him join in the conversation at last, and the thought appealed to me.

'I can imagine him, dressed in a velvet waistcoat and plus fours. Whiskers twitching.'

'Living in some underground office with tree roots across the ceiling,' Will said with a grin.

'Yes, but where are we going tomorrow?' Dennis said irritably. 'I haven't come here to talk about moles, I've come for the painting.'

Susan rummaged in her handbag and pulled out a sheaf of papers.

'It's all in the email she sent us, didn't you print them out?'

'I told you I never print things out,' Dennis said. 'It's a waste of the world's resources.'

'Then it's a good job I did,' Susan said, passing the paperwork across to him. 'Look, the minibus will collect us at nine thirty and take us to a spot along the coast where there is a ruined monastery. There's also a small café and information centre.'

'Have you been here before?' I said, turning my attention back to Will.

'No. Crete and Kos years ago, before it got too busy. I prefer somewhere quieter these days.'

A flicker of some emotion passed across his face, and he picked his sunglasses up from the table and put them back on again.

'I think this is lovely from what I've seen,' I said. 'So quiet and unspoiled. No famous people on yachts moored off the harbour. No huge villas full of celebrities.'

'Not yet,' Beryl said. 'It just takes one Oscar winner or television reality star to spill the beans about it. I can just about remember going to the south of France with our parents in the 1960s. An absolute jewel. Beautiful and stylish with hardly any traffic. Now it's very different.'

'If you'll excuse me, I need to make a phone call,' Will muttered, and he went back downstairs.

I was a bit disappointed to see him go so soon. I would have liked to talk to him some more. Still, there would be plenty of time in the days ahead.

The rest of us chatted quite easily about ourselves, what we liked about painting and what we were hoping to accomplish during our stay, and then Jillian appeared half an hour later, looking rather agitated.

'Where has Will gone now? I thought we could set off for our dinner now we are all together. The table is booked for six thirty.'

'I'll bang on his door as we go past,' I said. 'Where are we going?'

'*If* you had come on my guided walk earlier, you would know,' Jillian said rather waspishly. 'The Blue Sea restaurant, by the harbour. The one with all the Greek flags if you get lost.'

Anita and I exchanged a look.

'Told off,' Effie murmured.

'Will is in number nine. Now, let's get going,' Dennis said, 'or we will be late. And then they will give away our table and we'll have to scrape around for somewhere else with enough room for us all. And that will play havoc with my glucose levels.'

'I don't think he needs to worry,' Beryl said as we went down the stairs, 'it's not exactly high season, is it?'

I paused as we passed Will's room and tapped on the door while the others carried on down to the hallways.

He opened it after a few seconds and stood looking at me rather blankly. He was wearing a clean blue t-shirt and some rumpled shorts, and it looked as though he had been asleep.

'We're off to dinner,' I said. 'Are you coming too?'

'I think I'll give it a miss,' he said, rubbing one hand over his stubbly hair. 'I'm just catching up with a few things.'

*What things? I thought this was supposed to be a holiday?*

'That's a shame. I'm told you know all about the Minoans. Ancient history, that sort of stuff. And I'd love to hear all about it.'

'I know some of it, yes,' he said.

We stood looking at each other for a few seconds until the silence became a bit awkward.

'Do I know you from somewhere? Because you look really familiar.'

He hesitated and then imperceptibly started to close the door.

'I won't keep you. Have a good evening. I'll see you tomorrow.'

Well, my female powers of persuasion evidently needed a new battery. I left him to it and hurried to catch up with the others, who were already halfway down the road.

The thought that I knew him from somewhere nagged at the back of my mind. Had he been a neighbour of ours? Had he been in a boy band perhaps, or had he been a child actor or a disgraced politician? Nothing seemed to fit, and I was usually good at remembering faces.

* * *

When we arrived, The Blue Sea restaurant was empty except for us. And we did have a really pleasant evening. The group seemed to be already splitting into two smaller groups – Dennis, June and Susan had cosied up to Jillian at one end of the table and the four of us were down the other. Jillian evidently had not got over her resentment that we had not gone along on her introductory walk and occasionally sent tight-lipped looks down the table towards us.

'Now, this boat trip to St Joseph's beach,' Anita asked at one point. 'I like the sound of that. Where does that go from, Jillian?'

'Well, of course, and I hate to repeat myself, but *if* you had come on the guided walk this afternoon, you would know,' she called back with another of her frosty smiles. 'At the far end of the harbour. There's a little shed there with a red star painted on the door.'

'Does that mean it's also a Russian safe house?' Beryl chuckled, and Effie roared with laughter and leaned against her.

Jillian paused with a prawn halfway to her mouth and fixed her with a puzzled look.

'Don't mind me, Jillian, I've watched too many James Bond films.'

Jillian gave a heavy sigh. 'The Greeks believe red is associated with change, and of course I am hoping this is what you will all find here. Change for the better.'

'I hope so too,' Dennis said. 'I've been feeling my work is in need of inspiration.'

'And this is exactly the place to find that,' Jillian said with an approving nod in his direction.

'It's very beautiful, I must say,' Susan said. 'I think it's going to make all the difference.'

'As long as you don't just paint flowers and kittens?' Dennis said.

Susan pulled a face. 'There's nothing wrong with kittens—'

'Oooh, there are kittens that sleep on the canopy over my balcony,' I said.

Susan turned in her chair with a delighted smile and started telling me all about her cat who was nineteen and liked to sleep in the vegetable rack.

'Oh for pity's sake,' Dennis said with a sigh.

\* \* \*

I walked happily back through the warm streets to our hotel later that evening, full from my absolutely delicious meal (chicken souvlaki and tzatziki). I was feeling unbelievably positive and unexpectedly happy about the week ahead. Delighted to be here and excited about the prospects of the following day when apparently we would be treated to some wonderful views, a taste of ancient history and time to relax. It all sounded exactly what I wanted, and I began to wonder why on earth I hadn't done something like this sooner. I only hoped my limited artistic ability would improve as the days went on.

Some of the group were obviously taking the experience a lot more seriously than we were and had been earnestly discussing the various shades of blue needed to capture the essence of our Mediterranean dream. The benefits of indigo verses phthalocyanine, whether cerulean had any place here or should it be washed cobalt? I just nodded and looked thoughtful as these discussions went on, wondering if I should hide Nicky's school tin of watercolours from the possibility of scrutiny by Jillian. Perhaps I should have bought something more impressive than an empty Play-Doh pot to hold my water?

Back at Hotel Costas, the four of us decided to go back up to the roof terrace so that we could look at the night sky somewhere without light pollution.

When we got up there, all the lights were on and we couldn't see the stars at all.

Anita waved towards the wall. 'There's a light switch some-where, over there by the bins. I bet if we turn everything off we will see the sky far better. There aren't that many streetlights around here.'

Beryl and I went to look and found a bank of switches in a waterproof covering. We stabbed at a few through the thick plastic until eventually the roof was plunged into darkness. For a moment we all oooed and aahed appreciatively at the starry sky above us, but then there was a shout of outrage and what sounded like some very rude words from the pool area.

Switching the lights back on, we saw Costas in the hot tub, mercifully covered by the bubbles, which had started up again. He was resting back on a plastic cushion smoking a cheroot, a bottle of ouzo and a glass balanced on the edge of the tub.

'Costas! How did the darts match go?' Beryl asked to try to mollify him when it seemed our attempts at an explanation were not going down well.

Costas made a long grumbling noise and said a lot of words, which Beryl couldn't actually translate, but the gist of it was – not good.

'*Éna dýskolo paichnídi*. Such a hard game,' Beryl said sympa-thetically.

'I tried once, missed the board and stabbed myself in the foot,' Effie added.

At last, evidently annoyed at his end-of-day relaxation being disturbed, Costas hauled himself out, revealing two things. Insubstantial swimming trunks that were not up to the task required of them and the possibility that he had werewolf some-where in his ancestry.

The four of us scurried giggling to the other end of the roof terrace and tried to avert our gaze while he towelled down and then wrapped himself in a robe decorated with dolphins. After hearing the roof door slam behind him, we crept out and resumed our stargazing, lying down on some of the sunbeds for a better view of the night sky.

It was breathtaking, better than anything I had ever seen. The stars seemed to go on forever. In a funny way it made me realise exactly how small my problems were, and indeed so was I. If the garage couldn't fit my car in for its MOT next week, then I would just have to cope. I needed to paint my bedroom ceiling now that I had fixed the damp patch, but really it wasn't something to lose sleep over. The stars were here before me and would be here long after I had gone too.

'It's a sign, isn't it?' Effie said, following my gaze towards the glittering constellations above us.

'What? Not to disturb Costas in the hot tub?' I said.

Effie shook her head and chuckled.

'I've never seen a man that – what's the word? – hirsute,' Beryl agreed, and unfortunately at that point there was a great deal of childish giggling.

'I had a lip wax before I came here. It looked like I'd a small badger nestling on my top lip. I hate to think what it would entail if Costas... Do you think Nina has to comb him out?' Anita asked.

'Stop it,' I said, putting a hand to my throat to stop laughing, 'it's supposed to be very manly.'

'I think we need to go to bed,' Anita said, 'and prepare for the morning. Breakfast is at eight, and then we are off to the ruined monastery. Perhaps a few hours actually painting will settle us all down.'

'Good idea,' I said. 'After all, that is why we are here.'

Anita prodded at the light switch again and some of the bulbs around the roof glowed in the darkness.

'Serious, intellectual and creative thoughts, girls,' Beryl said. 'We need to find the higher plane of beauty and artistic endeavour.'

'Oh, I liked him. Endeavour. That actor, Sean someone, he was very watchable,' Effie said, her eyes lighting up, 'and I don't usually like the slim, frail, damaged types. I like a man I can get hold of. I'm a great feeder. I think I must have been a mother bird in a previous life. If I'd had children I would have been like a dear little hummingbird, with jewelled wings. Flitting from flower to flower. They are supposed to be the best bird mothers.'

Beryl gave a snort. 'Rubbish, you would have been a penguin. They leave the fathers in the Antarctic blizzards to incubate the eggs for weeks on their own, and when the mothers come back, they just vomit up a load of fish.'

\* \* \*

We trooped off downstairs again and went to our rooms.

'I'm so looking forward to tomorrow,' I said as Anita and I unlocked our neighbouring doors.

'Me too. I'm going to really focus and get something done which I can be proud of. Rick has already said he will pay to have my best one framed and has earmarked a space in the dining room where he says he's going to hang it. He has such faith in my abilities, which I fear are unfounded. See you in the morning.'

How nice, I thought as I made my way to my room. To have a husband who was encouraging and supportive. I could almost imagine the sneer Malcolm would have given as he struggled to find something positive to say about my paintings. For a moment I was almost envious of Anita, because apart from anything else, she seemed to really like her husband. Which sometimes – when the going got tough in a marriage – was more important than love.

The kittens were sound asleep on my bathmat again and woke when I closed the door, scarpering out onto the balcony in a flurry of paws and startled tails.

It had been a long and enjoyable day, and I was ready for my bed. Tomorrow, as Beryl said, we would get down to some work.

## 5

The following morning, I woke just after seven o'clock to see the beginnings of a beautiful day outside. The sun had risen over the roofs of the little white houses and the sea looked as though it was shimmering in the clear light. How lovely to live in a place where the climate was so reliable. Back home, the British weather was a constant topic of conversation.

Sunny summer days could never be relied on in England. People listened to the forecasts, kept umbrellas in their cars and checked apps on their phones as a matter of course. Here, I suppose it was very different.

I wondered what Greek people talked about instead. Politics perhaps, or their families. Food or the economy. Did Greek women have to hurry home from work because they had left a line full of washing, or worry about the cost of turning the heating on in the winter?

It was already quite a warm day and after I showered, I put on my one strappy sundress with a white blouse underneath it because I was a bit self-conscious about my upper arms, and then after taking a look in the mirror, I changed it for a red t-shirt, because I felt in need of a bit of colour. I wasn't in the mood to be predictable and safe any more. I wanted a bit of excitement.

Following the sound of excited chatter, I went downstairs feeling very much in the holiday mood. The others were already there, sitting at a long wooden table outside in a courtyard, which was probably the most delightful space I had ever been in for breakfast. There were terracotta pots of flowers everywhere, more of the bougainvillea blossoming enthusiastically across the walls, and the house cat and her kittens sitting hopefully on the dry, stone birdbath.

'We just help ourselves,' Beryl called across. 'It's really rather lovely.'

There were all sorts of teabags, urns of coffee and boiling water, cereals and milk, platters of cheese and ham, croissants and pastries and several glass pots of jam. I made a selection and went to sit between Beryl and Anita.

'Sleep well?' Anita asked. 'I was out like a light the minute my head touched the pillow, and I don't think I woke up until Rick messaged me at six, asking which bin needed to go out this week. He knows better than I do. I think it's his way of telling me he's missing me.'

'How romantic,' Effie said from further along the table.

'Rick says they are setting off for Scotland for their bird-watching break just after nine because they can't get into the hotel until three o'clock. He sounded terribly excited. He says there have been sightings of dotterels, Temminck's Stint and bluethroats. There's a loch nearby and they are hoping to see a garganey if they are lucky. I don't think he will miss me one bit in the face of all that excitement.'

I shook my head. 'Nonsense, Anita, you have your own appeal, the sort a garganey – whatever that is – couldn't possibly compete with.'

'True,' Anita said, buttering her croissant. 'I bet a garganey can't make syrup sponge and custard.'

Dennis was sitting at the head of the table with two cups of tea, a bowl of bran flakes and a plate loaded with pastries. He called over to us.

'I hope we will all be ready on time; the bus will be here to collect us promptly so don't be late. And don't forget all your painting things, and Jillian says a sunhat and bottles of water are essential. It's going to be a hot day. We don't want any of you ladies fainting.'

'You'll pick me up off the ground if I do, won't you, Dennis?' Anita said with a coy look.

Dennis looked flustered. 'I'd love to, but not with my dodgy ankle, I'm afraid. I fell down the stairs in Rackhams in 1980 and I've not been the same since.'

'Staircases can be so dangerous.' Beryl nodded. She looked wistful for a moment. 'I fell down the stairs at the White House in the early eighties. My heel got tangled up in my dress. Luckily there was a Marine there who caught me. He had the most savage haircut and muscles like iron bars. It was marvellous and almost worth doing again.'

'I shall paint like a demon today,' Dennis continued, flexing his fingers over his bran flakes like a concert pianist. 'I can almost feel the inspiration returning. Which means, I warn you now, I probably won't be very communicative. I get into a sort of artistic mindset when I forget everything, even mealtimes. My wife Sally says she loves to see me like that.'

'I bet she does,' Effie murmured.

Jillian came in, still holding her usual clipboard, and she ticked off a few things with a pencil, looking around and frowning.

'Will,' she said, 'where is he? Ah, there you are. I was wondering if you had overslept.'

Will came into the courtyard, made for the coffee machine and then came to sit opposite me.

'Not a bit of it, I was up at four thirty and went for a walk. There was a marvellous sunrise. The fishing boats were going out.'

Jillian ticked something else off.

'Wonderful, wonderful. Now then, nine o'clock, everyone. There is a lovely day ahead. Plenty of superb views and inspiration by the shedload. You absolutely *must* be by the front door with all your things.'

'What happens if we are a few minutes late, I wonder,' I said.

'Costas comes out and chucks a bucket of water over you,' Will said, and we grinned at each other.

'I'm looking forward to this,' I said. 'I've never seen so many gorgeous views in one place.'

'Greek islands are like that,' he agreed. 'They all seem so idyllic. But then so is Italy; the view over the Italian Lakes is breathtaking. Like something out of a film set. Have you ever been?'

'Never,' I said, 'but I'd love to if it's that good.'

'Then there is the Grand Canyon, the Norwegian Fjords, and even tourism can't spoil how mind-blowing the Niagara Falls are.'

'I need to go,' I said. 'I haven't travelled nearly as much as I would like to. But where should I go after this? Any advice?'

'The Rockies are wonderful. Not just because they go on forever, but the thought of people finding a route through them, building a railway, it's almost impossible to imagine. And the country is so young there are photographs of them doing it.'

I chewed on my croissant thoughtfully, trying to imagine myself seeing those things. Wondering how much it would cost; how would I deal with those sorts of adventures on my own?

Spending time on my own. I envied Beryl and Effie for having each other to travel with.

For a moment I could almost see myself sitting in the observation deck of the Rocky Mountaineer train, sipping a cocktail as I passed snow-covered mountain ranges and dizzying gorges. Would it matter that I was a solo traveller? Probably not actually, because by then I would be newly confident; I would have lost a stone and discovered a new sense of style which, up to then, had evaded me. But wouldn't it be more fun to share the experience with someone? Wasn't that the whole point?

And yet Malcolm had been my companion for so many years and never seemed impressed by much; in fact, he had been able to suck the joy out of many things by the time we divorced. Meals were never as good as he had hoped, holidays never as enjoyable, celebrations never really satisfactory.

But then I had a blinding realisation. If it was just me on my own, I could do what I liked and none of that would matter. I could go where I wanted and no longer feel as though I was responsible for someone else's experience. This was a new idea for me, and I sat considering it while around me, people chattered, drank coffee and ate pastries.

Beryl tapped me on the arm.

'Come on, Meg, time to get going. Today's bad decisions aren't going to make themselves.'

I cleared away my things and followed the others. I felt quite invigorated already. I was almost prepared to get on the next flight to – just about anywhere, really.

\* \* \*

Obedient as schoolchildren – well, 1960s schoolchildren – we were all ready and standing by the doorway at nine fifteen. The minibus was late and didn't arrive until after nine thirty, by which time some of our group had wandered off to the loo or to change their shoes or fill up their water bottles, and Jillian was ticking and crossing things off on her clipboard in quite a frenzy.

The driver – Gregor – was a sturdy-looking type with a black Captain Pugwash beard and he reacted to Jillian's twittering with a sigh and a dismissive wave of one hand.

'Kakí kykloforiakí symfórisi,' he said. 'Bad traffic.'

'A likely tale,' Jillian muttered, herding us all onto the bus after rounding up Susan and June from the hall where they were happily showing each other pictures of their grandchildren.

Gregor fiddled with the air conditioning for a few minutes and then the bus eventually trundled off in a great clashing of gears just before ten o'clock.

I was sitting in the seat behind Will, and I admired his profile a few times when he turned his head to look out of the window. He really was both very attractive and somehow familiar. I ran through the possibilities again in my mind. Was he a reclusive actor who had found and lost fame in the last few years? Or maybe a disgraced cabinet minister who didn't want his involvement with some terrible corruption to be remembered?

We headed through the town and up the hillside away from the sea, the scenery changing from the gardens and hard-won greenery to flinty-looking fields peppered with rocks, the occasional clump of cacti and some scraggy-looking goats.

Above us were high limestone crags and occasionally wire netting to stop boulders from falling onto the road. We went round hairpin bends and across deserted-looking tracks, passing petrol stations and bakeries in the middle of nowhere. There were clusters of little white box houses and a lot of tiny churches.

Sometimes we encountered another vehicle on roads that didn't seem to me to be wide enough for us both to pass. Gregor appeared to cope perfectly well, clashing the gears and forging forwards like a knight preparing for the joust into the most unlikely spaces and muttering under his breath. Words that Beryl said were at best unflattering regarding the other driver's parentage, appearance and intelligence.

Eventually, about forty minutes later, we pulled into a stony car park and Gregor opened the doors with a satisfied grunt.

Outside and away from the air conditioning, which had been unexpectedly aggressive, so much so that Susan had pulled on a cardigan halfway through the trip, the heat was already building and hit us like a wall as we clambered down.

The remains of the deserted monastery were just piles of stones in some places, and a couple of walls remaining in others. There was some welcome shade from a grove of trees which grew courageously in the rocky soil, but in front of us was the most breathtaking view over a little town below and the vast blue of the Mediterranean behind it. We all stood in silence for a few minutes, not quite able to believe what we were seeing.

We retrieved all our painting things and fold up chairs from the boot of the bus and Dennis strode out to pick a spot. Susan and June did the same and before too long, we were all settled in our preferred spaces, all of us mesmerised by the location. Was the sky ever that wonderful, intense shade of blue in Herefordshire? Maybe it was the way the light was reflected off the sea here, or possibly the clearness of the air.

A couple of seabirds wheeled above us before gliding effortlessly away.

I fussed about for a few minutes, wanting to find the spot to settle where I would discover previously unsuspected levels of talent in myself.

Will was obviously doing the same thing, and for a while we strolled around admiring the view of the ruins, the sea beneath us and the fabulous old olive trees which stood, bent and gnarled, casting shade over our group.

'Feeling inspired?' I asked at last.

We stood side by side looking out at the fishing boats far out to sea, and then he gave a sigh.

'I know what I would like to achieve, but I'm not sure I know how,' he said at last.

'Me too,' I said. 'Paintings can sum up so much, can't they? And I have found I remember far more about a place when I paint it than when I just take a photo on my phone. Don't you?'

'Yes, you're right,' he said.

'The trip our group took to Warwick Castle at the beginning of April; it really brought the feel of the place alive for me. This place is even better,' I said, warming to my subject.

Underneath the olive trees there was a crash and a bit of shouting. It seemed Susan had knocked Dennis's collapsible easel over and also spilled her painting water on his shoes. June was dabbing at him with a paint-daubed rag and Dennis was looking furious.

'We could go and help,' I said.

'Or we could stay out of their way and go over to that café and get a coffee or something,' Will said with a nod.

'Excellent,' I said and grinned up at him.

Well goodness me, I wasn't expecting that at all.

Effie was having a cigarette away from the group, but I could see Beryl and Anita watching us edge off, and Anita gave me an enthusiastic thumbs up.

It wasn't so much a café as a shack with a few metal tables and chairs arranged outside under a red and white awning. I sat down, my chair rocking slightly on the uneven ground.

'Greek coffee?' Will asked, and I nodded.

The owner busied himself with a mighty-looking urn and

after much hissing of steam and clattering of china, Will returned with a loaded tray.

'I got some *galaktoboureko* too. I hope you don't mind,' he said, putting a small plate in front of me. 'I've only recently re-discovered them. Filo pastry, vanilla custard and orange syrup.'

'I don't mind at all. What's the worst that can happen?' I laughed, pulling the plate towards me. 'Thank you.'

We sat in companionable silence for a few minutes, enjoying the rich smoky taste of the coffee, which contrasted so well with the sweetness of the pastry. Simple as it sounded, it was one of the most delightful things I'd ever eaten. To do so on the top of a sun-drenched crag overlooking the Mediterranean was an added delight.

And my companion somehow added to the event. I kept sneaking little glances at him, liking what I saw. He had a fine profile, clean jawline and close-cropped grey hair, so perhaps he had been a Marine. Or a secret agent. I could almost imagine him creeping into a deserted warehouse with his gun ready to dispatch the criminals within.

'Isn't this marvellous,' he said, 'exactly what I was hoping for.'

'Beautiful,' I agreed. 'Have you been here before?'

'Not to this island. I've been to some of the others as I told you. This is perfect.'

'It is, isn't it?' I said rather too enthusiastically.

We sipped at our coffee, which was hot and sweet, and I had almost plucked up the courage to ask him about himself when he turned to me.

'So, tell me about yourself. What brings you here, Meg?'

I swallowed my mouthful and wiped the sticky flakes of filo pastry from my mouth with a paper napkin, which unfortunately was one of the one-ply, cheap sort, and bits of it stuck to my chin very unattractively. I peeled them off and tried to look more comfortable than I felt.

'I moved to Lower Begley in January, following my divorce. It was quite traumatic actually because Malcolm – that's my ex-husband – kept hiding things from my solicitor and in the end we had to go to court' – *why did I need to tell him about that? Change the subject* – 'and I tried a few activities, because once I got the house straight, actually I was a bit bored. I quite liked the yoga class, and I'd even bought a mat and the little blocks you can use if you aren't very flexible, but then I got wedged – oh, never mind. Then I saw a notice about this art group in the village hall, which is only a short walk from my house, so terribly convenient. It's on a Tuesday morning, so that worked for me too. I needed something new to do. I was getting stuck in a rut of housework and gardening, you see, neither of which I'm very good at, and as I said, I was on my own too much. I wanted some company; a new hobby, I suppose. It's easy to make friends when one is young. You meet other women at antenatal classes, or toddler groups or at the school gates. At my age it is a bit harder. And Anita – the one over there in the yellow sunhat and the blue dress – she was there too and she turned out to be my neighbour. And she mentioned this trip soon after I joined. Apparently there was a spare place because Gwen was having her garden wall repointed...'

I realised I was rabbiting on and had hardly stopped to draw breath. Was I nervous? And if so, why?

'Anyway, enough about me, tell me about you,' I said at last.

'Nothing much to tell,' he said. 'I'm single, I'm retired, I just needed a break.'

'A break from what?'

'Everything.'

And that was that.

Oh. Well, didn't I feel a fool, going on about my divorce and Gwen's wall and yoga blocks. Although it was true; I had got stuck on the second afternoon when my back seized up, and it had been very embarrassing.

I wanted to change the conversation into a new direction, one where he would open up and tell me about himself and perhaps explain why he looked so familiar, but for some reason I couldn't think of anything sensible to say.

'This is delicious,' I said at last, 'thank you.'

'You're welcome,' he said, and I could tell that the brief moment of warmth between us had chilled. Perhaps because I was so often on my own, I talked too much when I had the chance. I tried a different tack.

'I'm looking forward to the wine-tasting evening,' I said. 'I've heard there are some lovely wines produced here.'

'Yes, that should be good.'

*Hmm.*

I wondered if he was regretting his decision to ask me over with him. What should I have done differently? And then I felt a bit cross. If he wanted to turn uncommunicative, it wasn't my fault. It really didn't matter if he liked me or not. I needed to stop worrying about such things.

'Well, perhaps we should get on with some painting?' I said.

He stood up and waited patiently for me to collect my handbag from under the table and he picked up my flimsy chair, which had fallen over when I stood up, and then we walked back towards the group, who looked as though they were already hard at work.

He paused and I turned to look at him.

'By the way, you've got a bit of paper stuck to your cheek,' he said. 'No, the other side.'

I did too, and hadn't realised. I pulled off a strip of paper napkin and shoved it in my pocket.

'There's a bit more on your chin,' he said.

I pulled out my handkerchief, licked the end of it and scrubbed at my face.

He took my hand and guided it to the right place, where it seemed I had a dollop of something. I was aware of two things: feeling a bit of a fool, but also the pleasant warmth of his hand holding mine. Heaven knew what he thought of me.

Honestly.

## 6

As I got back to my chair, Anita leaned over.

'I say, that was quick work. All the others are very interested that you nabbed him. He's rather gorgeous, isn't he? Nice shoulders.'

I found a wet wipe in my bag and scrubbed at my cheek again, which was still feeling very sticky.

'I haven't nabbed him at all. In fact, I made a bit of a tit of myself,' I hissed back.

Anita stood up and waved discreetly at Beryl and Effie.

'Let's go and pretend to explore the ruins. There's an information board over there,' she added loudly.

The other two stood up and followed us.

'What's going on?' Effie said, her face alight with interest.

'Nothing,' I said, feeling rather annoyed with myself.

'Something must be,' Beryl said. 'You were away for ages. Do tell.'

'Nothing. He bought me some coffee and a *galackto* something.'

'And then?' Effie said encouragingly.

'Then nothing.'

'That's boring, make something up,' Beryl said, 'just to satisfy us.'

'I droned on about my divorce and he clammed up,' I sighed.

'I thought men liked hearing about how other men behaved badly,' Effie said. 'It makes them feel superior. One day I must tell you about Francis. We were mere acquaintances for years, and then one day I told him about Rupert and what he did at Glyndebourne with the colonel's wife. Francis was absolutely thrilled and became a bit of a nuisance. Did I tell you, Beryl?'

'Many times,' Beryl said, 'and it was years ago. This fledgling holiday romance is much more interesting.'

'It's nothing of the sort,' I said, feeling myself blush. 'Now, tell me about this monastery which, after all, is what we are supposed to be doing.'

'You are a spoilsport,' Beryl said. 'It says on this noticeboard that it was built in the eleventh century and dedicated to Saint Nikolaos, the patron saint of fishermen and sailors. He gave gifts to children; I think that's the same saint who became Santa Claus. I like the thought of that. The monastery fell down after an earthquake in the twelfth century, was rebuilt and then abandoned. So not much else I can tell you.'

'It's very nice though,' Effie said, 'as ruins go.'

'If we brought our stuff over here we could paint this,' Anita suggested. 'It's very atmospheric.'

On the way back we passed the café and it took about five seconds for the other three to decide they wanted some refreshments. I didn't actually need anything after the first snack I had only recently enjoyed, but the others insisted I should try something, and so I gave in.

We sat down at another of the rickety tables and Beryl ordered for us in fluent Greek, which made us wonder what was coming. This time it was icy lemonade in tall glasses and four little cubes of baklava, which glistened stickily in the sunshine.

'I wonder how the others are getting on?' I said, my teeth a bit clogged with yet more filo pastry, walnuts and cinnamon. After the last time when I had apparently splattered food over my face, I would have to check my teeth for nuts this time.

Beryl straightened her yellow sunhat over her forehead.

'When I left, Dennis was waxing lyrical about his painting and said it was going to be the best thing he had ever done. But then he says that about everything. Remember that bowl of fruit he did last October? He said he was going to make it into Christmas cards and then his wife told him she had already bought some from the Cat's Protection League. He sulked for weeks.'

I gave a happy sigh as the laughter died down.

'This is exactly what I was hoping for. A nice hotel, sunshine, some new friends and a few laughs. I'd be crossing it off my bucket list if I had one.'

'I have a bucket list, I thought everyone did?' Effie said, sipping her lemonade. 'I've nearly finished mine. I just need a date with Colin Firth, to find a Vivienne Westwood original in a charity shop and a comfortable bra.'

'One and two are possible, three not so much,' I said.

Anita nodded. 'Isn't it ridiculous? That with all the technology and knowledge available, if you have any sort of bosom, bras still feel like straightjackets. I have a theory that at about seven thirty every evening there is a collective sigh around the nation as women remove them. My bucket list includes seeing the pyramids, crossing the Atlantic on a ship and having tea at the Ritz. Preferably with George Clooney. And I'd like to have a treehouse, with a ladder I could pull up so when Rick wants me to help with the weeding, he can't get me. And I'd like to go to a ball, a proper one with me in a big flouncy gown and proper dancing, which of course I can't actually do apart from square dancing and I don't think the Cumberland square eight comes up very often. You must have some things you'd like to do before you croak it, Meg?'

Effie stood up, brushed a shower of pastry off her sundress and wandered off to look at the view again.

I thought about it. I hadn't travelled much, and the places I had mentioned over the years that might be nice to visit, Malcolm had put the damper on. I had no need for designer clothes or handbags, and I didn't really appreciate Michelin-star meals.

'I wish I could surf,' I said at last. 'I used to when I was a child with one of those thin, wooden body boards with the curved end that nearly cut your feet off at the ankles if they hit you. But I mean the proper big-wave surfers you see on YouTube. Sliding down the waves at Bondi or St Nazaire. It never fails to amaze me how they do it, and how brave they are, with that huge thundering wall of water behind them. But perhaps more realistically I'd like to travel more. Go to Australia and watch the surfers there perhaps, or to Monument Valley to see if it's as impressive as everyone says. And I'd like to go on the Orient Express to Venice, but every time I look at the website I nearly faint at the cost. What about you, Beryl? You haven't said what's on your bucket list.'

Beryl pulled a face. 'Actually, I have an un-bucket list. Things I have done that I will never do again. It makes much more sense to me. Like getting married, drinking anyone's home-made chilli vodka, bungee jumping, ice skating – I did it once and fell over nineteen times in thirty minutes. The only good thing about it was the hot chocolate at the end. Then I'll never wear boots on a long-haul flight again; after ten hours, I couldn't get them back on. And that fish spa thing, where thousands of fish nibble the dead skin off your feet. I spent the whole time screaming and trying not to throw up. I could go on. Oooh, and sleeper trains. I always thought they would be so much fun but having been on one, I now know they are noisy, rackety and everything that can fall off a shelf will do so, but not until after midnight. My adaptor plug fell out of the socket and hit me on the head. And the one I was on went really slowly through built-up areas in Hungary and then packs of stray dogs chased after it barking fit to burst.'

'You always were such a drama queen. Look there,' Effie said, pointing at the sea and sounding rather excited. 'You could try that here.'

We all went to look. A speedboat was skimming across the sea, towing behind a young woman on water-skis. We watched in silence for a few minutes, admiring her slim figure in a red swimsuit, the way she swooped and turned behind the wake of the boat, her long hair flying out behind her.

'Wow,' I breathed, 'fancy being able to do that.'

'Not these days, not with my joints the way they are,' Beryl said, 'I'd probably dislocate both arms when the boat took off.'

'I'd just be dragged off my feet and faceplant into the water,' Anita said. 'I've seen those videos on Facebook.'

As we watched, another speedboat appeared, pulling behind someone in a giant inner tube which was bouncing and leaping across the water behind the boat.

'But we could do that?' I said, liking the idea. 'All you have to do then is hang on to the handles. That can't be difficult, can it?'

We discussed this for a few minutes. The only one of us who had ever tried anything like it was Effie, who had been on a four-person banana boat.

'I only lasted thirty seconds and then the speedboat took a

sudden turn and I fell off,' she said. 'It was fun. But I'm not sure I want to do it again.'

'Of course you could do that,' Beryl said, rummaging in her handbag and pulling out one of the many leaflets she had collected from the tourist information office. 'It's called ringos. Looks like they do two behind the same boat. Not me, obviously, I'll hold the bags and coats.'

'And I will watch and cheer,' Anita said, 'and take photos.'

'I'm going off the idea now, if I have to go on my own,' I said, pulling a face.

'Oh all right, I'll come with you,' Effie sighed.

Beryl frowned. 'Are you sure that's a good idea?'

'Of course it is. Then I can put it on my bucket list and cross it off,' Effie said.

'I don't think that's how it works,' Anita said doubtfully.

'Perhaps I'll think about it and do it another day,' I said.

Beryl wagged a finger at me. 'Nonsense. Now you've said it, and you have the chance, we have to organise it immediately. Otherwise, it would be very unlucky. And you might never get another opportunity. I went water skiing in the south of France when I was younger. You'll love it.'

'Will I?' I said, my initial enthusiasm dimming slightly.

'Only one way to find out,' Anita said.

'What are the others doing? Haven't we got this afternoon as free time?' Effie said.

I looked at my watch. 'Good grief, it's nearly quarter to one and the bus leaves at one o'clock. I haven't done a thing other than have drinks, gossip, eat cake and look at the view.'

'That sounds like a pretty good way to spend the morning to me,' Anita said. 'Like I said, we're not at school. We aren't going to get a detention for not doing our work, are we? There's always tomorrow.'

'Exactly,' Beryl agreed, 'and now we are getting a feel for the place, I'm sure it will imbue our work—'

'Imbue? You're getting posh in your old age,' Effie snorted.

'—with more confidence, and knowledge.'

'I have an increased knowledge of cake,' I said, licking my teeth to check I didn't have any fragments of walnuts stuck in my smile.

'A valuable life skill,' Anita said approvingly.

Beryl stood up and picked up her bag, and I looked around and wondered where Will had got to. I spotted him in the end, sitting underneath a tree with his bag, like mine, still unpacked. So he hadn't done any painting either. Perhaps he was deep in thought, planning a way to get away from us. No, why would he be thinking that? We were perfectly nice people, and there weren't that many of us. Surely a man of his age could cope?

'We need to pack up, get on the bus back to the hotel and get our things. Then we can have lunch first. Meg and Effie, I suggest you put your swimming costumes on under a sundress so you don't have to think about it and chicken out, and then we can walk down to the harbour and find a place that does ringos. This is very exciting indeed. I've never helped someone do something on their bucket list before.'

'Two hours ago I didn't have one,' I said rather weakly.

'Well, now you do,' Anita said. 'I don't think I've been this excited since Rick cleaned out the gutters and found three tennis balls, a rubber snake and a TV remote.'

## 7

I was beginning to realise that as a foursome we were going to spend a lot of time chatting, eating and drinking, and possibly not actually painting, which was what I had expected.

Still, I was definitely enjoying myself, and as we clambered up onto the minibus to go back to the hotel, I felt really happy with life.

The others in the group wondered what we had been doing and when Dennis heard that none of us had so much as dampened a paintbrush, he spent a lot of time telling us how well he had got on and how marvellous the light had been over the bay. He even held out his sketch book to show us some of his preliminary drawings, and next to him, Jillian beamed at her most enthusiastic student.

'Such a shame you wasted the opportunity,' she sighed when the four of us – sitting at the back of the minibus like naughty children on a school trip – admitted to making no progress on our artistic journey. 'After all, it's like anything else in life; the more you do it, the better you get.'

'That's what my first husband used to say,' Beryl said.

'I hope no one tells Rick that,' Anita murmured.

'It wasn't true anyway,' Beryl said. 'Charles had the seduction skills of a hippopotamus. But I didn't realise it for ages. Not until – well, never mind.'

The four of us giggled like schoolgirls and Jillian turned in her seat, sighed again and sent us one of her hard looks.

The minibus made its way back down the winding road to the town, where the streets were busier with tourists and traffic. As we drove along the seafront, we spotted a painted sign at the edge of the harbour which even had a picture of someone being towed on a ringo behind a boat and laughing and waving at the same time.

'We'll go there after a late lunch,' Effie said, 'and hope there isn't a queue.'

'Do we need lunch? I'm not really hungry after all that cake,' I said.

I had a horrible image of myself on a rubber ringo, far out across the blue sea behind a boat which was going somewhere near the speed limit, and me throwing up at the same time. It didn't bear thinking about and I began to regret my decision to do this even more.

'Oooh yes, you have to keep your strength up so you can hang on and not get thrown into the boat's propellers,' Effie said.

'Does that happen? I hadn't thought of that,' I said, panicking.

Effie patted my hand encouragingly. 'No, probably not, but it's the first thing I thought of. Now then, we're back. We'll go and get changed and then meet up in reception in ten minutes. Oooh, I'm quite excited. I hope my ringo doesn't tip over, I've heard that happens.'

'Tip over?' I said weakly.

'You're such a worrier. It'll be fine, you'll be wearing a life jacket so you won't sink,' Beryl said, 'and before you set off I'll make sure the driver has a kill switch, to stop the boat if he can't, and then it doesn't run you over by mistake.'

'*What?*'

'Stop it, Beryl,' Anita giggled, 'I bet that hardly ever happens.'

'Once would be enough,' I said, now visualising myself stranded far out to sea, bobbing like a cork on the water in my life jacket and watching the prow of an out-of-control speedboat hurtling towards my head. What should I do if that happened? Dive under the water? Swim out of the way?

What was the geometry involved in that particular triangle?

1) The speedboat 2) me 3) a place of safety.

How hard and fast would I have to swim? And in what direction?

I felt quite sick for a moment.

'Don't listen to them, they are just being silly. It'll be fine. I'll be there too, I'll look after you,' Effie said kindly.

'Are you a good swimmer?' I shouted down the stairwell as I reached my room and fumbled for my keys.

'No, never got past doggy paddle in the shallow end with one foot on the floor,' she shouted back happily. 'See you in ten minutes.'

* * *

We didn't see anyone else around in the hotel. There was only the faint sound of a radio playing some unfamiliar music from behind the reception desk. But no sign of Costas or Nina. Perhaps they were having a siesta. But siesta was a Spanish word, wasn't it? I wondered what the Greeks called it.

'*Messimeri,*' Beryl said when I asked her a few minutes later as we walked back towards the harbour. 'It used to be between two and five o'clock, but these days not many people do that. Not if they want to earn a living with a country full of tourists. And these days the Greeks have long working hours.'

'I love a nap in the afternoon,' Effie said, 'but I don't call them that. I think of them as deliberate life-pauses. Actually, I sometimes do doze off in front of *Antiques Roadshow*. It's so soothing, and everyone is so happy and smiling all the time. Except for that one time when the person thought the painting they bought for five hundred quid at a car boot sale was a Paul Gaugin and it turned out to be by Paul Goggin, who was a local plumber. And the morning chat shows are awful. Every single person is angry and shouting over each other. And the presenters are far more interested in voicing their opinions than listening to other people's. You said something about a late lunch, how about this place?'

We went into a little wine bar which had a few tables set out under a pergola and a bar with some barstools behind it.

'I'm not sure I want anything,' I said. 'I'm really nervous.'

'Better to have something rather than be retching on an empty stomach,' Beryl said. 'That's what my mother always told me.'

'She did, didn't she?' Effie said, delighted. 'She used to make us eat sandwiches all the way to Cornwall when we were kids. I can still taste that sardine and tomato paste now if I think about it.'

With this worrying advice echoing in my brain, I had some taramasalata, pita bread and a glass of water. It did strike me halfway through that although it was delicious, it wasn't the wisest thing to choose. The fishy taste did nothing to calm my uneasy stomach.

Effie seemed not to share my feelings and was tucking in to some dolmades and a glass of wine while the other two shared a platter of Greek snacks.

I looked out at the sea and took a deep breath. It was as Beryl had remarked – half an hour of my life and that was all. And if I didn't enjoy it, I never needed to do it again.

We paid the bill and carried on down to the harbour.

'Now then, this is the place, isn't it? *I say*, the chap in charge is rather lovely, isn't he?' Effie said, stopping suddenly so that we almost cannoned into her.

The man who was hiring out the ringos, the speedboat and my imminent imagined demise was a young Greek god called Tassos, who looked like he had muscles on his muscles. He spoke excellent English and wore white swimming trunks and a t-shirt which was sun and salt bleached but still bore the logo *Do not wash, this is my lucky t-shirt*, which in a way was mildly comforting. This was topped off with a baseball cap worn backwards which said *Don't worry, be happy. High chance of sunburn*. I grabbed the tube of sunblock and reapplied another layer.

Beryl dealt with all the paperwork and I handed over some euros.

'I think I'm well outside my comfort zone,' I said, tugging at the orange life jacket which was threatening to throttle me.

'I like to think outside one's comfort zone, a lot of very exciting things are happening. I wouldn't have climbed Kilimanjaro, gone along the Wall in China or tried wing walking if I'd thought like that. Now then, do either of you know your blood group?' Beryl murmured, holding up the biro with an enquiring look. And then she smiled. 'Only joking. Have fun. And don't forget to wave.'

'If you do wave, you're bound to fall off, in my limited experience anyway,' Effie said as we clambered into the boat and then sped away towards the open sea.

After a few minutes, Tassos stopped and encouraged us over the side and into the inflatables, which were being towed behind the boat on reassuringly strong-looking ropes. It all felt very silly to be leaving the relative security of a boat and getting into a rubber donut, and the whole procedure was accompanied by a lot of shrieking and yelping from us.

'Will be fine, absolutely safe,' he said with a grin as he tightened the straps on my life jacket, 'a lot of fun. Hold on tight, two handles, two hands.'

Effie and I sat, bobbing about in adjacent ringos, floating gently away from the back of the boat. I noticed Effie for all her bravado was clinging to the rubber handles with white knuckles and I did the same, waiting for the moment when the boat would start up.

Tassos gave us a cheery wave and a thumbs up and the boat started to move. Slowly at first and then faster until Effie and I started screaming in harmony as we sped across the blue sea.

When the water was smooth it was almost fun, but when the ringos slid across the wake of the boat, we started to bump about. At one point my craft started to fill with water from the spray, but then it gave an almighty leap across a wave and all the water slopped out into my face. I fell back and my legs flew up into the air over my head and it seemed I was going to completely part company with the boat.

I clung on to the handles, wondering for a moment if it was possible to yank them out altogether, in which case my inflatable would undoubtedly sink and I would be dragged on my face behind the boat on a flapping rubber disaster.

The noise of the boat engine, the rush of the sea, Effie's whooping and my own screaming effectively drowned out everything. My wet hair was in my eyes and the bottom of my swimming costume seemed to be attached to a pressure washer, which was very uncomfortable.

Why had this been on my bucket list? I might just as well

have opened all my windows and let everyone hurl buckets of cold water over me. Or walked into a car wash.

I looked over at Effie, who was making sort of howling noises, her head thrown back, and I realised she was enjoying herself. Outside my comfort zone, what had Beryl said? And suddenly I started to enjoy myself too.

All the same it was terrifying to start with. Wet, cold and noisy but exhilarating. The speed, the blueness of the sea and the brightness of the sun overhead, and I wasn't sitting in a deckchair sipping a cold drink; I was actually doing something extremely foolish. Something that surely only kids and teenagers would want to do.

It felt marvellous, and then I threw back my head too and gave Effie an echoing howl, and just for a second she turned to look at me and we grinned at each other. Seconds later, our ringos collided and we bumped off each other like some crazy, very wet dodgem cars. And I laughed as I hadn't done for many years, even when a load of seawater slapped me in the face. It just seemed the most astonishing thing I had ever done.

Perhaps this had been a good idea after all?

* * *

We got back to the harbour at a much slower and more acceptable speed, where we found Beryl and Anita waiting for us and cheering.

'You were marvellous,' Anita said. 'I don't know how you hung on when your ringo actually took off.'

'Did it?' I gasped as I dragged myself up onto dry land again. 'I don't think I realised that.'

'Oh yes, we saw it, clear daylight underneath you,' Beryl said cheerfully. 'I'm glad it wasn't me.'

'I think we deserve a drink after that,' Effie said as she hauled herself out of the boat. 'I feel as though I've been through a spin cycle in my washing machine. I'm not sure I will ever get all the water out of my ears, not to mention sundry other places.'

'Good fun, ladies. Yes?' Tassos called up at us. 'Very good fun, you enjoyed it, I know.'

He was coiling up one of the towing ropes as he spoke, obviously getting ready for his next customers, a dad and his teenage son.

'They could hear you screaming from here,' Anita said, 'but it doesn't seem to have put them off.'

I gave Tassos a little wave as we walked away.

'Thanks, Tassos, that was great fun,' I called, and I meant it.

\* \* \*

'In England we would have a reviving brandy,' Anita said, 'so let's have Metaxa.'

'Why do you need reviving?' I asked. 'You didn't do anything.'

'In support for your achievement,' she said with a grin.

We returned to the little bar and pulled ourselves up onto the barstools. Four small glasses of amber liquid were placed in front of us along with a dish of salted almonds.

'We didn't order those, did we?' Anita asked.

'They're complimentary,' Effie said.

'Oooh, you do look nice today,' I said, and the others groaned at the old pun.

Generally, brandy wasn't a drink I liked, but somehow in the warmth of a Greek afternoon and in the company of my friends, the Metaxa was delicious. It tasted of honey and spice and sunshine. Something else I had discovered; life really was full of surprises.

'You know we should be painting, don't you,' I said at last. 'None of us have done anything.'

'Dennis has,' Anita said. 'I heard him saying he had finished two paintings and several sketches. He will compensate for our sloppy ways.'

'Tomorrow,' Beryl said, 'we will set to tomorrow. I'd quite like to do a painting of the hotel. It's very picturesque.'

'As long as you put Costas and Nina in the picture too,' Effie said.

'And the kittens on my balcony.'

'They never come on to mine,' Anita said, pouting.

'Meg stole a slice of ham from the breakfast buffet for them. I saw her do it, so why would they bother coming to see you?' Effie said.

'Did you?' Beryl said. 'I bet they think all their birthdays have come at once.'

I decided to change the subject. 'I was looking at Costas this morning over breakfast. He really is quite lupine. All that hair.'

'Lots of testosterone,' Anita said, 'that's supposed to be what it means. Although Rick isn't at all hairy and I've got no complaints. Well, maybe a few but they are nothing to do with his level of chest hair. Gosh, I do miss him. I didn't think I would, but I do. I hope he's seeing lots of rare birds up in Scotland, that will really make him happy.'

'How long have you been married?' I asked.

'Thirty-seven years. I would have got less for murder.'

'And what about you two?' I asked Beryl and Effie, who were bickering gently about whether to have another round of Metaxa.

Effie chuckled. 'Oh, neither of us are married now. We've had several goes at that, haven't we, Beryl? I've had sandwiches I've enjoyed for longer than some of my relationships.'

Beryl huffed a bit. 'I remember when my second husband

introduced me at a party as a "domestic housewife", and I remember wondering if that meant there was such a thing as a "feral housewife" and if there were, that's what I was going to aim for. Anyway, after three attempts, I'm certainly not doing that again. Can you imagine us on Tinder or whatever it is people do these days to hook up?'

'Holidays are the place to find someone,' Anita said. 'My friend Kim met a really nice man in Mallorca on Juliette's hen holiday. That was a real gathering of the Old Ducks. There was a stag group in the villa next door to theirs and Vince was a friend of the groom. That looked such a gorgeous place. And so romantic. Kim met Vince and I didn't take to him at first when I met him. He was always going on about purple swamp hens and tits – the feathered kind, but then I realised what a nice man he was. And Juliette's cousin Denny – it was the strangest thing. She knew another of the stags from years before, and they have been together ever since. I think there is some sort of magic when one or more Old Ducks are gathered together. We will have to make sure you and Will don't break the run of luck.'

'Don't be daft,' I said, 'I don't think he is the slightest bit interested in me.'

'We'll see,' Anita said, and she gave a little smile. 'I think you're wrong. Anyway, that's your mission – should you decide to accept it, and let's be fair, you've got to because now we all want to find out more about him. All I know is he is an expert in ancient history and he wears sunglasses all the time. And quite often a Panama hat.'

'Like a celebrity, trying not to be spotted.' Effie nodded.

'He does look a bit familiar, don't you think?' I said, suddenly eager to talk about him.

'Perhaps he's been on television, talking about Vesuvius. I've seen a lot of programmes about Pompeii recently. Perhaps he's an expert on pyroclastic surges?' Beryl said.

'That sounds rude.' Effie giggled. 'He's very handsome. If I hadn't taken the vow of celibacy I might have some surges of my own in his direction.'

'Effie!' Anita spluttered.

'I'm old, not dead,' Effie said. 'There's nothing wrong with finding a good-looking man attractive. I may not have had much luck but there are plenty of fish in the sea, but then there are a lot of plastic bottles too, so you have to be selective. Now then, one more of this lovely Metaxa for the road, and then let's go back to the hotel. This swimming costume under my clothes is a bit restricting and damp. And if I want to go to the loo I'll have to strip off completely.'

'Agreed,' I said, wriggling in my seat.

And so, we sat there for another half an hour while the sun dipped low towards the sea, and once more I thought how happy I was to be there, swinging my legs on the bar stool, doing nothing particular. But then I realised, perhaps that was what friendship was all about, enjoying doing something with people or doing nothing, it didn't make any difference. It was the sharing of the experience that was important. The fun to be had in so many small ways which was somehow magnified when other like-minded people did it with you.

Laughter, new horizons, friendly encouragement and fun all mattered so much. I began to see how I had been cutting myself off from all that in the last few years, because I had lost confidence in myself. I might have declared that my divorce was a relief, that I didn't care very much, but I had to admit, it had affected me. Perhaps it was time to realise that there was life after divorce. It might be different and sometimes perplexing, but perhaps I needed to change the way I approached things. A challenge was also an opportunity after all.

I thought about Will for a moment, and yes, I did find him attractive, and more than that, interesting. There was something about him. I wanted to discover why, unlike everyone else in the group, he was so reticent; why, just as I had over the last few years, he kept himself to himself. He didn't seem ready to interact with the group with any enthusiasm, and yet I recognised something of myself in his shyness. I felt quite excited as we reached the hotel and I saw him through the doors to the inner courtyard, sitting on his own, his laptop open on the table in front of him.

'I'll be up in a minute,' I said, and I made a beeline for him, ignoring the chuckles from my three companions as I did so.

'Had a good day?' I said.

He looked up, slightly startled.

'Pretty good,' he said, 'you?'

'Effie and I have been ringo-ing. You know, sitting on a rubber ring behind a speedboat. I didn't think I would like it much, but I did.'

He smiled. 'Sounds like you had fun.'

'It was. You should try it. Knock it off your bucket list.'

'It's not actually on my bucket list.'

Feeling slightly emboldened, I pulled out the chair next to him and sat down.

'No, it wasn't on mine either, but – well, I ended up doing it anyway. What have you been up to?'

'Working,' he said as he closed his laptop and put his sunglasses on. Again.

Which was a shame in my opinion, because he had beautiful eyes. Closeup they were a wonderful blue flecked with green.

I think he realised that I had been trying to see what he had been doing, which was very nosey of me, but I couldn't help it.

There seemed to be a great many closely typed words and a spreadsheet with a lot of coloured squares.

'That's not on at all,' I said. 'I thought you said you were retired. You're supposed to be on a painting holiday.'

He gave a little laugh. 'Well, so are you!'

I sighed. 'I know, and I haven't done a thing yet. I should be ashamed.'

'And are you?'

'No. Not even a tiny bit. I'm having fun instead,' I said.

'That sounds great.'

He looked a bit sad then and I wondered if perhaps he needed the support and company of a friendly face, just as I had. I didn't think he would have much in common with Dennis, after all.

'You should come with us. We have a lot of laughs,' I said encouragingly.

He shook his head. 'I'm afraid I would be a bit of a spare wheel. I don't think I'm very good company at the moment.'

'I'm looking forward to the trip to see the Minoan excavation site one day this week. I'm told you know a lot about it. I'd really love to hear all about it.'

He looked doubtful. 'Would you? It's very dry stuff, some of it.'

'I would,' I said firmly, and he smiled at me, and for a few seconds we just sat looking at each other, and I swear the air between us fizzed with something.

Still, talking of things being dry, I was again aware that my damp swimming costume was riding up into places I'd rather it didn't. I really did need to go and get changed.

## 8

I'd only been in my room for a few moments when Anita tapped on the door and came in.

'What happened? What did he say?' she said.

'Nothing much,' I said. 'I asked him about the Minoans and he said it was pretty dry stuff. And he wasn't very good company at the moment.'

'I bet he is,' Anita replied. 'A man doesn't look like that and not enjoy life, surely? Perhaps he has just split up with his wife, and they have been through a terrible divorce. And she got the house, the children *and* the chihuahua. And he has come here to recover his peace of mind and plan the future away from the terrible rattle of the letterbox and more solicitors' letters.'

'He didn't say anything about that. Just that he understood things could be difficult,' I said, chuckling.

'Absolutely. He is probably a man battered by life, looking for tranquillity, and he has taken one look at you and seen you for the very woman he needs to restore his self-esteem and peace of mind.'

'I've never heard such nonsense,' I said. 'I think he really does want to be left alone.'

'In which case, what is he doing here?'

'I don't know, Anita!'

'You must find out, and we are only here for a few more days so there is no time to waste.'

'You ask him then.'

'Oh no, you are the one he wants to talk to.'

'Go away and let me get changed, this swimming costume is cutting off my blood supply. And I have sand in very inconvenient places.'

'Fair enough. Okay, I'll see you on the roof terrace later. I need to send Rick some pictures and let him know how we are getting on.'

Back in my room, I stripped off and showered and I thought about what she had said.

There were moments when Will actually did seem to want to talk to me. The trouble was he didn't seem keen on talking about himself, and that rather spoiled the flow of conversation.

Perhaps she was right and he was dealing with some terrible marital trauma, or maybe he was ill, or damaged in some way. It was very intriguing. And after all, after this week I would probably not see him again. He wasn't a member of the Lower Begley art class; he had come here independently. In fact, just like me, there was no evidence he painted at all.

I'd been married to Malcolm for so many years, and he had been a man who absolutely loved talking about himself. After nearly forty years there wasn't a thing I didn't know about his allergies (vanilla, cheap olive oil and kiwi fruit), his preferences (sheets and blankets, not duvets, and a hideously expensive duck down pillow), his special leather chair in the sitting room that no one else was allowed to sit in, incompetent colleagues (many) and his opinions on politics. Will was the other side of the coin, a man who didn't want to share the most basic information. So why in that case did I feel as though I knew him? It was very odd and increasingly interesting. Especially to an inquisitive person like me.

Up on the roof terrace, the daylight was fading and there were the beginnings of a beautiful, warm evening. The sky above us was a delicious violet with the first stars winking over the dark sea.

Effie was leaning over the balustrade and smoking; Susan and June were sitting at a table chatting, and next to them Dennis was rummaging importantly through his sketch book, peering at the pages in the glow from the terrace lights.

'I think I really got the sea right in this one, don't you?' he said, and June nodded and made appreciative noises.

'Tomorrow I'm going to really capture the spirit of this place,' he continued. 'I'm going to immerse myself in the local culture and splurge everything out on the paper.'

I wondered for a moment what this event would look like.

'Marvellous,' Susan said.

'How's your blister?' I asked.

Susan smiled happily. 'Oh, fine. Will asked how I was getting on and he had a lovely first aid kit, some special plasters and some antiseptic spray, and it seems to be healing up really well. But he says I need to be careful; at my age I don't heal so quickly.'

'Old age doesn't come easily,' Dennis said mournfully. 'The things we took for granted when we were young are different now. I've heard it said...'

He started on a long monologue about his ankle injury, his cholesterol levels and blood pressure and how his wife suffered from migraines, until I realised it wasn't just me; no one was actually listening any more.

June had pulled out some work from her knitting bag and her nimble fingers started moving. It looked like she was making a huge, stripey *Doctor Who* scarf.

'So the ancient ruins tomorrow,' June said when Dennis stopped to draw breath. 'I'm looking forward to that. I hear there is a lovely auditorium there that is very scenic. I hope there are some decent loos. That's always my first concern.'

'Ruins are hard to paint unless one gets the perspective right,' Dennis said.

'I'll sit next to you and copy you,' June said sweetly.

Effie came over to join us, flopping down onto a sun lounger.

'What are you knitting, June?'

'I was going to knit a scarf, but then it sort of got away from me so instead it's going to be a jumper for my husband to wear in the garden. I found lots of oddments when I was having a clear out in the garage, and Nigel is colourblind anyway so he won't even notice. So what have you been up to? I don't think we've seen much of you four. Jillian wasn't at all pleased.'

'We've been having a really lovely day,' Effie said, 'and we haven't done anything earthshattering, we've just been relaxing and enjoying ourselves and we've had fun and some laughs, haven't we, Meg?'

'Speak for yourself,' Dennis said, snorting down his nose. 'I'm quite worn out with it. Art can be exhausting when one is fully committed. You don't see Damian Hirst doing Iron Man challenges in his spare time, do you? Or hear about Picasso running marathons.'

'Perhaps he did it secretly? Away from the paparazzi?' I suggested.

'And I'm sure I read somewhere that John Constable used to like riding his bike,' Effie added thoughtfully. 'I like to think of him whizzing through that stream in the Haywain with his feet in the air.'

'Oh, I used to do that when I was little,' Susan said, 'and my brothers made a go-cart out of an old pram. Such fun we used to have.'

Dennis threw her an incredulous look and went back to his art folder.

'But Dennis is right,' I said, hoping to cheer him up. 'We must focus more on the painting part of this holiday, and perhaps a bit less on the other bits.'

'Absolutely,' Effie said, 'and we will start tomorrow. Meanwhile, are we eating this evening?'

'Jillian mentioned a place further up this road, where apparently they do great vegetarian food,' June said.

'That sounds great,' I said.

At that moment, Beryl, dressed in pink linen dungarees and a yellow frilly blouse underneath, appeared on the roof terrace with Anita.

'Did I hear you say vegetarian?' she said. 'I love vegetarian food. It always makes me feel very smug.'

'Jillian has booked us a table at six thirty, before the rush,' Susan said.

'I haven't seen any rush,' Dennis said, 'just a lot of waiters hanging about, looking at girls.'

'I expect later on it gets really busy,' I said. 'The Greeks like to eat later than we do, don't they?'

'Well, I don't think that's healthy,' Dennis said firmly. 'Sally says if I go to bed on a full stomach I'm a nightmare. Tossing about and fidgeting for hours. Quite often she goes to sleep in the spare room.'

'Can't blame her for that,' Beryl said.

'It's six fifteen. Where is Jillian anyway?' June asked, finishing one row of her knitting and bunching it up ready to start another. 'I'm going to change colour on this. I have a lovely purple all ready which will look nice next to this turquoise. I don't want to leave it halfway through.'

'There you are,' Jillian called from the door, looking rather flustered. 'It seems I can never get you all together in one place for long. I've never had this trouble before. People wandering off, it makes life very difficult. Now then, before one of you disappears, let's go down the road to Athena's.'

'What about Will?' I said. 'He's not here yet.'

Jillian pursed her mouth into a button of disapproval.

'No, well, I suppose someone should go and find him. Meg, you seem to be volunteering. The rest of you, follow me.'

'Go girl,' Anita whispered as she passed me, 'and take your time. By the way, I saw him sitting in the courtyard. I expect he's still there.'

I nudged her with my elbow. 'Stop being naughty!'

Effie touched my arm. 'We'll see you later, or perhaps not. See how things develop.'

I found Will sitting in the courtyard, once more with his laptop open.

'You're not still working, are you?' I said.

He looked up. 'Oh, you know. Just a few things to finish up.'

I went to sit down on the other side of the table.

'What things?'

'Did you want something?'

He sounded a bit tetchy. I decided I was going to ignore it and press on.

'Jillian told me to come and get you and take you to Athena's restaurant. The table is booked for six thirty, and if we eat too late, Dennis will be tossing and turning all night.'

He gave a grin. 'And this affects me how?'

'His wife sometimes has to sleep in the spare room.'

'I would too.' He slapped his laptop shut. 'I've got a better idea. Let's go to the Colosseum.'

I was confused for a second. 'In Rome?'

'Yes, I thought we could take a taxi. No, I mean the place I saw down by the seafront.'

'Well, I could ask the others what they think,' I said uncertainly.

I could just imagine it, bursting into one restaurant and trying to organise the group out of one set of chairs and into another at a different venue, while Jillian flapped and twittered her distress.

'I didn't mean everyone. I meant just you,' he said, 'unless you don't like the idea?'

He looked a bit anxious then, as though it had taken a lot to ask me in the first place and he was unsure of my response.

I felt a bit stunned at this point, wondering why I had been singled out like this and then rather excited at the prospect. I realised my mouth was gaping unattractively with the shock.

'Oh. Just me?'

'Absolutely,' he said, very earnestly and, gaining a bit of confidence, he gave me a rather unexpected, twinkling look that made my knees go wobbly. Gosh, I hadn't seen this coming at all.

Could I do this? Wouldn't I be seen as rather rude? And Jillian had already expressed her disapproval of us failing to stick together like a proper tour group. I drew in a deep breath, ready to voice these thoughts, to explain why the idea of the two of us forming a splinter group and going off alone wasn't a good idea.

'Oh, okay then,' I said. 'That sounds great.'

Honestly. Weak as water, that was me.

# 9

While he went back to his room to get ready, I changed into some smarter clothes, scattering discarded garments onto my bedroom floor like a teenager, and then hurried up the road to Athena's to tell the others we would not be joining them. I was rewarded with a tight smile from Jillian and some very immature comments from Anita and Effie.

I puffed my way back down the road to the hotel and found Will sitting outside on the wall, making a big fuss of one of the kittens that was sitting next to him. I approved of that. I always thought there was something attractive about men who were kind to animals. No wonder David Attenborough had such a huge fan base.

I'd seen a lot of posts on social media recently, of young men playing the guitar or the piano with their cats, and the little animals were obviously besotted with them. And without exception, the young men were delightfully attractive. I wondered why that was? Did the cats like them because they were good-looking, or did liking cats make a man more handsome? Another of life's important questions.

'Right then,' he said, 'let's go.'

The kitten stretched out a beseeching paw in his direction as he stood up and then reached down to scratch the little creature under the chin. I nearly melted.

The Colosseum was a lovely place, about a twenty-minute walk along the seafront from the hotel, and as we reached it, the sun was just setting into the horizon. The evening air was warm and scented with wonderful aromas coming from the restaurants we passed. I felt very happy and a bit nervous.

This wasn't actually a date, of course it wasn't. That was a thing I associated with teenagers and young millennials. Nicky had tried internet dating for a while and said it was fraught with danger. Phrases like 'roaching', which meant the other person was seeing multiple people, or 'kittenfishing', which meant the person was no stranger to Photoshop. In the end she had just gone out to the pub with a group of friends and accidently drank a pint of beer which belonged to Joe who was a physics teacher, and a year later they were married.

I hadn't really had much to do with unattached men in an *interesting* way for many years. It had usually involved paying a bill or trying to explain to a mechanic the odd noise my car made when I was reversing. He never did sort that out, and there had been a fair bit of eye-rolling between the patient Cain and the other chaps in the garage.

So of course this wasn't a date, but to all outward appearances it came pretty close to it. And nor had I expected to be doing this. After all, I had read enough articles about older men dumping their wives for the company of younger women. Trophy wife. Arm candy. I'd never heard of an ageing billionaire leaving his fashionista wife for a grandmother.

And to be honest, I might have done my best when it came to my appearance, but I definitely wasn't arm candy. At sixty-five I still hadn't really got to grips with managing my hair, under-standing my skin type or having proper manicures. And I'd never had my colours done, which had been a very trendy thing to do some years ago.

I did feel okay though. I was wearing a new shirt from Cotton Traders and some smart, pale pink trousers. And on the same shopping trip I had unexpectedly bought a dinky little pair of zebra-print kitten heels. I used to love wearing heels, but then it got to a point where I didn't seem able to balance on them properly.

These were holiday purchases which a year ago I would never have considered. I could still remember opening my wardrobe at home to a host of navy-blue and grey garments which really didn't seem to suit the prospect of spending a few days in the sunshine. Maybe that would go on my bucket list. Not to attempt to be fashionable, just not dreary in my clothing choices. Not so safe. This place had already shown me that colour could bring joy into a life, so why not to mine?

There were quite a lot of people about that evening, couples and families with small children who didn't need to be dictated to by school term dates. Everyone looked happy, no one seemed to be arguing or complaining about something, and I felt myself relax even more.

We were shown to a table under some fairy-lit canopies, across the path from the restaurant, and on a sort of gravelly beach area, which was a bit of a challenge with my new shoes, but by balancing most of my weight on the balls of my feet, I made it without incident. As Will took off his jacket and draped it on the back of his chair, I took the opportunity to remove the grit from my shoes. And having noticed that every other woman within eyeshot was wearing trainers or flip flops, I sat back with a smile on my face, feeling rather glamourous and slightly pleased with myself.

On one side of our table there was the pleasant sight of lights from local restaurants glowing in the dusk, and on the other the dark expanse of the sea. My chair sank down a little into the stones as I got comfortable, and I made a mental note not to fidget too much.

After a short wait, water and bread were brought plus two large menus which came complete with helpful photographs of the food, and the waiter lit the two candle lanterns on the table, and they flickered charmingly in the delicate breeze from the sea. How lovely to have that outdoors. It wouldn't be possible in Herefordshire; I was sure of that.

Fish, there was a lot of fish. But of course there was; after all, that's what this area was known for, how many of the population made their living.

Fish stuffed with vegetables, salad with octopus, squid stuffed with rice, squid and octopus with peaches for the adventurous diner. I turned the menu over and perked up a bit at the sight of the desserts.

'Would you like some wine?' Will said.

I looked at him over the top of my menu, thinking how flattering the candlelight was and hoping it was having the same effect on me.

'Love some,' I said. 'Something cold and dry and white.'

'What an excellent idea,' he said and called the waiter over.

We scanned the menus again and I wondered what on earth I was going to order. I didn't cook fish much because it was so easy to get wrong and so I didn't eat it much either. Fish finger sandwiches were the height of my culinary expertise. Here the fish came as an actual fish and I wasn't very fond of my food looking at me while I ate it.

I pointed at one of the pictures that looked like some sort of stew. 'Maybe I'll have baked fish with tomatoes,' I said. At least I recognised all the ingredients.

And then I decided that was a boring choice. And I stabbed at another illustration. Something I had always wanted to try and never had because it was always a dish for two people. Malcolm said it was disgusting and grumbled about 'bottom feeders' and 'scavengers of the sea' and 'heavy metal content', which always made me imagine prawns playing guitars.

'No, I won't, what about the Greek *paellera* with orzo,' I said. 'I rather think that is on my bucket list.'

'Good choice,' Will said. 'We can share a *paellera* between us.'

We smiled at each other across the table, and I felt a new leap of unexpected delight. How strange that simply going along to the local art group had resulted in this encounter. Proof that you never knew where life was going to take you. I bet my daughter would have been astonished to see me sitting here in my new clothes and cute shoes with an attractive man opposite me. At a nearby table, a couple were taking a grinning selfie and I half thought of taking a surreptitious picture to send to Nicky, and then luckily thought better of it. I would just enjoy the moment. Perhaps I could get a sneaky shot of him later.

'How's the painting going?' I said.

'I haven't done any,' he replied with a grimace. 'I've done a couple of sketches but that's all. How about you?'

'Not a thing,' I admitted happily. 'I've been having too much fun to settle to anything. It's a long time since I've been away on holiday like this, and I'm making the most of it. I don't think Jillian approves at all.'

'No, probably not,' he agreed.

I could almost hear Effie and Anita telling me to get on with it.

'So how did you come to be here? You're not from Lower Begley after all.'

He shrugged. 'Someone saw something about it somewhere. Probably on social media. And said it sounded like what I needed. I'll admit I didn't realise there was going to be a group. It's a long time since I've been on holiday too. What with one thing and another...'

*What thing? And what was the other thing? And was it a male someone or female?*

I decided not to push my luck; his expression had suddenly become just a bit guarded.

'It's certainly a beautiful place, and I like that the hotel is so simple and unsophisticated,' I said. 'I don't like a lot of fussing around with the towels being folded into animals. I went on a cruise once where the steward left a towel monkey hanging in the wardrobe. I nearly fainted with the shock.'

He laughed. 'And chocolate left on the pillow. You get into bed and there it is, and you have to clean your teeth again.'

'I slept on one by mistake once, and in the morning it was all over the sheets and I had it stuck to the side of my face.'

'I bet that looked attractive.' He chuckled.

'Not really. My ex-husband said I was a disaster and the staff would wonder what the heck I had been doing.'

'You're not a disaster, I think you're fun,' he said.

Well, that brought the conversation to a sudden halt, and for a moment both of us seemed a bit edgy, and he moved his cutlery about and I wriggled on my chair, so that one of the front chair legs sank deeper into the gravel. This meant I was leaning slightly to the right, and I had to plant my feet on the ground at a strange angle to steady myself. Perhaps I had congratulated myself too soon and trainers would have been a better choice after all.

Luckily at that moment the waiter returned with the wine, and close behind him was another with a vast metal pan of *paellera*. This meant there was a few minutes when we juggled with wine glasses, cutlery and plates until I couldn't wait until we were left in peace to get on with it. I didn't know about it being a meal for two; to me it looked like a family of four would have been quite happy to share.

China fingerbowls of water and a couple of cloth napkins were put down on the table a few minutes later followed by various implements and nutcrackers. Then the waiter did the sort of flourishing things waiters do with wine bottles and white napkins and poured some out for us to try.

'Assyrtiko, beautiful wine. An excellent choice,' he said as we did a bit of tasting and frowning and swirling.

At last we were left alone with the hot, metal dish filled with tiny, golden orzo pasta, various things like prawns, crab claws and mussels poking out, and the aroma of saffron and seafood was divine.

'Go for it,' Will said.

I dolloped a big spoonful onto my plate and started digging out the interesting bits. To be honest I wasn't entirely sure how to deal with a lot of it. I decided to watch what he did and follow his lead. In the end it was quite easy, and everything was delicious, even the bits of octopus, which I really wasn't sure about to start with.

The wine was going down extremely well too, and after a few minutes I began to feel more relaxed and even confident. This was going far better than I had ever imagined and the possible delights of Athena's – where the vegetarian moussaka was apparently the best on the island according to Jillian – paled into insignificance as far as I was concerned.

I stopped trying to get information out of him, and we just

chatted about light-hearted things. The weather, the island, a Netflix series we had both watched, what we were hoping to see at the ancient excavations the following day, and whether it would be possible to get a bus to the north of the island where there was a bigger town.

'I'm so glad we had this,' I said, washing my fingers in the china bowl, and unfortunately slopping some of the water over the table. 'I can cross this off my bucket list with a smile.'

I took my napkin and mopped the water up as best I could, stretching over to his side of the table where the rivulet was threatening to dribble onto his trousers. The leg of my chair shifted a little more, and I moved my feet again for stability. I hoped he wouldn't notice, but I was sitting very inelegantly, leaning forward on the edge of my chair, with my knees far apart and one of my beautiful new shoes completely buried in the dusty grit and gravel under my chair.

'I had this in Rhodes once. It was good, but this is better,' he said.

I felt unjustifiably proud to hear this; after all, I hadn't cooked it. Never mind, we were sharing a lovely evening, and I hoped he was enjoying it as much as I was.

'This is so much better than sitting at home watching television,' I said. 'There's just nothing on at all that I want to watch these days. Perhaps a few cooking programmes, and *Strictly*. But most of the time it's just people arguing with each other.'

He didn't look at me but concentrated on washing his fingers and drying them carefully. He had nice hands too, strong and well kept.

'What about dessert?' he said at last when we both had to admit that the *paellera* had defeated us. There were just a few clumps of orzo left and a lot of bits of shell.

'I don't think I have room,' I said.

'Metaxa then and coffee?'

'Perfect,' I said. 'I'll just go and...'

I made the sort of vague gestures that indicated I was going to go and find the loo, and turned in my chair to stand up.

Very unwise. The combination of the uneven gravel, one foot being buried and the best part of half a bottle of wine meant that my chair fell over and with a shriek, I sprawled full length next to my companion, narrowly missing hitting a passing waiter who was carrying a tray filled with massive pizzas on his shoulder for the family at the next table.

Will gave a cry of dismay and he and another very kind man who was sitting near us helped me to my feet, where I stood flushed with embarrassment, my knees together and my feet stuck out for balance. I brushed the dust off my clothes and fervently wished the ground could swallow me up. Indeed, it had actually buried one of my zebra-print kitten heels and we spent a few excruciating minutes looking for it, digging through the stones and the discarded pizza crusts and cigarette butts.

I had the awful feeling that everyone was looking at me and deciding I was either drunk or not safe to be out in the first place. I think a few sympathetic glances were thrown in Will's direction too, which made me feel even worse. What on earth would he think of me?

There were even a few muttered comments.

*What on earth...? Oh dear... Is she all right? Isn't that him?*

Back in one piece again, I tottered off to find the loo and spent a few minutes splashing my face with cold water and dabbing at my hot face with a damp paper towel.

I looked up to see my reflection, which was rather flushed and wild-eyed.

I patted at my hair, which was similarly looking a bit dishevelled, and wished I had brought a brush, peered closer. Yes, there were little turmeric stains around my mouth which made it look as though I had a nicotine habit. I washed them off.

*Isn't that him?*

I looked at my reflection thoughtfully. What did that mean? Were they referring to Will? And if so, why?

*Isn't that him?*

Had I heard that properly?

*Calm down, for heaven's sake.* I had probably just heard the tail end of someone else's conversation. It probably meant nothing.

I straightened up and took a deep breath. The waistband of my new trousers was feeling a bit snug because of the massive quantity of *paellera* I had eaten. Perhaps I needed a walk for a bit so that I didn't have a Dennis-type disturbed night. Or maybe the Metaxa would do the trick.

Back outside, I picked my way carefully across the gravel to our table and adjusted my chair so it was on more stable ground. There was a tray with two glasses of black coffee and some Metaxa in front of me, plus a dish of pastel sugared almonds. Pretty as they were, I wasn't going to risk it, not with all my fillings just waiting to snap off. A woman has to know her limitations.

'Okay?' Will said kindly.

I could feel myself blushing.

'Sorry about that, my chair tipped over. This gravel...'

'As long as you're not hurt,' he said. 'Have some Metaxa to settle yourself. It's very good, one of my favourites.'

I took a sip. Yes, he was right. And the coffee was good too, very hot and sweet in the way Greeks seem to like it.

I would behave as though nothing had happened, that was the answer.

'So tomorrow, the visit to the ancient ruins. What time do we have to leave?'

He gave me another twinkling grin across the table.

'You mean you didn't read Jillian's notes? That's just wilful disobedience.'

I laughed. 'I know, I've always been the same. It got me into no end of trouble at school.'

'I can't imagine that,' he said. 'You seem more the type to behave and do as you were told.'

I looked at him through my lashes.

'Ah, but you don't know me very well,' I said, with the astonishing feeling that I was actually flirting with him. It had been years since I had done that. I didn't think I still could.

'Not yet,' he said, taking a sip of his Metaxa. 'Let's wait and see what happens tomorrow morning when you are late for the bus, which, by the way, leaves at nine o'clock.'

'As long as Costas hasn't got a darts match this evening.'

'Good point.'

We finished our drinks and coffee and after a polite wrangle about who was going to pay, Will settled the bill.

'This was my idea. You can pay next time if it worries you that much,' he said.

I sat and thought about this, hoping I wasn't blushing. The next time. So, there was going to be a next time? Goodness me.

'That was really delicious,' I said as we finally escaped from the gravelled area and back onto more solid ground. 'A lovely way to spend the evening.'

I had to stop for a moment, leaning against a fence to take off my shoes and shake out the accumulated dust and grit. Will waited patiently, looking out to sea at the lights of a boat, and didn't mention my humiliating accident of earlier, for which I was grateful, and in a way, it made me like him more.

If it had been Malcolm, he would undoubtedly never let me forget *his* embarrassment, and eventually it would be turned into a story where my clumsiness and wine consumption would be exaggerated into his usual brand of gaslighting humour. I could almost imagine his ghastly ex-work colleagues from the bank, braying with laughter at my expense at the annual Christmas get-together.

As we walked back through the little town, the streets were busier. We had obviously beaten the rush, such as it was. At last, we turned into one of the little back alleyways which would lead us to the hotel.

'Thank you so much,' I said.

He gave a funny little bow in my direction. 'No, thank you.'

At this point I almost said *thank you for thanking me*, as a sort of joke, but mercifully I didn't.

I knew we were nearly back because I could see the lights from the Hotel Costas roof terrace ahead of us, and there was still a pile of moped parts on one side of the pavement, so evidently the man who had been working on it the previous day still had work to do.

I knew that once the others saw I was back, they would want to know chapter and verse about our evening. About him, what he had said, what I had said; it would be worse than being back at school. And I realised that despite our non-stop chatter, I still knew hardly anything about him apart from the facts that he was retired, lived alone and shared a cat with his neighbour.

I raked my memory for details. He obviously liked travel, seafood and white wine, and he was quietly elegant and had well cut hair. What else had he said? That he had once worked in London and had lived for a few years in Oxford where the traffic was terrible and parking spaces at a premium.

I had asked why he hadn't moved somewhere more rural with views over a lake and perhaps room for some hens. I had told him about my house, and he had made approving comments. And then we had talked about chickens and tried to think up funny names for them. Starting with fairly predictable ones like Henny-Penny, Chicken Little and Hen Solo and eventually deciding on Cluck Norris, Mother Clucker and Hennifer Lopez.

Then we discussed what would happen to them when he went off on holiday, and he picked up his phone and googled hen-boarding facilities, which I refused to accept even existed, and found Henidorm, What the Cluck and The Clucktastic Hotel within twenty miles of his house. By the time we finished I was almost weeping with laughter, and his face had lost a lot of the tension which had become so familiar. I could almost see the man he must have been when he was younger, and strangely enough he was even more memorable.

But apart from that? I went back through our conversation of that evening, looking for nuggets of information that the others would find titillating.

He let slip that he'd been briefly married in his thirties, a relationship which had ended after a few years. He had enjoyed sailing when he was younger, had once owned a boat, which I had found impressive until he told me about all the ropes and knots and having to pretend something akin to standing in the rain tearing up twenty-pound notes was fun.

'And how do you spend your time now?' I'd asked. 'What do you like to do with your retirement?'

'Dull things,' he'd said. 'Weeding my garden, reading old books, watching boxsets on television. Occasionally I cook. And as a side line I invested in a couple of properties years ago which I renovated and sold. I've just bought another one. That keeps me busy. I'm very keen on a spreadsheet, which is what I was doing the other day.'

'None of those things are dull, unless you think I am dull too,' I'd said.

'No, you're not,' he'd replied. 'I told you, I think you're fun. What else do you do?'

'Drink tea, sometimes coffee, eat biscuits, do the ironing.'

He'd pulled a face. 'Ironing? No one enjoys that.'

'I do. I love taking a basket full of crumpled things and creating order. And I can watch television at the same time. So that passes for multi-tasking I think.'

'Impressive. I like to clear my worktops in the kitchen—'

'Oh, me too!' I felt unreasonably pleased when he said that. Almost as though we were kindred spirits.

'—and I'm afraid I like to mow the lawn into precise stripes.'

'I can't do that; I tend to be more fluid in my mowing. I tried to mow my name into it once. The M for Meg was okay, but I had trouble with the E and the G. I did the little line on the G with a pair of kitchen scissors in the end.'

He'd laughed, throwing back his head at this. 'You're crazy.'

Funny; Malcolm had said much the same thing the day we separated and I had cut his new tie – which he had admitted quite proudly had been a present from his new lady friend – in half with the same scissors. But somehow this time it sounded different. As though being crazy might be a good thing. That someone like me, who laughed at silly things, who worried about the world, who cared about relative strangers and who suddenly wanted to live an interesting life again, was actually not a bad person after all.

'I think I am sometimes,' I'd said, 'and much good has it done me.'

'You've done me good,' he'd said. 'I haven't laughed so much for a very long time as I have this evening.'

And he bent and gently kissed my cheek, and I honestly thought I might explode with the shock. And considering how much *paellera* I had eaten, that would not have been a pretty sight.

## 10

Still in a bit of a daze and with a rather foolish grin on my face, I got back to my room and opened the doors onto my balcony. Looking across at Anita's, I was not surprised to see Beryl, and Effie sitting there with her in the dusk, a bottle of wine between them and the table lit with a candle lantern. When they saw me, Effie immediately stood up and shouted across.

'You're back! Did you have a nice time? What did you have to eat? Come and tell us all about it!'

From the racket she was making I would not have been surprised if other people in the street joined us, but bowing to the inevitable, I kicked off my lovely new shoes – one of which was now definitely a different colour from the other one – and put on my slippers. By the time I opened my door, Anita was already standing in the hallway, and she beckoned me into her room with some impatient hand waving.

'So? Tell us all about it,' she said, pressing a mug of wine into my hand and encouraging me to sit down at the table. There wasn't much room because it was only meant for two people, and Anita had found two other chairs from somewhere, so it was a bit cramped and the four of us banged knees for a bit until we were all settled.

I told them all about my evening, my meal and eventually about my accident with the gravel, the zebra-print kitten heels and the utter shame of being hauled to my feet by fellow diners.

Predictably – having ascertained I wasn't injured and nor had I crushed some other unsuspecting passer-by – they found this very amusing.

'What did he say? Was he embarrassed too? If that had happened to me when I was with Hector, he would probably have walked off, left me to pay the bill and not spoken to me for days afterwards,' Effie said with a kindly glance.

'I can absolutely sympathise,' Beryl said, shaking her head, 'but the great thing is that by the time you get to our age, just about everybody has done things that are equally as daft or even more embarrassing. I did worse than that in Portofino back in the late seventies. I was staying with the son of a gorgeous Italian Contessa at her villa on the lake, and I was flirting up a storm with him. I went to sit on the little wall at the end of his garden with the hope that I could lean back and look sultry and sexy and also get some information out of him—'

Anita leaned forward, her eyes wide. 'Goodness me, what sort of information?'

'Oh, the usual things. Interdepartmental government plotting, bribes, nothing really earthshattering. Anyway, I leaned back a bit too far and down I went. Into the water. Yves St Laurent dress, cocktail glass and everything. And even though it was June, it was frightfully cold. And the thing I was most upset about was Ernesto had just poured me an absolutely divine pear martini. Such a pity. But to be fair, his staff were so efficient about the whole thing. They fished me out quick as you like. Italians are so good about that, and spit spot, I was out and dried off and had a new drink in my hand in no time.'

'Oh my word, you had a St Laurent dress?' Effie breathed, impressed.

'I did,' Beryl said dreamily. 'Don't you remember it? Ernesto had bought it for my birthday. It was so beautiful. It was black with an emerald-green sash and huge purple sleeves. It sounds a bit odd describing it now, but I thought I was the cat's miaou. It was ruined, of course, which is a shame because it would be worth a fortune now. I was very fond of Ernesto; we spent a weekend in Venice and he was the only man who ever got me out of my clothes with just words.'

'Wow,' Anita said. 'Was he very romantic?'

'Not really. He just told me he'd seen a spider go down the back of my dress. Anyway, less about me and more about the handsome Will. So, what happened next?'

I tried to remember, drawing a little comfort from Beryl's story, which I had to agree was far worse than mine.

'I just emptied all the gravel out of my shoes and limped off to the loo. And when I got back, he didn't mention it again.'

Effie sighed with pleasure. 'How marvellous. Sometimes that's all we need, isn't it? For someone to do nothing. To *not* mention it. To ignore the daft things we might do or say.'

Anita topped up our wine glasses, emptying the bottle. It did cross my mind that we all seemed to be drinking an awful lot. Normally weeks could pass without me having any alcohol. And maybe this had been the reason I'd fallen over in the first place? I made a mental note of this and decided I would cut back from now on, otherwise I might well be going home with a tan and cirrhosis as well.

'And?' she said. '*And?* What then?'

'We had coffee and Metaxa, which I have to say I am getting quite a taste for, and then he paid the bill and we walked home.'

There was a moment of silence when all three of them looked at me with meaningful glances, and I could feel myself blushing.

'What?' I said, trying not to laugh.

'And?' Beryl said.

'He kissed you, didn't he?' Effie said with a sigh. 'I can tell. I remember the first time I was kissed by someone who wasn't my husband, and yes, before you ask, I was divorced by then. And it was like a bomb went off in my head. And it was a young man called Jeremy. And he wasn't a particularly good kisser or anything. Okay, quite nice really, but I mean he was no Warren Beatty. It was just the thought that a nice man wanted to kiss me. And it was sort of friendly and affectionate, which was something I'd missed. I'll never forget it.'

Yes, I thought, I could relate to that. And I wondered then how it was that a marriage like mine, which had started with such promise and had produced a loving and much-loved daughter, a comfortable home, and a good career, had slowly crumbled. The passion had died; the affection from Malcolm had been in an ever-dwindling supply and nearly always prompted by some other motivation. The need for his dry-cleaning to be collected in my lunch hour, or to make up for a birthday or anniversary missed, or occasional and forgettable sex.

Was the ability to be loved or even noticed something like the sand in an egg timer, which gradually ran through and disappeared with the passing years? Had this evening been the time when fate turned the timer over again and the clogged sand of my attractiveness began to run more freely?

I focused back on my companions who were now reminiscing happily about their own dating disasters. Anita had spilled wine down Rick on their first date and then done the same thing to his mother when they were introduced.

'Not on purpose, obviously, I was just so nervous. And she was not the sort of woman to laugh it off. The family called me "The Splasher" for years afterwards, and Rick's father Stan, who was a big bear of a man who liked slapstick and Carry On films, used to stand in front of me and ask when it was his turn.'

'Another thing, I fell out of my first boyfriend's car,' Beryl said. 'Luckily, we had parked up and we were getting a bit steamy at the time. It was a lovely green MG Miget. He did tell me the door catch could be a bit unreliable. I landed up on my back in a patch of nettles. Things were never the same after that.'

'Okay, so perhaps this wasn't as bad,' I said, laughing, 'but it's different to be a bit of a klutz at my age. For one thing, it's so undignified and it hurts more. I'm sure I must be covered in bruises. And what would the other people have thought of me?'

'Are you ever going to meet any of those people again?' Beryl asked.

'Probably not,' I said.

Beryl made a dismissive noise. 'Well then, what's the problem? Life is too short to worry about what strangers think of you. Have fun; if nothing else, give them something to think about.'

Yes, actually, she was right.

Effie nodded. 'Everyone says you should listen to your body as you get older. Well, my body says has anyone got any of that chocolate we bought in duty free left?'

I began to feel a lot happier about things as we all laughed together, and when Anita brought out a huge Toblerone, life looked even better.

About an hour later we decided it was definitely bedtime, and we began to clear up the wine glasses and the shreds of silver foil.

Beryl looked at her watch. 'Well, that's enough excitement for one evening. I've found the film channel on my television. I'm going to bed now with a nice cup of tea and Matt Damon.'

'Goodness, does Mrs Damon know?' Anita said, her eyebrows in her fringe.

'Not yet, but she would be furious if she did. There's nothing like a good spy thriller and a couple of car chases to settle me,' Beryl said cheerfully. 'So now then, synchronise watches, breakfast at eight, and then nine o'clock tomorrow, outside the hotel. Flat shoes, painting things, water and sunhats. I'm looking forward to our trip to the ancient ruins. And who knows, we might even get some painting done.'

'We were talking about it over dinner. Will knows a lot about the Minoans,' I said.

'Yes,' Effie said with a loud, wicked laugh, 'I bet he knows lots of interesting things.'

## 11

The following morning after a hurried breakfast, because we were a bit late getting up, the four of us refilled our water bottles from the water cooler in reception and went to wait obediently outside the hotel. The weather was perfect. Warm and sunny with a light breeze coming in from the sea. The forecast was for it to get much hotter later on.

A few minutes later, June and Susan arrived, both dressed in beige linen trousers, loose tops and broad-brimmed sunhats, carrying canvas backpacks and folding stools. This sent Effie off in a panic because she had forgotten hers. By the time she returned, the group was assembled, with Dennis at the back of the group in a white shirt and trousers, looking as though he was going to umpire a cricket match.

'You're looking very fine and summery this morning, Anita,' Dennis called over, touching the brim of his hat in salute.

Anita rewarded him with a nod and Dennis beamed and started telling her about his new tube of Dioxazine Purple and how he was looking forward to using it.

Then I saw Will sitting on the wall, once more making a fuss of one of the kittens, and I went over to say hello, feeling rather silly and foolish. Was this the beginnings of a daft crush? He looked up at me and grinned.

'Good morning. How are you today? I never could resist kittens,' he said.

'I'm more of a dog man, myself,' Dennis said, overhearing. 'Give me a chocolate labrador any time.'

'I had a chocolate rabbit at Easter,' Susan said. 'My grand-daughter gave me one. I could hardly bear to eat it. She bit off the ears for me in the end.'

'Ooh, I had one of those too,' June said. 'The ones with the little ribbon round the neck? I'm afraid I left mine in the sun on the kitchen windowsill and it went a bit soft. So my husband put it in the fridge to harden up again, and when I went to eat it, it looked more like the Easter Godzilla than the Easter Bunny.'

'Oh, for goodness' sake,' Dennis harrumphed, which seemed to be something he said on a regular basis. Luckily at that moment, the minibus pulled up and we all got on.

The drive to the ruins took us about half an hour, and we enjoyed the views as we drove along the coast road. It really was such an attractive place, with the white houses gleaming in the morning sunshine and the sparkling Mediterranean below them. We slowed down as we passed a little marina with some boats parked up, and I craned round to look as we passed.

There was a woman washing the deck of one of them with a mop and bucket. Perhaps she was going out for a sail later with her family, to a place where the water beneath the boat would be the colour of turquoise and crystal clear. Maybe there was a laden picnic basket on board with some Assyrtiko wine, a block of feta cheese and some rustic bread and a tub of perfect olives from a local grove. What fun, to be able to do that. I wondered if

Will had done things like that when he had a boat. Perhaps I would ask him later.

Occasionally, Gregor grumbled at some of the other drivers who made him slow down from his usual rackety speed, but we arrived in the car park without incident and clambered down to collect our belongings from the boot.

In just that short time, the day had heated up quite a bit, and we fanned at our faces and agreed it probably wasn't a bit like this back in England.

'I checked on my phone, it's raining and eleven degrees in Lower Begley,' Anita said. 'Raining and five degrees in Scotland.'

'They won't get much birdwatching done then, will they?' I asked.

Anita laughed. 'Rick and his friends have *all* the kit. Don't worry about them. Waterproof jackets and trousers, waterproof notebooks and pens, hand warmers, thermal base layers, camera covers. Waterproof chairs and portable hides. I thought bird-watching was quite a cheap hobby, but trust me, it isn't. Not to mention the tartan-strewn hotel they stay in near Inverness. In fact, this holiday is probably a lot cheaper than theirs.'

We left Gregor smoking and happily grumbling away to some other coach drivers in the car park and made our way up the track to the entrance. As we did, Will fell into step beside me and we both slowed our pace.

'Thank you for a lovely evening,' he said. 'I really enjoyed it.'

'Me too,' I said. 'Wasn't it fun?'

Now I really was feeling a bit fluttery and silly.

Well. It had been fun apart from the falling over bit, but I didn't mention that, and I felt a swell of gratitude towards him for not doing so either.

'We should do it again,' he said. 'Only if you wanted to. No pressure.'

I looked up at him, his eyes shaded behind his usual dark glasses and the rim of his hat, and smiled.

'I'd love that,' I said.

'Really?' He sounded startled, though why he should, I had no idea.

'Of course.'

'Oh, right then. Good. That's excellent. Splendid,' he said, sounding even more surprised.

'Come on, you two. Hurry up,' Dennis bellowed. 'Our private tour sets off in five minutes and June and Susan have already wandered off.'

'I expect they have gone to find a loo,' Anita called back, doing the universal explanatory gesture of hand washing. 'In fact, that's a great idea, let's do the same. Never turn down the opportunity, that's what I say.'

'Oh, for goodness' sake,' Dennis muttered, yet again.

'Your admirer is getting more and more tetchy as the week goes on. He will be going off you, Anita, at this rate,' I said.

'Good,' Anita said, 'I can do without listening to more of his tales of his time in India and his father's tea plantation and how his mother managed all the staff.'

'I don't think I'd like to have staff,' Effie said. 'I had a cleaning lady back when I was modelling in Milan, and I used to clean up before she arrived. I was always so embarrassed about the state of my apartment.'

'Not so bothered these days, going by the state of your flat,' Beryl murmured.

'A clean house is the sign of a wasted life,' Effie fired back.

We found the loos, which were spotlessly clean and well appointed, and I looked at myself in one of the mirrors as I washed my hands.

My reflection of course was familiar, but did I actually look old? I was nearly sixty-five. Which meant in no time I would be nudging up to seventy. I was no longer middle-aged, and I couldn't pretend I was. On winter days when it was cold and raining, and I hardly left the house unless I had to, I felt my age. I read a piece in the local paper recently, where there had been an interview with a lady of 101, and she was still apparently hale and hearty, and she put it down to good genes and a tot of whisky at bedtime. This morning, with the sunshine and blue sky above me, and the company of good friends, I felt quite hale myself, but I couldn't stand whisky. Perhaps this was the other secret. Being happy. Feeling positive and receptive to life.

Beryl came and stood at the sink next to me and peered at herself in the mirror too.

She patted her hair into shape and sighed. 'It's terribly annoying, isn't it. I've realised I don't look as bad as I thought I did a few years ago, because now I look worse. Oh well...'

Out in the clear air again, Anita, Effie and Beryl had pulled on their distinctive yellow sunhats patterned with ducks, and I suddenly wished I could have one too.

The Old Ducks Club, Anita had called it. They were so outlandish, and yet they were fun, they spoke of a new brand of sisterhood of which I wanted to be a part. To finally live my life the way I wanted to, and not worry about what other people expected of me. Not my friends, my family, even my daughter. After all, I'd been young and daft once, even though Nicky didn't seem to believe it. In fact, as time went on, I think I could feel my silliness levels rising for the first time in decades.

'Now then, let's put Dennis out of his misery and go and do this tour,' Beryl said. 'I can tell by all the fidgeting and nostril flaring he's getting impatient. And we can apparently leave all our bags in a locker by the entrance so we don't have to cart them round with us.'

We were greeted by our young guide, who introduced herself as Lydia. She was an archaeology student who was earning some money during the holidays explaining to people like us what we were seeing.

The remains of the Minoan settlement, which were still apparently being excavated, were wonderful. An ancient town, ruined by an earthquake and volcanic eruption thousands of years ago, was laid out before us under an impressive steel and glass roof. There was a wooden walkway so we could look down at the shells of kitchens and living rooms and imagine them as they had been before the island had been evacuated. The air was cooler than outside, and scented with dust and old stone and history. There were even clever seating areas where we could rest to listen to our guide, although some of the steps were quite deep and Beryl had to be hauled back up when that part of the talk was finished.

'Imagine what it must have been like,' Anita said. 'One minute you are a wealthy trader with ships and a family and a wine cellar and comfortable beds, and the next you are leaving all your things behind and heading out across the sea to live somewhere else.'

'I don't suppose there was much alternative,' I said, 'not if there was a volcano erupting behind you.'

'True.'

We wandered on, following Lydia to the next interesting thing where there was unexpectedly a very informative television presentation of life as a Minoan. And they had some lovely houses too, with windows open to the cooling breezes of the sea, bakehouses on every street and even quite sophisticated drainage systems.

Lydia patiently answered all our questions about ancient toilets and wall paintings in excellent English, and at the end of the tour we all dug deep into our pockets to give her a substantial tip.

'Now then, I think I'd like to go under those trees and paint the amphitheatre,' Dennis said. 'Marvellous shadows in those stones. My Dioxazine Purple is going to come into its own, I feel sure.'

June and Susan thought this was a good idea as the day was heating up even more, and they followed him to a little glade where there were some thoughtfully placed benches and picnic tables. Perhaps we should do something similar.

Effie had her own ideas. 'Perhaps later. I'd like to go into the gift shop first. Anyone coming?'

I was about to follow my three friends when I felt a touch on my arm.

I turned to see Will there.

'What about a cold drink or a cup of tea?' he said. 'There's a café over there.'

'Absolutely,' I said and smiled with pleasure. And this time I would not fall over or get my feet stuck anywhere.

'So, what did you think of it?' I asked.

'Fantastic,' he said, 'and so well done. It never fails to amaze me how clever some people are. I mean, one minute there is just a patch of scrubby land, the next someone has found a house or the stones of a street. It's very impressive. And much better actually seeing it rather than just reading about it.'

The café was like many of the others I had seen, small and really just a cabin with signs for foreign ice cream outside next to a freezer cabinet. There were some tables and chairs under a wooden canopy, which was covered in thick ropes of a burgeoning vine. Behind the counter was a young couple. He was wiping down the tables, clearing things away and taking the orders, and she was wrestling with a complicated coffee machine and piles of crockery. They both seemed very happy, which was lovely to see, and they called across to each other and laughed together when he dropped something.

'I wonder if they do this all year round,' I said, 'they seem a cheerful pair.'

'Perhaps,' Will replied. 'There are far worse places to work. Living a simple life is so much easier than the alternative.'

He sounded as though he knew the difference, which was an interesting insight.

'On the other hand, maybe after a while they will miss the bright lights and the excitement,' I said.

'I doubt it. After a while, the bright lights can give you a headache.'

He handed me a menu, which was handwritten on the back of a piece of cardboard.

I made my choice almost immediately. 'Ordinary tea if they have it and don't go bringing me any cake. I'm enjoying it too much and I'll be putting on pounds if I carry on indulging.'

'Nonsense,' he said, laughing, 'you're perfect as you are.'

I looked down at the menu, not really seeing the words. Never, not once in my life, had anyone told me I was perfect; and anyway, it wasn't true. I was, it had to be admitted, about a stone overweight, had an unpredictable knee which sometimes gave me trouble, and I needed reading glasses. I had lots of pairs of them too, bought online, which I kept losing. I estimated once that there were eight pairs around the house somewhere and occasionally, I still had to go out to the car and find the pair I kept there.

I took a deep breath. If he thought I was okay, then just for once I wasn't going to argue. In the past I would have been at pains to point out my flaws. Women were almost programmed to do so, to brush aside compliments and demean themselves.

Suddenly, I didn't want to do that. I'd had a lifetime of thinking I was ordinary and average. If someone wanted to tell me otherwise, then I wasn't going to argue about it.

He went to the counter to place our order and I watched him, liking what I saw. Tall and lean, a man who could be friendly and yet at the same time he was somehow reserved. Occasionally enthusiastic but then he could suddenly become closed in on himself. A man who liked to wear sunglasses and a concealing hat most of the time, who – the realisation struck me – always chose to sit with his back to other people.

*Is that him?*

Why would he do that? It was puzzling. He was the complete opposite of most men I had known, who would happily survey a crowded room, take the lead in conversations and push their opinions on everyone. Dennis for one. Malcolm for another.

Will wasn't like that; it was almost as though he was taking pains not to be seen or noticed. What did I really know about him anyway? He was about my age, maybe slightly more. He was attractive, had been single for years; he seemed a bit familiar to me; he hadn't been on holiday much recently; and he liked kittens and seafood. It wasn't much to go on.

He came to sit down, putting his wallet into the back pocket of his jeans. And that was another thing; how do men do that? When I tried doing that with my purse, I always ended up either forgetting it was there or sitting on it and bending it out of shape. The same went for my phone. I'd actually cracked the screen of one phone by sitting on it. Of course, men didn't have the unending curse of a handbag to worry about, and the pockets on women's clothes were always shallow and almost useless.

'They do have ordinary tea,' he said, holding out a paper bag, 'and I didn't buy any cake. But I did buy you an ice cream. I thought it might be a nice idea in this heat.'

He handed over a chocolate cone and I ripped the paper off with some enthusiasm.

'Exactly what I would have chosen,' I said, delighted, and he grinned.

'I thought so.'

We sat there quite content eating our ice creams and chatting about what we had seen, and after a while he relaxed enough to start telling me more of the things he knew about the Minoans and their history. He knew a lot too. How they had built up their maritime empire, centred around Crete where they had built the palace of Knossos, and how they had excelled at urban planning, writing and sophisticated art. And all about three thousand years ago.

'Such a tragedy, what happened to them.'

'No one can fight back against natural disasters, even now. Volcanic eruptions, tsunamis, the dominance of the Greeks back then. Nothing stays the same forever, and it didn't for the Minoans.'

'It doesn't now either,' I murmured. 'I found that out the hard way.'

I could sense him looking at me, his gaze curious and at the same time kind.

'It's never easy when a marriage ends, I know that. You sound as though you had a hard time of it.'

'Oh, no worse than a lot of other people,' I said, trying to sound offhand. 'We grew apart. He wanted something else; some*one* else. Someone who could make him feel better about himself, which apparently, I had failed to do, although heaven knows I tried.'

Was it a good thing to drone on to him about how another man had found me unappealing and unsatisfactory? No, probably not.

And what was it about Will that his wife hadn't liked? To me he seemed attractive, intelligent, well-groomed and polite. A veritable unicorn amongst men. I wondered why their marriage had floundered, and if she, or indeed he, had caused the split. Had she had an affair because he was away so much… doing what exactly?

'But anyway, that was years ago and luckily our daughter dealt with it very well. Sometimes kids don't, do they?' I said, licking a smear of chocolate sauce off my hand.

The unspoken question here was did he have any children?

I waited with unusual reserve and was rewarded for my patience.

'So I've heard. We didn't have children,' he said at last, 'so I don't know.'

It felt like a small triumph, to have found out something new.

I decided to change the subject, suspecting that if I pressed him for more information he would shy away like a startled pony and I would be back to square one.

I could see Anita and Effie in their matching yellow sunhats walking in the distance, and Effie stopped to do a little dance and pull a funny face at me, which meant I nearly snorted with laughter into the aforementioned tea. I changed it for a slightly wild smile as though I was just a bit overexcited.

'Good, isn't it?' he said. 'And the food too. I enjoyed our *paellera* the other night. I'm glad you chose it. I wouldn't normally eat a lot of shellfish. I always worry I'm going to give myself food poisoning.'

'Oh, exactly! Me too. And when I watch television cooks dealing with fish, they seem to hardly cook it at all.'

He finished his tea, tipping back his head to get the last few drops, and then he put his sunglasses back on.

'Shall we go?'

I'm not the most hyper-sensitive person but even I could tell the atmosphere between us had suddenly cooled yet again.

'Yes, okay,' I said, confused by his change of mood.

One minute we had been laughing together, enjoying ourselves, and without warning he had retreated back into his old, reserved ways. I could almost feel the chill between us, even though it was a hot day.

I left a few coins on the table for the owners, who were now dealing with a long queue for refreshments, and people were already hovering nearby, waiting to snap up our table.

I collected my things and hurried after him, still baffled by what I had done this time.

## 12

I caught up with Beryl and Effie a few minutes later. They were sitting under the trees on a bench, chatting away, although Beryl did have her sketch pad out and was doing something with a stick of charcoal. Well, at least one of us was trying to do something artistic.

'So the lovely Will singled you out again,' Effie said with a broad grin. 'This is getting serious. Have you found out more about him?'

'No,' I said, flopping down beside her in a battered but surprisingly comfortable wooden armchair, 'it's almost impossible to get anything out of him. He was married a long time ago, but it ended. He hasn't got any children. He's retired. I mean, that's the sort of basic information I could get in half an hour from Costas or Gregor.'

'So what did he do before he retired?' Beryl asked.

'He said he worked in business. What sort of business I have no idea. Although he has done some house renovations. And when I try with some more probing questions, he shuts down and goes quiet.'

'Perhaps he was a spy, or an assassin?' Effie suggested.

'No, I don't think so,' Beryl said. 'He's too memorable and handsome. Spies have to be forgettable, able to blend into a crowd. All this James Bond strutting around in a Hugo Boss suit stuff is nonsense. I used to work for the government and I never once had an Aston Martin or a speedboat. But I did used to like martinis, although you can't have a proper vespa martini like Bond used to order, because they don't make Kina Lilett any more.'

Anita reappeared at that moment carrying a paper bag from the gift shop, and she sat down.

'I knew it!' Anita said, overhearing the last of the conversation. 'I knew you were a spy. Everyone in the village thinks so.'

Beryl shrugged. 'Absolute nonsense, I just used to travel with various government departments. But I did have a gun. A dear little Glock. I kept it in the box with the Christmas decorations for a long time, and every year after I retired, I used to take it out and clean it. It became a seasonal ritual. On Christmas Eve I'd listen to the service of nine lessons and carols from King's College and get the Ballistol out. Even now when I get a whiff of it, I think of Christmas. But then I had to get a proper locked cabinet and – I don't know – it didn't seem the same.'

'Good Lord,' I said, 'the things one finds out. Did you have diplomatic immunity?'

Beryl chuckled. 'Oh no. Actually, I'm not sure; things were different in my day. Well, I never needed it. That's the thing. Don't get caught. Now then, let's talk about something else. If Meg has nothing more to tell us, what are we doing tomorrow?'

'We have the morning free and then in the afternoon, the wine tasting excursion,' Anita said.

'Jolly good,' Beryl said. 'In which case, I had better give my liver a rest and go to bed early tonight. All this eating out and sunshine, it makes it far too easy to knock back a few drinks, don't you think?'

We agreed it was. And we decided to stay off alcohol for the rest of the day in readiness for the wine tasting the following afternoon.

Beryl carried on with her charcoal sketch and I thought about getting my paints out, but in the end I didn't. I had a gorgeous view over the ancient town to one side and the sea on the other, so instead I took a few pictures on my phone and did some thinking. Not difficult thinking, just idly wondering about my surroundings and what colour I might paint the bathroom when I got home.

Sitting there in the sun was immensely relaxing and pleasant, and I felt properly warm right through which, after the months of horrible winter and disappointing spring weather back home, was a treat in itself. So often it had been necessary to turn on the heated seat in my car or pull on extra layers, a cardigan or jacket. Here none of those things applied. It made life easier somehow, or perhaps it was just because I was on holiday.

I liked being on holiday, I realised. And I hadn't before now.

So often in the past, holidays had been stressful things, worrying about the travel arrangements, the hotel we had booked in to, the reliability of the weather during an English summer. Would Malcolm like the food or the room we were allocated? Would there be some reason for him to complain, try to get an upgrade, or blame me when he realised he had packed the wrong clothes in his suitcase? Here, everything seemed easy. And that was because I was on my own, which was a delightful and unexpected freedom.

Yes, I had new friends to talk to, but if I wanted to go out for dinner with Will, or even strike out on my own, perhaps get a local bus to the bigger town on the island, or a ferry to somewhere, then I could. I didn't need anyone's permission or approval. I didn't need to take responsibility for anyone but myself. How absolutely marvellous.

*  *  *

Back at Hotel Costas, we clambered down from the minibus and the four of us decided to visit a very tempting bakery at the far end of the main street. So far we hadn't got there, but on the way back from the ancient town, Dennis had told us in great detail how good it was, how the sandwiches and cakes were all excellent and the prices very reasonable, so rather than going to another restaurant, we decided to give it a go.

'And at least they won't sell wine there,' Effie said, 'so we won't be tempted.'

'Good point,' I said. 'We need to be in training for tomorrow anyway.'

We all agreed this was a very good idea, and having left our bags at the hotel, we made our way through the little streets to the far end of town where behind a bus station, we found Artopolio.

I didn't know what we had been expecting, but it was marvellous, and apparently open for twenty-four hours a day. Inside it was as warm, floury and intoxicating as only great bakeries can be, and there were trays of all sorts of bread. Beryl was happily on hand to translate the names.

Rustic *horiatiko; psomi daktyla*, a large soft loaf covered in sesame seeds; *tsourekei*, a sweet, plaited loaf; *lagana* flatbread; rosemary-scented *eliopsomo*; and *kouloura* bread rings flavoured with olives, oregano or tomatoes. It was very impressive. Then on the other side of the shop were the ranks of cakes and pastries which were even more dazzling. Trays of sticky baklava, *portokalo-*

*pita and karithopita,* puffy, flaky fruit turnovers, sugar-glazed doughnuts of all colours and flavours, dozens of different cookies and things that looked like shortbread.

At the back of the shop next to some plastic doors, which I guessed led to the bakehouse, were racks of filled rolls and pitas. What on earth should I choose? Feta cheese with roasted peppers? Lamb, dill and mint tzatziki? Tuna with green peppers? It certainly beat my usual cheese and pickle choice back home.

It took us a long time but eventually we left the shop with greaseproof paper bags and huge, satisfied smiles. As we made our way back to the hotel, we passed the little supermarket and noticed a colourful, scribbled sign in the window: *Local wine – Ntópio krasi – €4.00.*

'Four hundred euros for a bottle of wine?' Anita spluttered.

Beryl went to look. 'Four euros actually.'

We stared at the bottles and we blinked a bit as we did the conversion.

'That's three pounds fifty,' I said at last. 'For a bottle of wine?'

Anita pointed. 'Actually, it's a litre of wine, not a bottle.'

We stood and looked at each other for a moment, slight frowns on our faces.

'I bet it's awful,' Effie said, and we all sort of agreed.

'Like battery acid,' Anita said.

'But if the locals drink it, and presumably more than once, it can't be that bad,' I said.

'Good point. And in my experience these things are usually better than you might think,' Beryl said. 'Well, there is only one way to find out.'

She handed me her lunch bag and went into the shop, returning a few minutes later with two bottles of the same wine.

'To be fair, it's got a nice label,' she said, holding one bottle so we could all see. 'It's got a screw top and these two came out of the chill cabinet, the man in there insisted. We had a lovely chat. He said the wine is from a vineyard near here and it's *zoirós*, very lively, and he's sure we will like it.'

'Lively?' I said doubtfully. 'I don't think I've heard that before. We'd better stand back when we open the bottle. Goodness me, we are living dangerously.'

'I remember not so long ago we used to answer the phone without knowing who was calling. Now that was living dangerously,' Beryl said.

We carried on towards Hotel Costas, arriving just as Dennis, Susan and June were leaving, their art materials in their shoulder bags.

'We are off to paint the sea,' he boomed. 'Don't you want to come too? It's such a fine afternoon and we have nothing planned.'

'Perhaps we'll catch up with you later,' Anita said, and Dennis tipped his hat towards her.

'I'm happy to wait if you like?'

'No, I wouldn't want to hold you up. We're going to have lunch first,' she said, holding up her paper bag by way of explanation, with a sweet smile that did little to dissuade him.

'It's no trouble,' he said.

Behind him, Susan and June were sitting on the little wall outside the hotel, apparently chatting happily. Susan took one sandal off and they both looked intently at her heel, so perhaps they were discussing the progress of Susan's blister.

'I think your friends are eager to get going,' Anita said. 'Mustn't keep the ladies waiting. After all, the weather may change. You know how clever you are at catching the light. It might rain. Or be foggy.'

We all looked at the clear, cerulean sky and obviously this was highly unlikely, but it seemed Dennis was persuaded, and after eliciting a promise that he would see us all later, he ambled off, June and Susan following at a statelier pace.

Having all agreed the rooftop terrace would probably be too hot at this time of day, we made our way to the lovely courtyard in the middle of the hotel. There it was deliciously cool, the shade from the hotel walls providing relief from the sun, and Costas had switched on the fountain in the middle, so the sound of splashing water added to the feeling we were in a little oasis of calm.

We opened our lunch bags and after a few minutes' quiet enjoyment of the delicious flavours, Effie went off to the water cooler in reception and brought back four plastic cups.

'Well, we ought to give this wine a try before it gets warm, don't you think?' she said. 'It would only be polite.'

Beryl unscrewed the lid and poured a tiny amount into each one, and after touching our beakers together and shouting '*Yamas*', we tried it.

Then we pulled faces at each other.

'It's not what I would call *lively*.' Anita coughed.

'Probably deadly,' Beryl suggested, 'still, I am sure it will take the tea stains off my tooth enamel. I'll ask my hygienist if that's even possible the next time I see her.'

We took another sip.

'Sherbert lemons?' Effie suggested.

'Mixed with salad dressing,' I added.

'But actually, now I'm getting used to it, I quite like it,' Anita said, holding up her beaker and squinting at the wine. 'It's sort of… brisk.'

'That's a good word. Brisk and efficient,' Beryl said, 'and a bit lively. That sounds like my hygienist too. It's certainly woken up my tastebuds.'

Effie stuck out her tongue and patted the end of it. 'I think mine are a bit numb actually.'

'Probably good with fish,' I said, and I pointed at my chocolate-glazed cream puff. 'Not *kokakia*.'

Beryl filled up our beakers. 'Let's give it another try. It reminds me of something I drank in Peru years ago, made by such a lovely family. But they didn't really know what they were doing. Anyway, I'm sure this is much better than that. It doesn't taste particularly wine-ish though, does it?'

She picked up the bottle and squinted at the label.

'It just says wine from local growers, nothing about alcohol content. But the good thing is we are supporting the local economy so that's fine. It's growing on me actually. Which is just as well as I bought two bottles. Two litres. That's a lot of wine.'

'Go big or go home, isn't that what people say?' I said.

Beryl gave me a look. 'People who say that seriously underestimate my enjoyment of going home. Now then, did anyone get any good pictures this morning? Even if we didn't paint anything.'

We all took out our phones and scrolled through them. Mine seemed to have a lot of pictures of food, some great views over the sea and a few from the ancient village that morning. Including – I felt a jolt of shock – one with Will in the background. Goodness, I hadn't even realised he was there.

I enlarged the photo and zoomed in to look at it more closely.

Yes, it was definitely him. And he had been smiling. Sunglasses off for once. The others had been standing by the remains of an amphitheatre, chatting away quite comfortably by the looks of it. Dennis had been holding out one finger, presumably pointing out the perspective he hoped to capture. Will was standing in that easy, rather elegant way that was so hard to define.

I stared at Will's face. For once he had his hat off as well as the sunglasses, and I thought again what a nice face it was. A face you could trust. A face that was new to me and at the same time annoyingly familiar.

I sent some of the pictures on to Nicky, plus a couple of selfies I had taken of the four of us about to eat, another sitting on the minibus, all of us looking excited.

MUM

> Just so you can see where we are and what we have been up to, although not much painting done yet. I've been having too much fun exploring. As you can see I've made some new friends. The weather is gorgeous and the food is excellent. We are in the middle of drinking a bottle of local wine, 4 euros for a litre! It's different but I don't think I will bring any home. How is work going? Any updates on if the library is closing or not?

An hour later, we had finished the bottle of wine and all of us were thinking it was probably stronger than we realised.

'I need a little nap,' Effie said, 'and I need to commune with my conscience about not having any alcohol today. Perhaps I will call it in-depth training, so when we get some of the good stuff tomorrow we will realise the difference.'

'That's a great take on things,' Beryl said. 'We are now informed. We can make our own choices.'

'My choice is to have a lie down,' I said.

I looked at my watch; it was three thirty. Had I changed it to local time or was that GMT? For a moment I couldn't remember. We had a discussion about this and decided it was right, so there was still the opportunity for a bit of a – what had Beryl said? A *messimeri*. A siesta.

I thought of my clean, comfortable bed upstairs, the bedroom which would have been straightened up and hoovered by the cleaning staff, my own little bathroom, and the lovely view out over the twinkling Mediterranean, and I sighed happily at the prospect.

The big windows onto the balcony would be open to allow the breeze from the Mediterranean in, but the shutters would be closed and the sunlight would be filtering through, casting dappled shade onto the bed. Maybe the kittens would be out there, snoozing in their canvas hammock. Perhaps they would poke their little furry faces over the edge when they heard me come in. The whole thing sounded irresistible.

'In fact, that's a great idea,' I said, standing up.

The other three followed and we made our way to our rooms to sleep off the *ntópio krasi* and gather our resources together for another evening.

Back in my room, I undressed and slipped into my dressing gown. I'd have liked a cup of tea actually, and for a moment I looked over at the little cupboard in the corner where there was a kettle and my plastic zip-lock bag of proper teabags brought from home, but in the end I decided I couldn't be bothered and lay down on my bed with a sigh of relief. This was absolute bliss, and I felt marvellous.

As I closed my eyes and felt myself relax deliciously into a snooze, my mobile buzzed with a text, and of course I looked. As a parent there is always the tiny thought at the back of one's mind that back home, *something might have happened*. Although even if it had, what I could do about it was anyone's guess.

It was from Nicky.

NICKY

Looks like you're having a brilliant time, good for you. No more news about the library, we are going to start a petition and also try and think about doing new things to make the place more visible. The weather here is horrible, it's cold and raining on and off. I had to stand on the edge of a muddy pitch the other day watching Joe play in a football tournament. It was hours of purgatory. #badwifealert

Ivan is fine, he hoovers up his food like a good 'un. I took him some leftover sausages this morning, and he was delighted. I sat in the kitchen for an hour yesterday doing some paperwork, and I thought he might like some company. Ivan came and sat on my lap and purred like mad. And then he kept lying across my laptop and getting in the way, it was so funny.

By the way, I showed your pictures to Joyce just now (you met her, she was retired and then volunteered to come in and help with the pre-schoolers reading group) and she said what is Doctor Bill doing there? She says he hasn't been heard of for years. I can almost remember him but I wouldn't have recognised him. He's devilishly attractive. Joyce asked if he was filming?

# 13

I sat up so fast that for a moment I felt quite dizzy, although of course that might have been the effects of the wine. I hung on to the edge of the bed until everything calmed down and then I reached for my laptop. I'd left it on top of the dressing table in a jumble of adaptors, plugs and cables, and it took me a few minutes to untangle everything. Then I made the cup of tea after all and sat back down on my bed with my laptop on my knees.

*Search: Doctor Bill*

Even as I waited for the information to load up, I could suddenly vaguely remember him. And then I wondered why it had taken me this long to put the pieces together and realise who he was.

Morning television had been in its infancy back then in the 1980s. All I could remember was a lot of loud, rather smug presenters (*look how early we've got up, aren't we marvellous*) plus some irritating, childish entertainers making a racket with sock puppets. Malcolm had hated it, saying it was annoying and patronising, and for once I had agreed with him. It was something that we therefore didn't see very often, although sometimes when I was at home with Nicky when she was little I'll admit I had switched it on. There weren't that many channels back then, and not much else to watch.

As time went by, some of the presenters became more well known and had begun to appear on other programmes as celebrities. And Doctor Bill had been one of them.

He had started out as the resident doctor on *Marvellous Mornings*, popping up from time to time to talk about flu and immunisation, or perhaps giving expert advice on varicose veins or the problem of glue sniffing in schools. He had always been well-dressed in a suit and tie, well-spoken and polite, even when faced with the most outlandish theories. He'd had a fan base of women who should have known better who sent in silly questions to his 'Ask Doctor Bill' spot.

He became quite a celebrity himself, appearing on cooking shows and panel games where he would be pawed rather embarrassingly by other female panellists, the sort of thing that these days would never be allowed.

And then he had simply disappeared from screens everywhere, almost overnight. There had been no explanation, no scandal, no awkward photographs of him emerging bleary-eyed from hotels or nightclubs. No claims that he had been something of a predator or unpleasant to work with. And not that I would have read them, but I couldn't remember any kiss-and-tell exposés in the Sunday papers from fading starlets desperate for attention who had hooked up with him. Nothing.

I scrolled through the links to find out more. There were images of him, with longer, dark hair. He's been much younger, of course, obviously taken in his television days, some with celebrities grinning next to him. There were pictures of him with the rest of the *Marvellous Mornings* team when they celebrated their first anniversary, and there was a very brief Wikipedia post which said nothing very much.

Dr William McKenzie James, born in Dorset, qualified from medical school in Oxford, worked for Médecins Sans Frontières in Europe and Africa for several years before pursuing a career in media on Marvellous Mornings. He appeared several times on Ask the Doctor, Medical Matters and a regular on Your Health Your Choice, and then left to pursue other interests. Married Selena Montgomery 1988–1990. No children. Update needed on this post.

There were a few old posts from people wondering what had happened to him. And that was all.

I frowned, wondering what the mystery was, and then I drank my tea and opened the shutters. A kitten came zooming in, scuffed up the bedside rug and went out again.

Perhaps Will had just gone back to being a doctor, and there was no mystery at all. But then I discovered there had even been a fan club, The Bill-Lovers, started by a woman called Fifi in the West Midlands who, for a small yearly fee, would send updates and photos, allegedly signed by him. I clicked on the most recent link, which was from nearly a decade ago.

No news to report this year, Bill-Lovers. And sad to say I'll be closing down this site. Remembering Doctor Bill with love and hugs. Or should that be Heimlich manoeuvres? Haha! I'm sure you miss him as much as I do. Sad face.

I had a message last month from a Bill-Lover in Spain who thought she saw him at the beach in Marbella, but having seen the photo, I don't think it was. And I'm sure Doctor Bill wouldn't have been serving ice cream anyway. Even if he did give her an extra flake. Which of course is exactly what he would have done. If it had been him.

I know you lovely fans will miss talking about our favourite Doctor Bill moments. I think the best one was when he was spotted in Waitrose buying asparagus. I never eat it now without thinking of him. Wasn't he gorgeous, ladies? Signing off for now, Fifi.

I looked back at the images of him as a young man again, recognising the same lovely eyes, kind face and tall frame. There were even some of him at awards ceremonies in a DJ, and didn't he scrub up well. In a couple, the elegant blonde woman beside him was identified as his wife Selena. My word, she was a stunner – tall, willowy and gorgeous. What a fantastic couple they made, and yet...

I sat back and stared into space. Flipping heck. I'd discovered the whereabouts of the elusive Doctor Bill, and he had resurfaced all these years later here, on a painting course when he wasn't actually doing any painting as far as I could tell. He'd taken me out to dinner and been incredibly friendly. And he'd kissed me. Goodness, that would give the Bill-Lovers something to think about.

What should I do next? Should I tell the others, confront him with the news that I knew who he was?

No, of course not. I wasn't going to do any of those things. Apart from anything else, it would undoubtedly mean that Dennis would want a long consultation with him about his ankle, his cholesterol medication and who knew what other medical problems. People always did that to doctors, didn't they? Try and get some free advice. I pulled a face in sympathy.

The best thing to do was nothing. I would carry on as though

I didn't know. And treat him exactly the same. But would I be able to do so when I had just now seen photographs of him smiling as he met the Queen, a couple of prime ministers and two of the Spice Girls?

I would do my best. And I definitely wouldn't mention my problems with my knee or ask him what he thought about statins.

\* \* \*

That evening, Jillian was determined we would all go out together. Why she kept on trying to round us up, I had no idea. We had all been quite happy spending time with the people we liked and really didn't need to be treated like an unruly school party.

Just after six thirty we assembled around a table in Trofi ton Theón, which Beryl said translated as Food of the Gods.

Jillian stood at one end of the table, while the waiters hovered with menus behind her. She wanted to explain about our trip to the vineyard the following day, and had even printed out some sheets of paper explaining where it was and what to expect.

'Everyone enjoys this tour,' she said, a bright smile fixed on her face. 'Everyone.'

'Even the tee-totallers?' Effie murmured, taking one of the sheets and passing the rest on.

She was rewarded with a hard look.

'And I know you will enjoy it too. It's just a short ride in the minibus and we will be leaving the hotel at two o'clock, so don't be late or Gregor will go without you. He's a great fan of the place.'

'I hope he won't be joining in?' Dennis said. 'His driving is bad enough without adding a wine tasting into the mix.'

Jillian gave an exasperated sigh.

'No, of course not, but apparently his daughter was married there a few years ago. It's a gorgeous place with lovely views, of course. A great location to take pictures, perhaps to use later for a painting, if some of you ever get round to doing any,' she added quietly.

'She means us,' Effie muttered. 'Well, I'm definitely not going to do any painting now, just to annoy her.'

I smothered a snort of laughter.

'There is no actual meal, just a few tasty nibbles which have been specially selected from local suppliers to complement the various wines,' Jillian said. 'I have quite a good palate.'

'Me too,' Beryl said, 'although mine is covered in acrylics. Perhaps I should clean it off, although I don't think Van Gogh ever did. I saw his at a museum once, it was a right old mess.'

'I mean *palate*, not *palette*,' Jillian said, annoyed.

'Of course, I'm just being silly,' Beryl said.

'And then you can buy bottles of your favourite wines at a discount if you want to. Some of them are really good value. An absolute bargain.'

'Are they more than four euros?' Effie asked, her expression innocent.

'Well, yes, of course they are,' Jillian said. 'But some of the bin-ends are very reasonably priced.'

'Not that great then,' Beryl murmured.

Jillian rapped on the table with the back of a fork to hush everyone.

'Now that I have you all here *for once,* and it's obvious that my work with the handouts has been a waste of time, I am just going to remind you that tomorrow morning is free time, and late afternoon we will be going to the vineyards for the wine-tasting experience. The day after that I have arranged a still-life session, which will be for *everyone*, and will be up on the roof terrace at ten thirty. I do hope *all* of you will be there.'

Jillian sent a sharp look down to our end of the table.

Will was sitting almost opposite me, and we exchanged quick glances. I gave him a rather nervous grin, and he smiled back. Could I think of him just as Will any more, or would I forever imagine him standing by the lovely Selena outside a London theatre at the Royal Variety Show, getting a Blue Peter badge from presenter Yvette Fielding or having an interview with the programme's canine sock-puppet mascot Marvellous Monty about going to the vet.

Hmm.

'That sounds like a group directive to me. We'd better comply or she might turn nasty. Have you had a good afternoon?' he said as we scanned our menus.

'We had some local wine. It was four euros from the supermarket.'

'And was it nice?'

'It depends what you mean by nice,' I said. 'We didn't have any tasty nibbles specially selected from local suppliers to complement it.'

He chuckled. 'That's where you went wrong, obviously.'

I laughed too, feeling more at ease.

'There is a lovely looking menu in their actual restaurant. I was looking on their website,' he said at last. 'I thought we might go there one evening, if you like? It was just an idea.'

'Count me in! That sounds great,' I said, and I took a deep breath, hoping the others hadn't overheard him. 'But how would we get there? We don't have a car.'

It was funny talking like this with him, using the 'we' word about a man again. It made me feel rather odd.

'Local bus? Taxi?' he said.

He turned back to his menu, and so did I.

'Fish with purple potato salad and black garlic ketchup,' Dennis announced loudly from his end of the table. 'That sounds colourful. I bet you wouldn't get that in Lower Begley.'

'Steak and asparagus,' Will said. 'I like the sound of that.'

I was reminded of the mournful Fifi in the West Midlands, who undoubtedly would have blown a gasket if she had heard this.

In the end I decided that as I was wearing a black t-shirt, I was safe ordering linguini with tomatoes and clams. Undoubtedly I would splatter some of it over myself, but no one would notice.

It took a long time to take the order for our food, as people kept asking for substitutions and changing their minds when they heard what other people were ordering, but at last we were left alone with some carafes of iced water and house wine.

'I'm not drinking this evening,' I said. 'I think I've had enough for one day and my taste buds need a chance to recover from the wine we had earlier.'

'Good idea,' he said, 'me too.'

How nice that he didn't think he had to persuade me to change my mind. Unless I was the designated driver, Malcolm had always protested when I said I didn't want a drink. Calling me a killjoy or boring. Which perhaps I had been. To me, wine had been something to do with a celebration, not just something to be knocked back.

'Done any painting yet?' Will asked.

I pulled one of the long, thin breadsticks out of the jar on the table and bit off the end.

'Nothing,' I said defiantly, and he grinned.

'Drawing? Sketching? Creating the outline for something?'

I shook my head. 'None of the above.'

'Thought about it?'

'Nope.'

He took a sip of iced water.

'Jillian would say we are lazy.' He grinned.

'Not lazy, I prefer to think of it as selective participation.'

He laughed. 'Good for you. That sounds far more acceptable. But we will be getting a very bad end-of-term report from Jillian at this rate.'

'I don't care,' I said, 'I'm just enjoying myself. Isn't that what holidays are supposed to be all about?'

He nodded.

'She will ask why we signed up for a painting tour when we obviously aren't doing anything remotely artistic. So, what are you getting out of it?' I said, suddenly bold.

He didn't speak for a moment and was obviously thinking very carefully about what to say in response to this. It made me feel uneasy, as though I was treading on dangerous territory.

'I haven't had a proper holiday for a while,' he said at last. 'I was – well, I was away for a long time, and then when I came back I had a few issues I had to deal with.'

'You were in a Guatemalan prison for armed robbery?' I said with a grin.

He chuckled and his face relaxed again. 'No, nothing like that, I can assure you. It's just sometimes – I don't know, one falls out of the habit of thinking of a trip abroad as an actual holiday.'

Ah, yes, I remembered, of course, the Médecins Sans Frontières years, mentioned on Wikipedia.

'This is the first time I have enjoyed a holiday for years,' I said. 'I don't know why exactly. Just the freedom to do what I like, go where I like, think what I like.'

I accompanied the last few words with a jaunty wave of my breadstick, like an orchestra conductor, and of course, it broke in two and half of it fell into his water glass with a splosh.

I looked at him, agonised, concerned what his reaction would be and wondering what I should do. I couldn't exactly go delving into his water with my fingers and grab it. Malcolm would have been immensely annoyed, I knew that.

'Gosh, I'm so sorry,' I said.

'Good shot.' He chuckled and fished it out.

'Shall I ask for a clean glass?'

'No, no need for that,' he said and took a sip of water. And then he fished another crumb of breadstick out and winked at me.

Such a silly little thing, but somehow it was important. I could do something daft and not be sneered at. It was a refreshing moment, and it made my poor old, battered heart sing.

The food arrived then, four waiters carrying our meals out from the kitchen with a lot of noise and bustle, and the head waiter came over to supervise them with a lot of theatrical gestures as he congratulated us on our choices and offered additional condiments and sauces.

It wasn't like this back home; they seemed genuinely pleased to have us there, and happy with what they were doing. Perhaps they weren't, and when they went back through the swing doors, their shoulders slumped and they resumed their grumbles and arguments. But for us, that evening, it was delightful and somehow added to the experience.

The head waiter stood there for a few moments, with a wistful smile on his face, fretting about refilling the water jugs. Did everyone have the right cutlery? Could he do anything more for us?

My pasta was delicious, just the right mixture of sweet and spicy, and although I did leave a few splatters of sauce on the tablecloth, I don't think any landed on me.

At the other end of the table, Dennis was telling Jillian a story that the rest of us had heard several times, about his family in India. How a very important local dignitary had wanted to marry his mother and adopt the cherubic baby Dennis, and how his mother had refused because, after all, she was already married to Geoffrey and also had young Ronald to think about. But the very important local dignitary didn't want Ronald, so it all came to nothing. And how often Dennis had wondered what might have been.

'This tale differs every time I hear it,' Beryl murmured. 'If we hang around long enough it will be the Maharajah of Jaipur who wanted to adopt him. This food is absolutely marvellous, isn't it? And yet so simple, and one almost thinks it would be possible to make it at home.'

'Except you never cook,' Effie said. 'I don't think you know how to turn the oven on.'

'Here's a life hack. If you don't ever turn the oven on, you never have to worry about whether you turned it off or not,' Beryl said. 'I expect I could cook this if I wanted to.'

Anita thought about this. 'But then you wouldn't have the warm evening or the sea over your shoulder, or someone else making it and clearing up afterwards.'

'Or the company,' Will added.

Beryl's eyes sparkled. 'Yes, that's true. And how are you enjoying yourself, Will?'

'Very much,' he said, turning his attention back to his steak. 'Very much indeed.'

'And what do you do? Are you still working?'

'Retired, I'm glad to say,' he said. 'What about all of you?'

This of course neatly deflected the conversation away from himself, as people told tales of their working lives and families and how much more pleasant it was to have given up work.

I thought about what I knew – that he had, after all, been a bit of a celebrity a long time ago – and then I wondered why he was still reluctant to discuss it at any level. After all, there were twenty times as many so-called celebrities these days. They were always crawling out of the woodwork on television game shows, in advertisements, on reality programmes when their opinions – however ludicrous – were earnestly discussed and reported and given credence.

I looked up at one point and Will did the same, and in that moment when our gazes locked, I knew he had done this deliberately, and he knew, for want of a better phrase, that I knew too. It made me feel somehow more connected to him, as though we shared something, a little secret, an awareness of each other. And then he gave a little smile and looked away again, and the moment was gone.

I finished my pasta while around me the conversation had drifted away from the restrictions and responsibilities of a working life and on to what makes a good painting.

This, predictably, degenerated into a fairly heated discussion about the balance between technical skill and intellectual depth and then only more dangerous territory about whether a painting should be realistic or not.

'I mean,' Dennis boomed, 'all this nonsense about modern art and blank canvases with one blue dot on them. Who wants that in their living room? Sally wouldn't give them house room, she's more likely to give them to the grandchildren to finish off with their crayons. I have five granddaughters, have I told you?'

This of course successfully opened up the conversation to grandchildren – who had the most, who had the cleverest, the cutest, the most outstanding. Everyone scrolled through their phones to pull up pictures of the little tots, and naturally Will and his past history was forgotten.

Paying the bill took a long time. There was no way the group was just going to split the bill, and so Jillian took out a notebook and pen and asked for a menu to be brought back so that she could work out who owed what. Then there was the problem of the added things which might or might not have been shared between people, who had drunk red wine, who had ordered white.

And then there was the worry of a tip and how much were we expected to leave. By the time Dennis had told us for the third time that it was bad manners to tip at all in Japan, I think most of us had endured enough, and I almost wished that I could have whipped out my credit card and paid for the lot so we could get out of there.

After thirty minutes of that, I pulled out some euros and put them on the table, enough to cover the cost of my meal and a hefty tip, and at the same time, Will did the same.

'Good idea,' Beryl said approvingly. 'I've had enough of this nonsense.'

'It's like Daddy totting up a mess bill,' Effie added.

'Oh my goodness, do you remember that time he told us about Cowley Camp in Egypt...'

They pulled out their purses and added to the little pile of notes on the table, and then Anita followed suit and the five of us stood up to leave, much to Dennis's confusion, because he thought we were doing a runner.

'I say, you can't just leave,' he said.

Beryl shuffled the notes together, rapidly counted them and handed them over like a bank teller.

'I think you will find that more than covers our share of things,' she said sweetly.

'Well, now we're in a right old beggar's muddle. Jillian will have to start again,' Dennis grumbled as we made our excuses and left.

## 14

The following day, we had the morning free to 'find a place that thrills you,' as Jillian put it, and then at three o'clock we were due to go to the much-anticipated wine-tasting experience.

Beryl and Effie decided the place that thrilled them most that morning was the roof terrace where they were planning on sketching the view while Costas made them endless cups of coffee and brought them plates of Nina's baklava at regular intervals.

Anita and I decided to go down to the little harbour where we found a café where there were comfortable chairs and charming waiters who didn't seem to mind us hanging around for two hours.

Anita did a few rough sketches of a fishing boat, while I drank coffee and closed my eyes against the sunshine, which gradually peeked out from under the shade of the yellow parasols. I didn't think I had been this comfortable within myself for months. And I was contented, right through to my bones, with a gentle breeze from the sea, the restful sounds of the water and lazy chatter of the few people who were about.

Why couldn't life be like that all the time? Were all the people around me just generally cheerful and it was all a coincidence that we had come here at the same time? That man with the two teenage sons, the woman with her toddler in a stroller, that family eating ice cream; all of them looked happy. Perhaps it was easier to be content in a warmer climate. But that couldn't be the sole reason. So what was it?

'You look very relaxed,' Anita said, looking up from her sketch pad, 'more so than I've ever seen you.'

'I like it here. I'm so glad I came,' I said. 'The hotel, the company, the food; it's all lovely.'

'And Will?' she asked, giving me a sly look. 'You two are getting along famously, aren't you?'

'Oh, I wouldn't go that far,' I said, feeling myself blush.

'I can tell,' she said, making some sweeping strokes of her pencil over the paper. 'It was just the same with Sophia when we went to Rhodes, and she met Theo. A sort of sparkle between them. It was very sweet to watch.'

'And what happened?'

'She sold her house and bought one in Rhodes. You could do that reasonably easily back then, and they are still together.'

'Well, obviously that's not happening,' I said with a little laugh, 'but I do like him. And I'm curious about him, he gives so little away.'

'I expect he wants to put his past behind him, all things considered.'

'What things?' I said, rather sharply.

'Well, his days as Doctor Bill on that awful morning television programme. Didn't you recognise him? I knew I remembered him from somewhere,' Anita said. 'I like what I've done here. I might even have a go at doing a watercolour wash when I get back to the hotel.'

'I thought I was the only one who realised who he was,' I said.

'You didn't say anything.'

'Well, nor did you! And I didn't watch that programme much, because Malcolm didn't approve of it. So what do you know about him?'

'Who, Malcolm?'

'No, Doctor Bill of course, don't be daft.'

Anita shrugged. 'Only that he was everywhere once upon a time, and then there was that business with his wife—'

I sat up, alert to find out more.

'What business?'

'Golly, where have you been hiding? Don't you remember? She ran off with that bloke, the one in that thing. That pop group. You know who I mean; nasty little mouth, and didn't seem to own a hairbrush, thought he was God's gift. He was always in the papers coming out of nightclubs with some twiglet young enough to be his daughter. Benjamin something. Barker? Ben Johnson? No, he was an athlete, wasn't he. Benjamin Franklin? No it can't have been him. Um... um...'

'And then what happened?' I said rather breathlessly.

'I think he just gave it all up and left. I hadn't heard anything about Doctor Bill for years and then he pops up here. There was no mistaking that jawline and those eyes. Beryl and Effie had never heard of him, so they weren't that interested when I told them. Look, if you're that concerned, why don't you ask him?'

'I'm not. And I couldn't,' I said.

'Why not? It's not as though you're asking for his autograph across your bosom like they used to. I suppose those were the days before social media, and the newspapers actually published the news back then, and didn't fill their column inches with celebrity gossip and pictures of girls in bikinis with – what do they insist on calling them? – pert *derrières*. Can you catch the waiter's eye next time he goes past? I'd like some more coffee.'

I thought about this for a while. Wondering what it would have been like for Will back then. Did he enjoy the fame or did he find it a burden? Did he still have a lot of famous people for friends? Did that make us rather boring as a result? He evidently didn't want his past life to be brought up again and discussed. He had been so considerate when I made a fool of myself falling over that evening; perhaps I should show the same sort of discretion.

'Can we not talk about this to the others?' I said. 'If he has spent such a long time avoiding being noticed, perhaps we should respect that?'

'If you like,' Anita said with a shrug, 'although it's been such a long time.'

\* \* \*

I thought about it a great deal that morning. In fact, it was so much on my mind that I was quite surprised when we were joined just before one o'clock by Beryl and Effie, who had been wandering around the town buying souvenirs and exploring the many little churches in the town and were now looking for a snack.

'Do you know there are over a thousand churches on this island alone,' Effie said as she settled down to read the menu. 'That's about one for every twenty people who live here. The curator of one of them told us people used to build them to cele-brate their favourite saint. And on the saint's day, the family had to hold a *panigyri* and invite all their relatives and the neigh-bours. It must have cost them a fortune.'

'I was told that people built them because a church doesn't

have to pay the electricity company to connect them. And then after a while they quietly add on a house,' Beryl said.

'Yes, that makes sense.' I nodded. 'You wouldn't get away with that in Lower Begley.'

'Nor would you get grilled Halloumi with fresh pomegranate seeds,' Anita said, looking at the menu. 'I'm definitely having that. And some water. Absolutely definitely no wine.'

'I wonder how my daughter is getting on at home,' I said after our order had been taken. 'She says her library might be closed at the end of the year. It's such a shame; they are doing all they can to get people in and it's always busy when I go there. I don't understand it.'

Beryl nodded. 'You know what Albert Einstein said. "The only thing you absolutely have to know is the location of the library." And he didn't do too badly, did he? Before the internet, people used to think the cause of stupidity was lack of access to information; well, now we know it wasn't that.'

'You need someone with influence, the mayor or the local MP or something. To take a stand,' Anita said.

'I don't think either of them would lift a finger,' I said, 'and I don't actually know either of them. I see the mayor in the paper occasionally, giving awards to local businessmen. And there was a television crew in Begley Mortimer not long ago, filming an episode of the *Antiques Roadshow*, and he was there, centre stage, in his robes. Other than that—'

'A protest march then?' Effie said.

'You know society is seriously messed up if librarians start marching,' Beryl snorted, 'and people today just seem to find out things on their phones rather than books.'

I held up an admonishing finger. 'Nicky says a good librarian can find something more accurately than a search engine.'

'You're right. Ah, here comes our food. Gosh, do we really

need more to eat?' Effie said. 'My trousers are getting tighter by the day.'

'We have specially selected snacks to go with the wine tasting later,' I said, 'which means we will fall out of the place absolutely stuffed.'

'I bet it won't be a beige buffet either,' Beryl said. 'I've not seen a sausage roll since I arrived here.'

* * *

We returned to Hotel Costas just after one thirty to find Susan and June, wearing almost matching sundresses, already sitting outside waiting for the minibus.

'I hate being late for anything,' June said. 'It's genetic. I can't help myself. I'd rather be an hour early than a minute late for something.'

'Me too,' Susan agreed. 'If I say I'll be somewhere at nine o'clock and I'm late, you'll know I've had an accident. I'd probably be lying on the kitchen floor unconscious.'

'Or your car will have had a puncture.' June nodded.

'Or I've had a stroke, or burglars have broken in and are holding me hostage.'

'Have any of these things ever happened to you?' I asked.

'No, but it happens all the time in Los Angeles. I watch that series. And the one in New Orleans. Drug cartels and men with guns all over the place. It's very worrying, to think they might come to Lower Begley, looking for drug donkeys.'

'I think it's drug mules,' June said. 'I always worry when I go through security that I'm going to be searched for cocaine. I'd be hopeless with a lie detector. My pulse rate rockets at the sight of sniffer dogs in case they mistake my perfume for something else. My husband bought me Opium perfume in duty-free once; I didn't dare use it. And I'm just as bad with traffic wardens.'

Beryl snorted. 'I don't need any drugs. At my age I can get the same effect just standing up too quickly.'

Susan flapped a hand. 'That too; anyway, Gregor will be here soon, so you'd better get ready. I am looking forward to this. Apparently there is a wine called Vin Santo, which is like communion wine it's so sweet. I'm very partial to that. I think it's the highlight of the Sunday service sometimes. Hurry up, we won't let him go without you.'

We went off to our rooms to freshen up and in the spirit of holiday enthusiasm, I put on a new sundress I had bought in one of the shops in town. It was quite flouncy and very pretty with a pattern of pink roses. I paired that with some white trainers and admired my reflection in the wardrobe mirror for a moment. I didn't look sixty-four, did I? Maybe I did. And actually, perhaps it didn't matter.

I went back downstairs, liking how the full skirts of my new dress swirled around my knees. I would be more adventurous in future with my fashion choices, although if I was honest, I couldn't really see myself wearing that dress into the local super-market or opening the door to the postman with quite the same confidence. Still, I had enjoyed buying it, making a choice for myself without having to ask someone else's opinion, and that had been part of my satisfaction.

'Right then, the gang's all here,' Beryl said from her seat by the front door.

'And here comes the minibus,' Anita said, shielding her eyes from the afternoon sun as she looked down the road. 'Gregor is right on time for once. I expect he is looking forward to visiting the vineyard. Perhaps he gets a preferential rate?'

'I don't know much about wine, but I know what I like,'

Dennis said. 'I can't be doing with all this hints of gooseberry or chocolate or vanilla. Just give me a nice glass of decent plonk and I'm happy. Anyone agree?'

'Absolutely right, Dennis,' Anita said, earning herself an approving nod. 'And I tend to choose the one with the prettiest label anyway.'

'As good a reason as any,' Dennis said.

'But I don't think I'll ever like a wine as much as I liked Tizer when I was a kid,' she added.

'No, well, Ronald and I weren't allowed fizzy drinks when we were children. That's why I've got my own teeth,' Dennis said.

'I've got my own teeth too,' June piped up, 'and I brought a spare set in my washbag.'

'Oh, for goodness' sake,' Dennis muttered.

\* \* \*

The drive to the Ampelónes Apóllona – the Apollo Vineyards – took about an hour, along another picturesque road that hugged the coast. Past boats and little villages and several tiny churches of course, situated in the middle of rocky fields. I'd counted eleven before, at last, the minibus pulled through some impressive metal gates and we stopped outside the doors to the shop.

It wasn't what I had been expecting at all. Everything was very modern with an attractive décor of shining glass and new wood, and there were wonderful shelves full of wine bottles. There was a lovely warm scent everywhere. The faint drift of garlic and herbs, mixed with wine. Even the air seemed a bit intoxicating.

We spent a few minutes outside on the terrace, admiring the view down over the sea, where we could see three speedboats swirling their wake behind them, and a couple of cruise ships moored up. It was breathtaking. What a fabulous place to see, to be a part of with other people who were obviously equally as enchanted as I was.

Eventually, having taken lots of pictures and selfies with the sea twinkling behind us, Jillian rounded us up and led us to a long table which had been set for our group.

'I've never been anywhere like this,' I said. 'It's just beautiful.'

'The Italian Lakes are like that.' Will nodded from his seat opposite me. 'They take your breath away. I remember looking out over Lake Eseo when I was there for a wedding. It was like being in a film set. And no painting or photograph could ever capture it. You had to be there, to really experience what the world can be like.'

How true, I thought. All the photographs and documentaries I had ever seen of places like the Grand Canyon or the pyramids probably didn't show just how awe-inspiring they were in real life. I felt even more determined then. I would see them. I would go and find out for myself.

Shortly after that, a charming waitress came to our table and the usual discussions began about what we were going to order. There were several possibilities. One actual glass of wine for those who preferred to keep things simple. Or three different sample sizes. Five samples. Seven or nine for the people taking it seriously.

'Three glasses of wine? You'd have to carry me to the minibus. And then take me to a hospital to recover,' June said, wide-eyed.

'They aren't full glasses,' Jillian said, 'just little measures for you to sip and then you refer to the tasting notes.'

'I don't think I could manage five. And does anyone ever order nine?' Susan said. 'Surely that would be dangerous. I mean, I'm practically teetotal. Just the occasional sherry or a port and lemon. That's about my limit these days. My mother was the same, except she used to like a Babycham at Christmas, or a snowball. And then she would sleep on the sofa all afternoon after lunch.'

'They aren't full glasses,' Jillian sighed, 'I told you, and it's in the handout.'

'And what's this about food?' Dennis called from his end of the table. 'Don't we have to order that first?'

'It's not actually a meal; it's the specially selected local delicacies that they provide. It's in the handout,' Jillian said.

June held up her hand as though she was at school. 'So do we have to order starters as well as main courses? Because Susan and I had quite a big lunch. We went to that place we went to the first evening. The Blue Sea. We had calamari. Absolutely lovely and fresh, not a bit like the own-brand frozen ones I've had from the supermarket.'

Jillian's smile froze a little.

'It's just a platter of small nibbles. Not a meal. It was all in the handout...'

'Well, I'm not driving anywhere so I think I'll go mad for once and have the nine glasses. But will there be dessert?' June asked.

'If you have nine glasses of wine, you won't have room for dessert.' Susan chuckled. 'You'll be in the back of an ambulance.'

'It's sample sizes,' Jillian said through gritted teeth, 'it's all in the handout. I don't know why I bother sometimes.'

'Perhaps I'll just have a sweet sherry,' Susan said, looking down at the menu again, her face puzzled. 'I don't have to have all this, do I? As I said, I'm not much of a drinker. Although I was when I was younger; cider and blackcurrant, that's what I used to like. I don't suppose they do that, do they?'

Will and I exchanged a glance across the table and both of us were obviously trying very hard not to laugh. Next to me, Beryl had no such reservations and she and Effie were by then leaning against each other laughing, Effie dabbing at her eyes with her napkin.

'No, I shouldn't think so, this is a vineyard, where they make wine,' Jillian said faintly. 'Honestly, I'm losing the will, really, I am.'

Eventually, and with commendable patience, our waitress took the orders and went off with a sigh of relief to fetch them. A few minutes later, they started arriving. Oval wooden platters with the requisite number of wine glasses on them, plus some china bowls of nibbles.

The tasting notes were clear and informative and we picked up our first glasses and tried to make the sort of faces we had seen wine experts make. Thoughtful, faintly bemused and slightly puzzled.

'It says dry on the palate, faintly zesty and with a hint of salt,' Anita said.

'And crispy,' I added, referring to my notes.

'I'm getting white wine,' Beryl said, 'and it's not at all dry, it's quite wet.'

Jillian bent forward and gave her a look.

'The old jokes are the best, aren't they?' Beryl smiled back at her.

We worked our way through the different little glasses of wines and picked at the nibbles, which included some salty pistachios, chopped-up cured meats and slices of pita bread and fava bean hummus.

'I don't know if these complement the wines or not,' I said, 'but they taste jolly nice. Did you have some of the Vin Santo, Susan? You said you like communion wine. I think you would love this.'

Susan looked down at her tasting notes. 'I'm not sure I would. It says it's got cinnamon, cloves and a vicious palate.'

'Viscous palate, Susan, viscous,' Jillian said.

Susan perked up. 'Oh well, perhaps I'll give it a go. I say, I feel a bit tiddly already and I've only tried two.'

'Which is your favourite?' Will asked.

I swirled the remains of some white wine around in the glass.

'This one. Assyrtiko, the same as we had the other evening. I like the – what does it say here? – flavours of toast, vanilla and complex herbs.'

He raised his eyebrows. 'Do you indeed?'

'And it says here that it would have a long ageing potential. Well, it wouldn't if it was in my fridge.'

'I'm sure you're right,' he said, and we smiled at each other. 'Perhaps we should buy some to take home?'

'Well, I would but I know if I did, the bottle would break inside the suitcase and I'd never get the smell of wine out of my clothes.'

'Then we would have to drink it here,' he said. 'Problem solved.'

I looked down again at my tasting notes, and then picked up a different glass, one containing a little sample of wine which was a beautiful pink blush, like the bridesmaid's dress at Nicky's wedding. Kissiris Rosé. I sipped it and looked thoughtfully into the distance.

*We*. It was a long time since a man had included me like that. To somehow make me a part of a partnership. And that definitely included Malcolm, whose pronouncements usually started with 'I'.

Yes, I was part of a group here, and *we* were having a fine old time, friendly and companionable, but it was a different sort of thing when it came to Will. Exclusive but also somehow inclusive. I couldn't quite get my head around it.

Did I want to be included in the more exclusive plans Will might make for us? How did I feel about that? I wasn't sure.

'I think I've had enough wine for a while,' I said, putting my glass down. 'I think my liver needs a little rest.'

He nodded. 'I know how you feel. I'm a great one for tea though. Proper builders' tea with one sugar.'

'No sugar for me. I prefer tea with a couple of chocolate digestives,' I said.

'I'll try and remember that,' he said.

This comment sent me into a bit of a spin, which of course might have been due to the seven tasting glasses of wine I had sampled, but then in my defence I hadn't finished any of them.

He was doing it again. Saying things that drew us together. I had spent the last few years pulling away from that sort of thing, from the suffocating control of Malcolm. And since we had divorced, I had gradually learned to be my own boss, to organise my days and not worry about what to make for dinner based on his preferences.

I looked around me. This was a lovely place, a perfect setting. It wasn't just me who needed to rethink my life and find my place in the world. Perhaps all of us did. Did I have long ageing potential too, like the wine?

This group might be a disparate bunch who didn't co-operate as Jillian would have wished, but they were without exception law-abiding, decent people. No one was obnoxious or rude. Everyone was trying their best. And who knew what private traumas or problems they were dealing with? It wasn't just Will who was the unknown quantity here; all of us probably had difficulties, unspoken worries, illnesses and disappointments. I felt a sudden and unexpected affection for all of them.

Perhaps it was just the occasion, the glorious setting, the sea air, the long days of sunshine and relaxation I had enjoyed. It all added up to a slightly unfamiliar feeling of being happy for no particular reason, and at the same time I was enthusiastic for what each day might bring. Anticipation.

Although I had been reasonably content with my daily life as a rule, I hadn't felt that way for a long time. And I liked it.

There was a burst of noise from the other end of the table as Dennis told one of his stories, and June, Susan and Jillian leaned in towards him, laughing.

I suddenly needed a breath of fresh air; I got up from my seat and went to walk on the stone terraces outside with the superb views over the rocky coastline. It felt as though this was the moment, the new beginning I had been seeking after so many years of feeling directionless and unfocused. I had a happily married daughter, maybe the prospect of grandchildren. I had a decent home and pension. I had my health. I had a great deal to be thankful for. It would be wrong to let opportunities pass, to allow the future to slip past unremarked and unremarkable.

I shouldn't take it all for granted. And I wasn't going to. I had behaved and conformed and paid my taxes. I had earned my place. I deserved to be happy as much as the next person.

From today onwards I was going to say no if I felt like it and not explain why. And I was going to say yes to things too, broaden my mind to possibilities and opportunities. Did that include Will? Was he a possibility or an opportunity? Did that sound a bit cold blooded?

Over the last few years with Malcolm, I could see that my life had become predictable, dull and a bit sad. I'd put up with things, gone along with his plans, allowed myself to play second fiddle to his marching band. Well, now I knew what independence felt like.

From now on I was going to find my own way, look for

warmth and lift my face to the sun. The prospect of this made me feel very excited.

# 15

The rest of the evening passed very pleasantly with everyone discussing the wine in quite sensible terms. New parties arrived, settling at their tables and chattering excitedly over the tasting notes just as we had. Occasionally people would wander off to look at the view again, which was changing with the early evening light. The sky changed, dimming to a luscious grey velvet colour over the dark satin sea as the sun set, and then the lights of the houses in the little coastal villages began to twinkle.

I went to lean my warm arms on the cool steel rail of the glass barrier separating me from a plunge down onto the rocks below and took a deep breath of the sea-scented air. I wondered what the people in those houses were doing.

Perhaps some would be returning home from work, preparing an evening meal. Playing with their children or maybe arguing with a partner. Some would be laughing, crying, elated or despairing, and still life would go on. In just a few days I would leave and return to my everyday life and there would be new people sitting here looking at that incredible coastline. Just as people thousands of years ago had done.

'You look very thoughtful,' Will said behind me, and I blushed to think he had followed me. After such a long marriage when I had been largely ignored and then forgotten, it felt strange and yet rather exciting to realise that he wanted to seek me out.

I looked back over Homer's 'wine-dark sea' and sighed with pleasure.

'I'm just wondering what it was like all those years ago when the Minoans left forever. And did people stand here hundreds of years ago and watch invading ships from Greece or Italy and wonder what on earth was happening? Are there people in those houses who right now are taking their first breath or even their last? It's made me think about the future in a way I don't think I have before.'

He leaned his hands on the railing next to me and looked out at the sea.

'And what conclusion did you come to?'

'None really, except I shouldn't be held back by the mistakes I've made. Or more importantly by the actions of other people. You know what it's like when a marriage ends. Was it him? Was it me? Could things have been different? Well, now I think I've been wasting my time fretting and rehashing the past, but now it's time to think about the future.'

He nodded. 'That's a very good way of looking at it.'

'I suppose I am beginning to realise that I can be in control of my life. As long as I don't offend anyone or break any laws, I can do what I like. In future I'm going to do really exciting, epic things. Unless I get too tired, or it's too expensive. In which case I'm going to do more affordable, epic stuff, and make time for naps.'

He laughed then, a proper loud laugh, which made a few people turn round to see what was going on.

'Marvellous,' he said at last. 'You're a tonic. Perhaps they should bottle your spirit and sell it here too.'

'I think I would be a dry white,' I said, 'with fruity undertones and hints of irony and washing up liquid. Good with salads, fillet steak and chocolate digestives.'

'I think you would.' He chuckled. 'In an elegant bottle with a beautiful label. A picture of the sea, a rocky coastline and one perfect seagull wheeling overhead.'

'Not so sure about the seagull,' I said, grinning. 'You know what they're like for stealing your chips or worse.'

'*Chateau Meg. Vin* not *ordinaire* at all. I'd buy a case,' he said, and he put one hand over mine.

'Would you?' I said, half laughing, half breathless with surprise.

'I would,' he said, 'definitely.'

And he looked just for a moment at my mouth, and we all knew what that meant. He was thinking about kissing me. Properly this time.

All sorts of inappropriate, wine-linked thoughts went through my head. Screw-tops and tasting and lying down. Ageing well. Full bodied.

'Homer said wine gives a man fresh strength,' he said, 'and I think you would be that sort of wine—'

*How amazing, I was just thinking about Homer too.*

'You've certainly made such a difference to me, even in this short time.'

'Gosh, have I?' I said. 'I thought the possibility of being an influencer was over.'

'Not at all,' he said, and he took his hand away.

And suddenly I missed the warmth of it, the feel of it. I hadn't expected that at all.

'Remember I said we should come back here for a proper meal one evening?' he said. 'What do you think?'

I swear my heart gave a little thrill of excitement. After an afternoon walking around a shopping mall, Malcolm had once claimed he had atrial fibrillation. I hoped it wasn't that.

'That would be really nice,' I said at last.

*Nice.* What a weak word to use.

'Good. Shall I go and book us a table?'

Wow, I was being consulted too. That made a change.

'Yes, that's a great idea.'

He went off towards the restaurant and I looked around for the signs to the ladies' room. It was downstairs underneath the building, spacious and absolutely spotless with delightful pictures of the island on the walls, light shades made out of wine glasses and some wonderful handwash that smelled of the sea breeze.

I looked at myself in the mirror over the sink as I washed my hands and somehow this time, I looked younger, more alive. Perhaps this place had better lighting than I was used to.

What a perfect evening this had been. And most unexpectedly, I had a date. What should I wear?

'There you are,' said a voice behind me, and Beryl, Effie and Anita barged in through the door, all trying to get in at once.

'What have you been doing?'

'What happened?'

'What did he say?'

'Tell us everything.'

I laughed. 'Honestly, you lot, beak out of it!'

Beryl went to sit in a charming little armchair in one corner, her handbag on her lap.

'We watched you going off and he followed you. And you were talking for ages. I wish I'd had one of my old listening devices in my handbag, I could have tuned it in. You must have said something.'

'He suggested coming back here for dinner,' I said, 'one evening.'

'Oooh,' Anita cooed, 'what a brilliant idea, that would be lovely. I took a look at their menu on my phone; it looks really impressive. I'll choose the scallops to start with, then the smoked duck with plum sauce. And then the chocolate and pistachio souffle.'

'Down, girl! We aren't going too,' Effie harrumphed. 'This sounds like a proper date. Again.'

The three of them looked at me rather mistily for a moment, and I looked away and washed my hands again for something to do.

'Stop looking at me like that,' I said at last. 'Honestly, it's just dinner.'

'Dinner with Doctor Bill,' Anita sighed, her head on one side.

I sent her a meaningful look.

Effie looked confused. 'Is he a doctor? I didn't know that. No wonder he was so good with Susan's blister. She said he had a proper first aid kit too. Not just one of those daft ones from the chemist with a triangular bandage and too many cheap plasters that don't stick properly. Fancy that. Perhaps you could ask him about your knee, Beryl.'

'He's on holiday and he's retired,' I said firmly.

'Well, a knee is a knee, isn't it?' Beryl said. 'Anyway, much more importantly, we have a three-line whip from Jillian for tomorrow and the still life class. I think perhaps as we have been so unruly, we should comply. It might cheer her up. She does seem a bit exasperated with us. What do you think?'

'On the roof terrace at ten thirty,' Effie said with a little salute.

'Synchronise your watches, ladies. It will be a bowl of fruit I expect, or some of the bougainvillea.'

'To hear is to obey,' I said, returning the salute with a grin.

\* \* \*

We got back to the hotel just before nine o'clock, and while the others wanted to go up to the rooftop terrace for a nightcap, I just wanted to go to my room and think. And investigate the clothes I had packed to come here. To try to find something suitable to wear.

And then I told myself to stop being foolish and went to have a cool shower before bed, as the evening had been rather warm. When I came back into my room, I saw someone had pushed an envelope with the hotel's logo on the back, under my door.

*I have booked a table for the day after tomorrow. Six-thirty-ish for seven o'clock. I hope this suits you? If not please tell me. I will arrange a taxi to take us there, leaving here just after six. Again, if this doesn't fit in with your plans for the day do let me know at the still-life class tomorrow morning. Kind regards, Will.*

O.M.G.

I calmed myself down by sending Nicky a long email and some of the many photographs I had taken on my phone over the last couple of days. I didn't mention the forthcoming dinner date. It wasn't anything she needed to know about anyway. As a teenager she had always been banging on about people respecting her privacy; well, now, rather surprisingly, it was my turn.

It was frustrating, though, not to be fifteen again, not able to sit on my bed with some giggling friends and discuss every word of his message, read into it things that probably weren't there. To be young enough to be properly silly.

But then women of my age, who had been single for a while, were probably hard to impress. I hadn't thought for a moment about ever having another relationship after my divorce. A man would have to be seriously remarkable to make me change my mind about that. And most men I had encountered of my generation seemed to be a bit like Dennis. Perfectly all right but set in their ways, a bit grumpy, firmly attached to someone, and there weren't many of them in the first place. And then there was the emotional baggage both of us would be dragging behind us. Our families, our pasts, our suspicions and assumptions.

What would a man like Will bring into my life? What would I bring into his? There had to be some reason, surely? Did this step actually count as one of the epic things I had been planning, or was it, in the grand scheme of things, nothing?

I had a lot of thinking to do. And meanwhile, I needed to pick all my discarded clothes up and put them back in the wardrobe.

## 16

The following day dawned just as all the others had, clear skies and sunny, with the promising warmth and slightly fresh edge of an early summer morning.

I made some tea and sat in bed for a while, looking out of the open windows. There was a scuffle in the bougainvillea and one of the kittens fell onto the balcony and started sniffing around the place where I had started leaving some scraps from my breakfast ham.

'I'll bring you some later,' I said, and it stopped, startled at the sound of my voice, and scampered away.

I wondered how Ivan was getting on without me back home. Not that he was the sort of cat to fawn around me when I was there, and undoubtedly I would get the cold shoulder from him for several days on my return. It was surprising that Nicky was getting on so well with him, but knowing Ivan, he was canny enough to be doing it just to be ornery.

I pulled on some loose linen trousers and a clean shirt and then found my sunhat, which was plain white and a bit boring compared with the jaunty Old Ducks hats Anita, Effie and Beryl wore.

Out in the courtyard, the breakfast was set out as usual and the table was nearly full. Will was at the far end, my friends at the other. I went to sit between Beryl and Effie with my croissants and coffee.

We had a discussion about what our painting task would be that morning. We wondered what Jillian had in mind.

'This would make a good still life,' Effie said, pointing at her plate. 'A glass of orange juice and five grapes. I could call it *The Joy of Six*.'

Beryl pushed her toast and apricot jam around the plate for a few minutes.

'There you are – mine would be called *This Picture is Toast*.'

'I wish it could be the kittens,' Susan said, 'but do you think they would stay still for long enough?'

Reminded by this comment, I wrapped a piece of ham in a paper napkin and sneaked it into my pocket.

**\* \* \***

Bang on ten thirty we all assembled obediently on the roof terrace, where Nina had kindly put up all the parasols and placed several carafes of iced water and some glasses on each table. And we would need them; it was shaping up to be a hot day.

'So now then, what are we supposed to be painting?' Dennis said, hands on hips, surveying the terrace like a captain on the bridge of his ship.

Jillian, who was already there with her usual clipboard and a worried expression, settled us all down.

'One moment, and it will all be revealed to you,' she said. 'I think you will be amazed. And possibly a bit surprised.'

Will and I exchanged looks at this point, neither of us knowing where this was going.

Moments later, Costas appeared, wrapped in his dolphin-patterned robe, bowed extravagantly towards us and went to sit on the sunbed in the middle of our group. Before doing so, he unfastened the belt and rather theatrically let the garment fall to the floor in a heap. And then he struck a sort of Usain Bolt lightning pose, the sunlight glinting on his oiled torso and a rather startling green thong.

Then in a final flourish he did a slow rotation to give us the full benefit of his physique and held out his arms to us and shook them.

'Ha!' he said. 'Is Apollo!'

It was a scene which could have come straight out of *Zorba the Greek*, and for a second the whole group was shocked into respectful silence.

Then we gave a collective gasp and Costas laughed.

'My goodness, I haven't seen anything like it, not since I was having dinner in the Crazy Horse in Paris in 1977,' Beryl breathed.

'I'm definitely amazed,' Effie said.

'And surprised,' I said.

Unable to look away, we stared as Costas settled himself on the sunbed and took out his cigarettes, lighting one with a sigh of pleasure.

'Thank heaven he's wearing that thong,' Anita whispered.

'Well, I must say, this is an unexpected development,' Dennis said. 'Let's get to it, folks. Costas, can you uncross your legs?'

'Please don't,' Effie whimpered, 'not from where I'm sitting. I don't think my blood pressure would stand it. I might have to move.'

'He's very brave,' I said.

'I've never drawn an actual person,' Susan said, 'and certainly not a man in his – you know – a tiny little *thing* like that.'

'It's not a thing, it's a thong. I think we all need some water,' Beryl said, reaching for the carafe.

'And so, I thought this would make an interesting change from the last few days of glorious landscapes and views,' Jillian said very firmly. Perhaps she had seen the looks on our faces. 'And there is nothing to it. Just let your materials flow across the paper, meld with your imaginations. You don't have to be anatomically accurate in order to be inspired.'

'That's good news,' Will said. 'It's a long time since I've done this sort of thing.'

'We don't?' June said hopefully. 'Be too – you know – *anatomical*, I mean?'

'Absolutely not. This is just another opportunity to try a new medium perhaps, allow your inner Francis Bacon to fly. Perhaps focus on one thing. Draw it in detail. Really study the shape and line of it.'

We watched as Costas got settled. He was a big, muscular man with legs like tree trunks and unsurpassed and rather endearing body confidence. He took a big dollop of suntan oil and slapped it on his chest, rubbing it into his fur with a broad grin on his face, and then held out both arms towards us in triumph again, shook them and shouted, *'Hey!* Is Apollo, no?'

'Abso-blooming-lutely,' Effie drawled.

I could smell the bergamot tang of the oil and almost sense the heat of his tanned skin from my chair. You wouldn't see that in Lower Begley.

I sighed. 'Well, as my builder said to me when I wanted the shower moved, I've not seen it done before...'

I had no idea where or how to start. Then I noticed Costas

had large beautifully shaped feet, like something from an ancient Greek statue, so I decided to draw one of them.

I looked around at my companions, all of whom had expressions of intense concentration on their faces, apart from Susan, who was sitting back in her chair frowning thoughtfully and sipping water.

'Simply marvellous! He really is quite majestic when one gets over the surprise of seeing him *déshabille*,' Beryl said. 'My mother used to say it didn't matter how handsome or muscular a man was, she said the acid test was could he put some shelves up for his mother, and I think Costas fills that brief very well.'

'He could probably put a house up, never mind some shelves,' I said, head ducked down, focusing on Costas's big toe.

'That's an awfully attractive trait, don't you think?' Effie sighed, sucking the end of her pencil and leaving black marks around her mouth as a result. 'For a man to do manly things. Building houses and digging holes and mending cars. I've always found mechanics and lumberjacks desperately appealing. And firemen.'

'I have a calendar of firemen,' June said in a loud stage whisper, 'with their shirts off. I'm particularly fond of August.'

'Is that the one with kittens?' Susan said. 'I've got that one too. It's always a little boost to my morning. My favourite is February; he has the nicest seal-point Siamese kitten perched on his shoulder. But then they are so wide he probably has room for a couple of labradors.'

We worked on in silence for a while, and occasionally Costas shifted about and lit another cigarette, settling again with a smile on his face, obviously delighted to be the centre of attention.

About an hour later he signalled to Jillian that he needed a break, and he stood up and stretched his arms up towards the sky. And then he snapped the two sides of his thong against his sides with his thumbs and for a moment we held our collective breaths as it seemed as though his barely there thong might fall down, but happily it didn't and we all downed pencils and scurried off for coffee and more baklava, which Nina had kindly supplied next to the bar. As we helped ourselves, she nodded and smiled proudly, obviously delighted that her husband was being so well received.

'*Eínai kalós ánthropos*. He is a fine man, my Costas,' she said, looking at him with hungry eyes. 'He can unblock the drains faster than any man I know.'

'I think this was a marvellous idea,' Dennis said. 'I'm thoroughly enjoying doing something different. I might suggest to Cassandra that she do something similar in Lower Begley when we get back.'

I thought about this. It was all very well for someone to do this on a Greek, sun-drenched roof terrace, where the temperature was still rising and the rest of us were getting very hot and sweaty. And at least we had the possibility of a dip in the pool afterwards to cool off.

I tried to imagine someone stripping off in Lower Begley village hall, where the curtains at the windows didn't quite close properly and the heating was unreliable. I didn't think she would have many volunteers.

'How are you getting on?' I asked Susan, who hadn't been talking very much but had been bent over her sketch book all the time, with fixed concentration and a little smile.

'Marvellous,' she said, beaming. 'I think it's one of the best things I've done since we came here.'

'I'm so pleased to hear that,' Jillian chipped in, overhearing. 'I'm thrilled. Sometimes it's all we need, isn't it? To look at our work with a fresh perspective and new ideas of what is possible. Let's have a look?'

Susan put down her coffee, went to fetch her sketchbook and held it out proudly.

'I've just drawn a tiny, important bit of Costas as well, for scale—'

I think there was a loud intake of breath at this point.

'—and then I focused in on this...'

She had indeed drawn the top of Costas's head with just a few of his vigorous, grey curls in the corner of the page, but the majority of her picture was taken up with the hotel cat, who had been peacefully sleeping on the wall behind him.

'It's jolly good,' I said, 'terrifically lifelike. Especially the whiskers.'

'Unexpected,' Jillian said.

Dennis wandered over to see what the fuss was about.

'You haven't drawn Costas at all, you've drawn the flaming cat again! For goodness' sake!'

Susan stuck her tongue out at him.

'I like cats, I like drawing cats. So there. Yah boo sucks to you with knobs on.'

Costas meanwhile was standing with his back to us at the roof terrace rail, smoking a cigarette, sipping an espresso and proudly surveying the little street below. Occasionally he gave a little shimmy of pleasure. Evidently this was his idea of a morning well spent.

I think we were all fascinated but trying hard not to stare too obviously.

'Imagine back in the day, thousands of Costases invading from the Greek ships,' June whispered, 'climbing up the cliffs and marauding. No one would have stood a chance.'

'I don't think they would have been wearing green thongs though,' I whispered back.

'No, probably not,' June said, and she dabbed at her throat with a wet wipe. 'Pity really.'

* * *

We carried on sketching and painting until Nina eventually had a word with Jillian and the proceedings came to a halt.

'Costas has to go off now, to a very important meeting with the local council, so I think we should give him time to – you know – get ready.'

'Get dressed,' Beryl murmured.

With great dignity, Costas pulled on his robe and, with a polite bow, left us.

'Well now, let's see what you have achieved,' Jillian said. 'It's been so nice to have you all here, working together. For once.'

We went to look at each other's work, agreeing it had been an enjoyable and enlightening session.

Dennis had concentrated on Costas's profile and done very well, sketching out his noble nose, broad forehead and determined chin.

'I would have liked longer; after all, it's just a work in progress,' Dennis said modestly.

My efforts to draw Costas's foot were admired, and I had to admit it was quite realistic. Effie had tried to do Costas full length and even coloured in his green thong with a watercolour pencil. Beryl had focused on one of Costas's arms, the one that wasn't involved with the smoking. June had been quite perturbed by the whole thing and spent most of her time drawing the structure of the sun lounger behind his reclining figure.

Anita had drawn Costas full length too and had been very successful in capturing the essence of the man, although as she herself said, his nose had gone a bit wrong. And she hadn't drawn his hands or feet because they were too difficult.

Susan's picture of the hotel cat was much praised, and Will, who had been sitting opposite me in our circle, had done well with the outline of Costas's muscular shoulders. But also, I noticed, he had drawn beyond his view of Costas and included me in the picture. I had been hunched over my sketchpad, my legs slanted to one side, my hair a mess by the looks of it, and surely I was neither that stylish nor that trim?

'I like this,' Jillian announced, holding up Will's picture. 'Including someone else in the picture gives a real depth. Movement and perspective. Some charm and rustic honesty. What prompted this, Will? I am sure we would all be able to learn from your ideas.'

Will looked embarrassed, and I sent him a little grin.

'Someone once said that by drawing a picture, you remember it far more than just taking a photograph. So, I wanted to remember it properly.'

'How very true,' Jillian said, delighted, 'and I'm sure your friends and family back home will be amazed at what you have all achieved.'

'I don't think Rick will want to pay to have a picture of a glistening, nearly naked man framed unless it was him, and in any case, it certainly wouldn't go into the dining room,' Anita murmured.

\* \* \*

After a quick snack at the taverna a few doors down from the hotel, Beryl and Effie decided they needed an afternoon nap as the morning spent with such concentration in the sun had worn them out, and Anita said she was going to stay outside in the shade of the courtyard to finish off her sketch of Costas and try to give him a better nose.

Left to my own devices, I set off from the hotel towards the irresistible pull of the sea. It was such a beautiful afternoon and I felt for once that I needed some time on my own. I wanted to keep thinking about the future, what I might do with it and how to achieve my fledgling ambitions.

Sitting under the shade of a straw-fringed parasol with an icy lemonade, I thought of all the things I would like to see. For a moment I could almost visualise myself on that luxury train, boarding in Vancouver and speeding off through the Rockies. Maybe I would be standing somewhere in the Alps overlooking wonderful mountain ranges, taking deep breaths of the crystal-clear air.

Hang on, why the heck would I be there? It would mean I was on a walking holiday, wouldn't it? That would be most unlikely.

I closed my eyes and tried to visualise myself in some sturdy walking shorts with lots of pockets down the legs and a pair of stout walking boots. Add to that a backpack filled with maps, water and Kendal mint cake, and my father's binoculars round my neck like a ton weight. Nope. Not in a million years.

So where would be a nice place to visit? Somewhere less energy sapping.

The Italian Lakes. Will had said they were lovely. Like a film set. Or the Grand Canyon. Standing on a viewing platform, looking down at the Colorado river. Marvelling at the way it had patiently cut its way through the rocks over millions of years.

Or what about Paris in the spring? I imagined myself sitting at a café table where the bright, new leaves were unfurling from the trees around me. There would be a snake-hipped waiter bringing me black coffee and pastis. But I didn't like pastis. Okay, perhaps he would bring me Kir Royale instead and a single perfect almond biscuit.

This scenario had almost morphed into one where I was wearing Audrey Hepburn sunglasses and had a white poodle on a leash beside me. I wondered what Ivan would think about that? Not much.

Maybe I would board a cruise liner, setting out from Southampton towards New York in style. People would be leaning over the edge and throwing paper streamers to the people standing on the dockside. No, I didn't think that had been allowed for years. People were fined for dropping a sweet wrapper these days.

And there was another thing. Would I be brave enough to drive on the other side of the road in Europe or America? What if I broke down? It might take a while for the AA to reach me if I was marooned in the Lincoln tunnel with a flat tyre on my way out of Manhattan.

Perhaps I would stick to trains. After all, if the Rocky Mountaineer got stuck in a snowdrift, no one would expect me to help dig it out. I would just sit back with another cocktail and smile at the rather attractive man sitting nearby and we would agree that it wouldn't be long until we got to Kamloops or Whistler or wherever it was we were going, and then we would strike up a conversation.

Then magically we would be standing on a wooden balcony overlooking a snowy New England landscape and somewhere Frank Sinatra would be softly crooning *Moonlight in Vermont*, which has always been one of my favourite songs. The air would be as clear and crisp as iced water, and perhaps I would be drinking mulled wine from a glass cup. Inside there would be an open fire, blazing with logs.

No, actually, it would be Christmas, and there would be a tree in one corner sparkling with coloured lights and underneath it a pile of beautiful presents with ribbons and tags which hadn't fallen off. Nicky and her husband would be there too, and perhaps some of my new friends from this holiday. Gosh, it would have to be a massive house to fit us all in. Like the Pine Tree Lodge. It was a place that every time I watched *White Christmas*, I wanted to go. To a mountain lodge with friendly people and glorious views. And snow.

And then I had a more realistic image of myself in the massive kitchen, rooting about in the giant fridge for something, and realised I'd probably be doing all the catering, so no, I wouldn't think of that.

I went back in my imagination to the Rocky Mountaineer. I would look fixedly out of the window at the lovely scenery until the track was cleared of the snowdrift, like something out of *Murder on the Orient Express*, and we got going again.

Then it struck me that the handsome stranger of my imagination in the train looked an awful lot like Will. That wouldn't do at all. I had already decided I didn't need a man to make my life complete. I just needed my own self-belief for a change.

I would turn away from my fantasy travelling companion and read my book, which I would have bought in the airport. It would be an improving, literary novel about important things with a dark, sensible cover, not the sort of jolly escapism I usually read where women had fun and sat on beaches and got the better of their disloyal husbands.

'Hello,' he said.

I turned to see Will standing next to me, looking very relaxed and a bit dishevelled in cargo shorts (with a great many pockets down the legs) and a blue polo shirt that matched his eyes.

'Oh, hello,' I said, feeling very flustered. Good job he didn't know that he had only recently been the object of one of my daydreams.

'May I join you?' he asked politely, one hand on the back of the chair opposite me.

'Of course,' I said with a little laugh to show that this didn't bother me at all.

'I've just been exploring,' he said. 'I walked down to the far end of the beach. I think I must have found the place where you went on that ringo. There was a bit of a queue.'

'Oh, it was great fun,' I said, remembering how it felt to be smacked in the face by a lot of seawater, almost have my arms wrenched from their sockets and pay for the privilege. 'You should try it.'

The waiter came up at that point, balancing a round tray on his fingertips. Will ordered a lemonade like mine after asking me if I needed anything else.

'It's lovely here, isn't it,' I said. 'I've enjoyed it far more than I thought I would, even if I haven't really joined in with the group activities.'

'Nor have I, I'm afraid,' he said, and grinned. 'I've never been much of a conformer. I was the same at school; not one for team games.'

'Nor me,' I said. 'And it was no good picking me for a side. I had the co-ordination skills of a panda. Have you seen the clips on Facebook? They are always falling off things and tumbling out of trees, aren't they?'

He laughed. 'Cute cubs though.'

'Absolutely, although I think I would prefer a quokka. They have such smiley faces. I'd love to see one of those.'

'In which case you need to go to Rottnest Island near Perth. It's well worth a visit.'

Australia. Yes, that would be a good place to see, and they

drove on the proper side of the road too. I could almost see myself in a broad-brimmed hat, and one of those rather unattractive t-shirts which claim to 'wick moisture away'. Which is rather an unpleasant thought as the moisture surely has to go somewhere?

So the only drawback would be the length of the journey to get there. Not to mention the cost because there was no way I was going to spend hours and hours on a plane in an economy seat with not enough room and my feet shuffling about in all the debris a long-haul plane flight produces. Horrible blankets and bits of plastic and possibly someone else's feet poking through on my armrest.

How marvellous it would be to go in the posh seats just for once. To be welcomed into one of the nice lounges at the airport instead of someone frowning at my boarding pass and waving me away, as had happened once when Malcolm and I were travelling to Austria for one of his tedious financial conferences and he had wrongly assumed he had been upgraded.

'Maybe I will one day,' I said. 'Go to Australia, I mean.'

'So where next after this?' Will said, sipping his lemonade.

'Home,' I said, pulling a face. 'Do the washing, mow the lawn, try and get my cat to talk to me again.'

He laughed. 'Same thing.'

This little interaction was making me bold. 'Where do you live now?'

'In the Cotswolds. A little village not far from Bicester.'

'Ah, the big outlet shopping experience.'

'Never been, although I did get a really great kitchen installed by a firm there. I can recommend them if you ever want one.'

'I've just had a bathroom refitted,' I said. 'I need to get over one mess and muddle before I start on another.'

I wondered then about him having a kitchen fitted, and how

he had dealt with it. Had he made countless cups of tea and bought special biscuits for the builders as I had? Did he pore over his spreadsheets and costings and question every decision and tap and door latch? Or had he just let them get on with it?

'I'm looking forward to tomorrow evening,' he said. 'Our meal out at the vineyard.'

'Me too,' I said, 'and this time it's on me.'

'Oh, I don't know—'

I interrupted his protests. 'We agreed when we had dinner last time that the next time I would pay, so don't argue.'

He held up his hands in submission. 'Okay, whatever you say.'

I thought about my bank balance then. It was all very well being firm and independent, but how much would a meal in that place cost? How much was the wine? How much was the taxi?

No, I was sure it would be fine. My pension had just gone into my bank account, and if the worst came to the worst I had a credit card.

We sat in companionable silence for a while, looking out at the sea, the children playing on the rather gritty beach, four young men playing volleyball at one of the nets set up there.

I gave a deep sigh, pleased to be seeing all these things, knowing that this would not be the last time I went somewhere different and looked out on new places. It was a very liberating sensation. I wondered how Will was feeling. Had this week brought him a new sense of freedom too?

I suppose I had always thought that men like him lived their lives and dealt with changes and losses and doubts very differently from the way women did. Women were able to confide more in their closest friends, draw support from each other. They could sympathise without feeling they needed to provide a solution.

Men on the other hand didn't seem to do that. He had friends, he already said as much, but were they the sort of people he would split a bottle of prosecco with and to whom he could unburden himself? Where did men get their support mechanism when they needed one?

I'd always assumed the male of the species had things easier than women, but now I wasn't so sure. I suddenly felt rather sorry for him, which wasn't an emotion I had ever felt for a man before. Certainly not for my ex-husband, who had managed to turn each success into a personal victory and every failure into someone else's fault.

I wanted to learn so much more about Will, to discover what made him tick and perhaps more importantly, why a man like him, who had been successful, was good-looking and well-mannered, sometimes had such a look of sadness in his eyes.

'It sounds as though you have travelled far more than I have,' I said. 'Where's the best place you've ever been?'

He took another sip of his lemonade and pursed his lips thoughtfully.

'Australia is great. But then so is Italy. And France for that matter. But if I think about it, and if I had to choose, I went skiing once, a few years ago with a couple who are still really good friends. They had helped me get through a difficult time and I needed to get away. It was unforgettable. We rented a glorious log cabin overlooking a wonderful view of endless hills and valleys. There was a broad wooden balcony all around the first floor and one night I stood out there, just looking out at the moon shining on the mountains. I felt at peace for the first time in ages. It had been snowing and everywhere was so crisp and clear, and there was a bright, full moon that seemed so close it almost felt as though I could reach out and touch it. Vermont,' he said. 'That's my favourite place.'

Gosh. What a coincidence. How marvellous.

\* \* \*

I encouraged him then, to talk about small, everyday things. The way he spent his leisure hours, what sort of food he enjoyed, did he support a particular football team (no, thank heavens).

His nearest neighbour was an elderly woman called Mrs Haliburton, who had apparently owned ten cats over the years, all called Fluffy. Will shared the company of the latest Fluffy, a cat who took advantage of both of them, pleading hunger and settling down comfortably on its own blanket next to Will's wood burner on cold winter nights while its other owner called fruit-lessly at her back door and rattled bags of treats to try to lure Fluffy back.

'I like cats,' he said, reinforcing my earlier view that men who were cat-lovers either were or became more attractive as a result. 'I think I would like Ivan from what you tell me of him. He sounds the independent type.'

'Irascible might be a better word,' I said. 'He has only sat on my lap once, and I have never shown that cat anything but kind-ness. Still, he does bring me gifts from time to time. Mice and a couple of shrews as a treat.'

'I think Fluffy is too fat and lazy to catch anything, and why should she when she has two of us feeding her?'

'What about cooking? Are you a maestro in your new kitchen?'

He laughed. 'Hardly. And now I have a new one, I don't know how much of it works, but occasionally when my sister comes to visit with her family, it's nice to try. But then she will shove me out of the way and take over, as all much younger sisters do, I think.'

So, he had a much younger sister.

'Nephews and nieces?' I asked.

'Twin nephews. Emlyn and Huw. They are in the middle of their A levels. What about you?'

'I have one sister who works for the World Bank in Washington. Bridget is married to an American called Cole, and they have a son called Newt, after Sir Isaac Newton, not the amphibian, and I have one daughter. She doesn't have any children yet, although I remain hopeful. Nicky is a librarian, but her library is in danger of being closed at the moment, and there doesn't seem to be anything they can do about it.'

He shook his head. 'It's such a shame; libraries are important places for so many people. Is there nothing that can be done?'

'They are planning a protest or a sit-in.'

'Oh dear, you know things are bad if librarians are protesting.'

'That's exactly what Beryl said.'

We sat in easy silence then and watched the sea. People were packing up their picnic bags and young children and obviously getting ready to go back to their houses or hotels. Groups of teenagers were gathering instead, the girls lithe and pretty in their skimpy clothes, the boys loud and yet cautious around them. A tale as old as time.

I felt a surge of frustration. *Make the most of it*, I wanted to say to them; *don't take this freedom, this confidence, for granted. Never doubt yourselves. Be the best you can be.*

And yet those same thoughts were dominating my mind. I wanted to stop thinking of myself as abandoned to old age, gradually feeling my usefulness decline. I should seize my newfound self-reliance and run with it as far and as fast as I could. Which at my age with a dodgy knee would not be particularly fast or far.

I looked at my watch; it was three thirty and I needed time to get a shower and put on some fresh clothes ready for the evening's outing. Added to this, I had the feeling that if I kept on asking questions and probing him for information, he might clam up again and I would be back to square one.

'Right then, I'd better go back to the hotel and freshen up.'

He looked a little disappointed. 'Must you? I was enjoying this.'

I wavered for a moment and then stuck to my guns. What had P.T. Barnum said? Always leave then wanting more.

'Absolutely,' I said. 'I'm looking forward to this evening. Did you book a taxi? You said you would ask Costas and after seeing him in his thong, I didn't feel quite up to it to be honest.'

He laughed. 'I did. It will be outside at six o'clock. I'm going to stay here and finish my lemonade and do a bit more thinking, but I could see you safely back to the hotel if you want me to?'

Very gentlemanly, I thought, but I didn't think anything was likely to happen in the hundred yards between the café and Hotel Costas.

'No need, I'll be fine and I'll see you later,' I said.

Walking back, I felt quite optimistic and pleased with the way things had gone. Unlike most men I had known, he didn't want to talk about himself all the time, which was refreshing but also slightly annoying, because just like Fifi in Manchester, there were things I wanted to know. Why had he left his blossoming career and where had he gone anyway? What had he been doing to fill those years, and with whom?

## 17

Back in my room I checked that the kittens had finished up their breakfast ham – of course they had – and then I went and had a long, cool shower.

What day was it anyway? I normally had a hard enough time remembering what day of the week it was, but here, where one sunny day blended into another and I didn't have to remember when it was Friday and time to put the bins out, it was even more difficult.

I thought for a moment and then decided it was Thursday. Which meant we only had two more days to go until we went home again. Back to my house in Lower Begley where the grass would need mowing. There would probably be a pile of uninteresting post and flyers for retirement villages on my doorstep, and Ivan, well fed and adored by Nicky, would not run up meowing to greet me with his tail held high, but fix me with one of his withering looks.

I sent off a quick email and some more pictures to my daughter and then turned to the pressing problem of what I was going to wear that evening. Perhaps my new rose-printed sundress, or maybe the one I had brought with me which was pale blue, and I still had a clean white t-shirt to wear underneath it. But that was a bit informal, wasn't it? Maybe some smart, dark trousers and a blue linen blouse? I looked as though I was going for a job interview. Jeans and a polo shirt? Too casual. Dark trousers and a striped, green top. There was a small red wine stain on one side of the neck which scrubbing with handwash had failed to completely remove, but I could cover that up with an artfully draped scarf. Would my zebra-print kitten heels bear another outing, even though one of them was still a slightly darker colour than the other one?

I bet Will wasn't worrying about such things. I expect he just slung on the first clean shirt he found in his suitcase and thought no more about it.

So what would I feel most comfortable in? Never mind what he might think of me.

In the end, hoping to avoid detection, I sneaked quietly out of my room to go downstairs just before six o'clock in dark trousers and a clean pink top, my kitten heels clacking on the marble stairs. I was reasonably confident although I held firmly on to the handrail as I went, because I was sure one of the shoes could skid out from underneath me and send me flying down to the bottom. Not a good first impression at all.

'So,' said a voice behind me. 'You're off with the divine Will again.'

I turned to see Anita hanging over the banister at the top of the stairs, and I realised she must have been listening for my door to open. It did have quite a distinctive squeak.

'Oh, just off for that meal I was telling you about,' I said airily.

'Excellent news. I shall take great pleasure in telling Jillian when she is flapping around trying to round us all up for the ouzo tasting evening at the Poseidon bar. She'll be very annoyed.

You must tell us all about it when you get back. Unless it's after midnight, in which case we will all be asleep and not interested enough to wake up. On the other hand, if you end up locked in a passionate embrace in his room, I insist you do bang on my door when you finally get back to your own bed and tell me all about it. I will want to know every titillating detail.'

'It certainly won't be that late and I certainly won't end up doing any of that stuff!' I said.

'I live in hope,' Anita said.

'Oh, you!'

I resumed my careful way down the stairs.

'Have fun!' she called after me, her voice echoing down the stairwell. 'Don't do anything I wouldn't do. Actually, I've always thought that's a bit meaningless, isn't it? Do *all* the things!'

I flapped a hand at her to stop making such a racket and reached the front door where Will was waiting for me, two of the kittens playing with a twig at his feet.

'Ah, marvellous,' he said. 'You look lovely.'

'So do you,' I said rather foolishly. Well, he did. He was wearing some well-pressed chinos (I hadn't noticed an iron in my room; perhaps he had brought one with him?) and a brilliantly white shirt with the sleeves rolled up to show his tanned forearms. I love that; it's one of my favourite looks on a man. We were off to a great start.

The taxi came moments later, apparently driven by Gregor's brother Hector. He was equally as uncommunicative and large as our usual driver was. He also seemed to share the same disregard for speed limits and other vehicles, and the journey to the vineyard flashed past with me clinging, white-knuckled, onto the door handle.

We arrived in record time and Hector got out of the car and went to chat with a group of other taxi drivers who were huddled

around an ancient olive tree in the car park, smoking and probably complaining about the state of the roads or the government.

At the door everything looked very different from our last
visit. Inside and out the place was lit with hundreds of fairy lights
which were strung along the walls, around the windows and out
along the steel and glass barrier on the terrace. It looked magical.
I almost didn't care what the food was like; the setting and the
feeling I had this evening were something I would probably
never forget.

We decided to start with a glass of Lefteris Glinavos Brut,
which was the Greek equivalent of champagne, and it came in
slender glasses, the bubbles winking enticingly at the brim.

'*Yamas,*' Will said, and we clinked our glasses as the lights
from a departing cruise ship far below us moved silently off into
the evening.

'Cheers,' I said. 'I think I would like to learn a new language. I
often feel it's a bit arrogant, thinking that English is the only one
worth bothering with. I did French at school; I wasn't clever
enough to do German. I'd like to learn Italian, so when I go there
I can ask for things, not just the bill in a café.'

'You'd like Italy I think,' he said. 'I met some lovely people
there. But then I've realised there are kind, decent people all over
the world. People who don't care if you are rich or poor. It's very
grounding, if that's not too lofty a word.'

'It's reassuring,' I said, sipping my wine and enjoying the
slightly flowery taste. And the hint of citrus. Perhaps that wine
tasting had done something for my understanding of wine
after all.

At the back of my mind was the small amount of knowledge I
had gleaned from Wikipedia about Will. He was a doctor, a
proper medical professional even if he had spent a lot of time on
television discussing potty training and chickenpox. He had

worked for Médecins Sans Frontières, and I would have been genuinely interested to hear about it. Common sense told me I would have to bide my time and let him bring it up.

'I'm hungry,' I said, 'are you?'

'I didn't have lunch, so yes,' he replied.

We were shown to our table, which was in an enchanting little booth overlooking the sea, and as usual Will chose the seat with his back to the room. Which of course, knowing what I now knew about him, was predictable but really a bit silly. The evening was warm and the air scented with herbs, warm flowers and the faintest drift of his aftershave, which was lemony and delicious.

We looked at the menus, me wishing I had brought my reading glasses, because without them a lot of the finer points of the dishes went unseen. I would have to hope for the best.

Eventually I decided on scallops to start with followed by a delicious-sounding crispy chicken, until the waitress gently pointed out that I had chosen something from the children's menu. Flustered, I pointed at the first thing on the fish offerings, which was catch of the day. Who knew what I was going to get?

'Ah, *bourtheto*,' the waitress said approvingly, 'you like this – um *aromatódis*? Hot?'

'Oh, yes,' I said confidently, 'very hot.'

Surely there would be nothing worse than tepid fish?

'Good, good,' she said, making a note on her pad.

Then there was a bit of a discussion with the wine waiter, and eventually we decided on some Kontarades, which was apparently 'crisp and dry with stony minerality' and would go well with fish.

All that business out of the way, we sat back to enjoy our sparkling wine and the view. The restaurant was getting busier, with smart couples and groups settling themselves, even a few children who would probably also choose the crispy chicken.

We fitted in, I realised with a little thrill of pleasure. Will and I were just like these other people, out for a pleasant evening. I was just as entitled to be there as anyone. If other people noticed us, they might assume we were a couple, perhaps married, enjoying a holiday together.

It was so much easier being part of a couple, I realised. Having spent several years on my own or tagging along with other people, a lone woman could, for absolutely no reason, be seen as an oddity, or on one occasion, even a threat.

I remembered one evening some years ago, I went to a retirement party for my old headmaster at the school where I had been the secretary for so many years. Madge Clifford had been sure I was desperate to latch on to her dull husband and lure him into the stationary cupboard with my evil wiles. Which I hadn't been, and my wiles, such as they were, could be safely ignored by all concerned. I could find little common ground with a man whose sole topic of conversation that evening was Richard III and how he was much maligned. Roger Clifford might have wanted to discuss the tactical importance of the Battle of Bosworth, but I didn't.

'What unusual shoes,' Madge Clifford had said as she steered the hapless Roger away from me. I'd been wearing heels that evening, and the implication was: a) that I was too old for that sort of nonsense, and b) therefore a bit of a floozy.

Anyway, here I was now, just a woman out for the evening with a man. A very attractive man actually, who wanted to spend time in my company and talk to me.

Our starters came quickly and I tried not to greedily hoover up my scallops as though I was starving. Instead, I ate daintily and slowly, taking sips of water and paying attention to our conversation. And my word how we talked. We talked about so many things in a way I hadn't done with any man for years. We even disagreed about things without anyone taking offence or storming off jangling the car keys as had happened once with Malcolm when we fell out over Brexit.

The wine waiter brought over our bottle of Kontarades, and a few minutes were spent messing about with corks and white napkins before we were left in peace to enjoy it.

'Definitely stony minerality,' Will said, and he winked at me.

I grinned back. 'And crisp and dry.'

'Perfect,' he said, 'just like this evening.'

I gave a happy sigh. He was right. Everything about it was lovely. There was enough space between the tables so no one was tripping over my handbag, we were not privy to other people's conversations and there was no terrible background muzak playing.

The main courses arrived. He had chosen some beautifully presented lamb dish with what looked like potato cakes and green salad. Then my catch of the day arrived, and my confidence took a tumble.

In front of me was an oval dish containing a bed of mixed vegetables and on top of that a huge fishy something, and it was looking at me with quite a resentful expression which, under the circumstances, was understandable.

'*Bourtheto*,' the waiter said with a wistful smile, 'so delicious. A speciality. *Éna fili sef* – a chef's kiss.'

Oh well, I'd better get on with it and not meet my dinner's gaze. I took a dollop of the vegetables with my fork and covered up the accusing face.

It took me one mouthful to realise it was incredibly fiery and it nearly blew my tastebuds away. The waitress hadn't meant did I want my food hot as in hot, she'd meant spicy. If this was a kiss from the chef I wouldn't want to meet him in a dark alley without some sort of a weapon.

I gamely pressed on, concentrating on the vegetables and taking frequent sips of iced water, which I didn't think was the right thing to do. I'd read somewhere that a glass of milk would be better, but I'd look a right fool ordering that, wouldn't I?

'Mmm,' I said to Will's enquiry, 'full of flavour; in fact, lots of flavours but a bit peppery. How's yours?'

'Terrific,' he said, 'absolutely delicious.'

I gazed enviously at his meal for a moment and then dabbed at my face with my napkin. The spice of the meal was bringing heat to my face and tears to my eyes. Which meant my mascara was probably running. Just great.

'Very filling too,' I said, leaning back in my chair, 'I think I need a little breather.'

Perhaps I could get some fresh air and go to the loo. I knew where it was after all.

'Would you excuse me for just a moment?'

I stood up and went downstairs to the ladies, hanging my tongue unattractively out of my mouth as I went so it could get some fresh air. A couple passed me on the stone staircase and gave me an odd look.

'Lovely evening,' I said brightly.

'*Nai, kalispéra,*' the woman said doubtfully, grabbing her companion's arm.

The ladies' room was empty and I sat for a moment on a little chair, hanging my tongue out and panting for a bit longer and then standing up to wash my hands. What an idiot I was. If I had brought my reading glasses with me, things might have been very different. What should I do?

There was nothing for it. I would have to try again.

And afterwards I would have ice cream for dessert. Yes, that was a great idea.

Back at the table, I made a gallant effort to eat some more, and in the end after having hidden as much of the fish as I could under the sauce, the remaining vegetables and my cutlery and napkin, sat back and gave a happy sigh.

'That looked like it was a bit of a challenge?' Will said.

'It was a bit spicy,' I admitted, and then realised I had a fishbone stuck somewhere in between my side teeth. This was getting worse by the minute.

There was a little pot of cocktail sticks on the table and in an ideal world I would have taken one and gone poking about between my teeth to dislodge the fishbone, which as the seconds passed seemed to have taken on the size and shape of a darning needle and was sticking into my lip.

I couldn't sit there in front of him and do that. It would be disgusting.

After a while, the waiter came to remove our plates and I watched him go with some relief, my tongue still probing as daintily as I could.

'I'll just go and freshen up and then perhaps we can have some dessert?' he said. 'The menu looks wonderful.'

Within seconds of his leaving, I had grabbed a toothpick and was prodding at my teeth, trying and failing to dislodge the fishbone. I closed my eyes and tried to visualise my premolars, hoping I didn't have any fillings there that I might displace, and then I sloshed some of the lovely wine about like a mouthwash.

Will would be back in a minute. I needed to hurry.

I had another quick poke about with clumsy fingers and after a few seconds, the toothpick snapped off. As Will reappeared, heading back towards the table, I realised to my horror that the situation had worsened and I now had most of a cocktail stick sticking out into my lip from between my teeth.

I covered my mouth with my hand and looked up at him with a frozen expression as he sat down.

'Something wrong?' he said.

'Sort of,' I admitted, lisping slightly.

He bent his head towards me.

'I've got half a cocktail stick stuck between my teeth and I can't get it out.'

He bit back a smile.

'Can you get it out with another one?'

I had a sudden horrible vision of myself, ending the evening with a veritable forest of sticks protruding from the front of my mouth, or failing that, strapped onto an ambulance gurney being taken to a hospital with a fit of hysterics.

I took a deep breath. Okay, I could do this. I would not let this spoil the evening.

I grabbed a few more cocktail sticks and hurried back downstairs to the ladies' loo, where I spent an embarrassing few minutes prodding, wincing and delving until eventually, with my head spinning and gums aching, I managed to dislodge it. And the fishbone too, which of course was actually so tiny as to be practically invisible to the naked eye.

I swilled out my mouth with a handful of tap water and spat it out with a loud exclamation of relief, which sounded like an angry *gaah*. At that moment the same woman who had seen me airing my tongue earlier on the staircase appeared in the doorway, gave me a slightly frightened look and backed out again.

'*Yassou!*' I said, trying to look normal and unthreatening. 'Hello!'

Then as she edged back in, I gave an embarrassed smile and looked away. At least the burning had gone. I glanced at myself in the mirror over the sink. Yes, my mascara had run so one eye had a sort of sad clown dollop underneath it. I grabbed a paper towel and cleaned myself up, wishing not for the first time that I was more elegant, more sophisticated and less of a klutz.

'Everything okay?' Will said when I returned.

'Fine,' I said with a bright smile. 'Sorry about that.'

I grabbed my wine and took a good, reviving slurp. It really was delicious even though probably half my tastebuds weren't working properly and never would again.

'So now then, dessert?' he said.

I felt a wash of relief and affection for him at that moment. Just as he had done when I fell over on the gravelly beach, he was going to tactfully ignore what had happened. It didn't matter; his kind eyes were saying, *It could happen to anyone.*

Yes, but why did these things happen to me? That was twice we had been out together and on both occasions I had embarrassed myself.

'What about sorbet,' he said, 'if your mouth is a bit tender. Although healing is always quick. It's surprising. The mouth heals up faster than anywhere else.'

'Ideal,' I said, 'and I'm so sorry.'

'You don't have to apologise,' he said. 'Lemon, mango and raspberry? Would that be nice?'

'Perfect,' I said, finishing off my wine. Immediately, our waiter was back to top up my glass. Perhaps I should take it easy. At this moment I felt I was capable of anything, and a good slug of wine wasn't really going to help.

What with one thing and another it had been a strange evening, and yet, it didn't feel as though he was going to call Hector back early so that we could go home.

'And then some Greek coffee?'

'Yes please.'

All this dodging around was irritating and getting increasingly difficult. I needed to remember the snippets of information he had let slip without knowing the full picture. And I liked him, and I wanted to understand him better than I did. Perhaps I would take the bull by the horns and say something.

I waited until my dessert had been delivered, a beautiful glass bowl with three scoops of delicately coloured sorbets and decorated with fresh mint leaves, and then I looked across the table at him.

'So tell me more about yourself. We only ever seem to talk about me.'

He looked down at his dessert.

'I don't like talking about myself,' he said. 'To be honest, there's a lot in my past history I'm not very good at explaining.'

'I'm a good listener.'

He didn't reply for a moment, and I blundered in to fill the silence.

'I know you used to be a doctor. I didn't know at first, but then someone said something and of course then I remembered you.'

He looked down at his dessert and dabbed at it with the spoon.

'Oh dear,' he sighed.

I felt a plunge of anxiety. Had I spoiled everything?

## 18

I glanced at my watch. It was just after eight thirty and Hector was due to pick us up at nine o'clock.

I should have waited. Any conversation we could have now was going to be one where we were interrupted. The bill needed paying too.

I signalled to the waitress and did the usual scribbling in thin air that people did in every country when they couldn't speak the language. She gave me one of her brilliant smiles and a few minutes later, I was presented with a discreet, green leather folder containing a printout.

Will and I had a short, polite discussion about who was going to pay, which I won, and of course the next few minutes were taken up with the slowness of the card machine while I worried that it was going to decline the payment, our discussion about leaving a suitable tip, and then the business of Will getting his jacket on and making our way through the gift shop to the front door. They had some lovely fridge magnets and tea towels too, which under other circumstances I would have bought.

We went outside into the warm, dark evening, where the

skeins of lights were illuminating our path, past the old olive tree, and out into the car park. Hector was there, smoking a cigarette and still chatting with the other drivers. I wondered if he had been there all the time, waiting for us. Surely not.

Hector's expression brightened as he saw us, and he stubbed out his cigarette and opened the back door for me with elaborate courtesy.

'Good meal, heh?' he said. 'Good food?'

'Excellent, thanks,' I said, and then unexpectedly, bearing in mind my rather rattled mental state, I remembered the words, '*Éxochos efcharistó.*'

Hector smiled, pleased at my efforts, and started the car.

The drive home through the patchy darkness seemed to take twice as long as it had on the way there, and we didn't talk much. It felt to me as though there was a distinct tension building between Will and me in the car, and I wondered if he felt it too. I should have kept my curiosity under control. What difference did it make after all? If he wanted to keep his life private, what right did I have to pry?

But human nature wasn't like that, was it? Newspapers and magazines made a great deal of money rehashing other people's secrets and scandals. How many column inches were filled with details of unwise behaviour and lawsuits by irrelevant soap stars or footballers? And hardly anyone cared, not really. It was just gossip; pathetic fodder. And most of the people I'd never heard of and would never meet in my local supermarket. Had Will been subjected to this, back in the day, I wondered?

Eventually, we saw the lights of our little town appearing in front of us. Past the petrol station, the supermarket, the bakery and the shop where we had bought that terrible wine, and then we turned into our road and stopped outside Hotel Costas at last.

I could hear music from the roof terrace bar, and all the lights up there were blazing. There was laughter and someone shouted, 'Oh, Dennis, don't be daft!'

I think it was Effie.

Will and I watched the taillights of Hector's car disappear down the road and then we looked at each other.

I felt uneasy, unsure of what was going to happen next. I think I assumed he was going to say something polite about having had a lovely evening, and thank me, and then disappear back into his room. And I would do the same. I certainly didn't feel much like going up and joining the others on the terrace.

In fact, I felt a bit sad. It wasn't what I had expected from this evening at all. One that had started so well and gradually got worse until the two of us were barely speaking.

Will took a deep breath and jerked his head up towards the noise from the party that was going on.

'I don't think so, do you?' he said.

I shook my head. 'Absolutely not.'

'What do you think? Let's get a nightcap, shall we? Are you warm enough?'

And when I said I was, he reached out, took my hand and tucked it into the crook of his elbow. Just like that. So he couldn't have been thinking negative thoughts about me after all my angst and overthinking, could he?

We walked off together down the street towards the sea, the noise from the hotel fading behind us. After a few steps, he adjusted his long stride to my pace. And my thoughts were tumbling over each other in a way they hadn't done for a long time.

It wasn't that I was pleased to be getting a man's attention after so many years of being practically invisible, it was that he was another human being treating me with kindness and respect. Two important things I had missed out on. Small acts mattered.

Little gestures of consideration were what made my heart soar that evening, and the way that we were together, communicating as new friends.

* * *

It was surprisingly crowded as we walked down the little coast road. Most of the restaurants were open and looked busy. The older people like us had gone, and it was time for the tribes of younger holidaymakers to come out. Groups of young men passed us in a cloud of aftershave and hair products. No jeans and t-shirts but smart trousers and shirts. They twitched nervously at their cuffs, smoothing their hair down, casting glances at the girls as they passed. The girls in white trousers, ruffled crop tops and hair extensions which they tossed about like weapons of mass destruction.

Was it easier for young women these days? I'd thought so once, with all their freedoms and expectations, but perhaps it wasn't. Maybe underneath the nail treatments and flicky eyeliner, they were just as insecure and confused as my generation had been at that age. The boys too, not knowing what was expected of them. What to do to catch and hold a girl's attention, all of them wondering if they were attractive enough, buff enough to pair up with someone.

And yet even at my age I guessed people felt much the same. I might have decided that I had no interest in a new relationship, but was that true? I had blithely discounted the idea, noting the drawbacks of older men. 'Set in their ways' was the expression most of my friends used about their husbands, but wasn't that true for older women too? Perhaps I was set in my ways as well, unwilling to change. If I wanted my life to improve in the ways I had imagined, then I would need to do something about that.

In my head I might have felt about thirty-five, but one glance in the mirror showed that wasn't true. Perhaps it was the same for men.

I sneaked a look up at Will's profile, seeing traces of the young heart throb he had once been, but this evening of course he looked older too: his hair grey when once it had been dark; there were wrinkles on his face, crow's feet around his eyes accentuated by his tan.

I thought not for the first time how annoying it was that these things somehow made a man better looking while women were urged to buy expensive creams and potions or 'get a little work done'. I bet no one ever suggested that to George Clooney or Patrick Dempsey.

Sensing my gaze, he looked down at me.

'Okay?'

'Yes, fine. It's busier now, isn't it?'

He laughed. 'All the young people coming out to play. Not sloping off to bed early with a good book and a cup of tea like I usually do.'

'Me too,' I said, delighted to think he agreed with me. 'There's nothing I like better than a cold winter's evening, the electric blanket on full power, a cup of tea and a biscuit. Sometimes my cat will even curl up on my feet if he feels like it. I'd rather he did that than be out hunting and the risk that he might bring me a late-night snack of his own choosing.'

'Does he often do that?'

'Unfortunately, yes. Twice recently he brought in mice and let them go under the bed, which of course makes for some very entertaining moments. And he is always so furious when I take the poor things away from him. Then he will sit at the end of the bed and glower at me.'

'I like the sound of Ivan.' Will chuckled. 'I'd love to meet him.'

'Knowing Ivan, he would be all over you like a rash, and you would think I had made up the story of his baleful nature and bad behaviour.'

'I like that about cats. Dogs always seem to be consistent and uncomplicated, happy to please, but cats can be very sneaky.'

Interesting, I thought. He was talking about a time after this holiday was over when it sounded as though we might keep in touch. Even if the thought had been prompted by my slightly sinister cat.

We got to the far end of the beach road where the wine bars and restaurants had almost petered out, and still we hadn't stopped for that nightcap. At last, as the only thing in front of us was a boat yard and a few ramshackle sheds, we turned round and retraced our steps.

'What about here,' he said as we passed a café which was still open but practically empty apart from a man behind the counter who was hunched over a newspaper and sipping something cloudy and white that was probably ouzo.

'What do you think?' Will said, and I nodded.

'Not ouzo,' I murmured, 'or retsina. They don't agree with me.'

'Oooh yes we do,' he said in a silly voice, and I laughed.

The room was enlivened by a small electrically powered water feature in the middle where a waterfall trickled onto the figure of Poseidon complete with his trident. They really shouldn't put these things in places where older women were going to be sitting. Did I need to go to the loo? No, I was okay for the moment.

We sat down at a table in the corner and the boss came over with two menus and his notepad ready.

'A Greek mojito,' I said, pointing at the picture. 'It's got Metaxa in it and I'm getting a taste for it.'

'Good idea, two of those,' Will said, and the boss wandered off through the tables again. 'Perhaps you should take a bottle home with you in your luggage.'

'But what if it broke? We discussed this before, didn't we? I'd never get the smell out. I'd spend my next holiday pursued by sniffer dogs.'

'And where will you go next?' he said.

'I think I will go and visit my sister in Washington; it's a while since I've seen her. And then perhaps Carcassonne,' I said, imagining myself wandering through those medieval streets and learning all about the Cathars. 'Or maybe a transatlantic crossing. The trouble is when I get to New York, what would I do? I wouldn't know where to stay or how to get there, that's the problem. It's the travelling I like the idea of.'

'You could always join a tour group?'

'Hmm, I'm not very good at being herded around by someone,' I said with a rueful smile, 'as you may have noticed.'

'Me neither,' he said. 'My sister made me come on this trip. She used to go to the Begley Mortimer group a few years ago and she's still on their Facebook group. I think she was fed up with me refusing to book anything, so she did it for me and paid the deposit and presented it to me as a fait accompli. If I'm honest, I didn't realise there would be such an emphasis on the group as a thing, or I wouldn't have come. And before you ask, no I haven't done much actual painting since I've been here. A few sketches, the picture of Costas.'

'That was hilarious,' I said. 'What a character he is. Tell me some more about your sister?'

'Lorna is twelve years younger than me, she's a doctor, and married with twin boys. She lives in Banbury now, with her husband Oliver.'

I seized my moment.

'So you were both doctors.'

He shot me a look as though he knew where I was going.

'Yes, following in a family tradition.'

Our drinks arrived at that point, in long narrow glasses decorated with mint.

I took a sip through the straw. 'Look, you can either tell me or not tell me about what happened when you stopped doing television work, I don't mind. Although I am mildly curious, but that's all.'

He stirred his drink with the plastic stick which had a tinsel cocktail umbrella on the end and looked thoughtful.

'Have you ever had people photographing you through the windows of your kitchen? Or chasing your car down the street, banging on the windows so much that you had to move house? Or people going through your rubbish bins? Invading every aspect of your life so that nothing was safe and you didn't know who to trust any more?'

I shook my head. 'None of those things. I'm very uninteresting.'

'I wouldn't say that, but I know what you mean. One minute I was just a doctor who had worked in general practice and then gone to Africa, doing my best there against terrible odds of poverty and disease, and the next I was in a television studio with a girl patting make up on my face, interviewing celebrities I'd never heard of about their weight loss or smoking or pregnancies. Sometimes all three at the same time.'

'A bit of a culture shock, I imagine?'

'It was ridiculous. There are so many medical professionals out there quietly getting on with their jobs, and yet because I looked a certain way, had a certain background and had been approached by an agent who was married to one of my patients, I was invited to premieres and openings, celebrity events and the sort of parties you and I would normally run a mile from.'

'It must have been exciting though?'

'For about a year, I suppose it was. But then after we got married, all sorts of ridiculous stories started coming out. Rumours and lies – click-bait, I think they are called these days. And my wife was beautiful and incapable of having a bad photograph taken, designers lent her clothes, the press interest got worse. And then you know what happened.'

'Well, no, actually, I don't,' I said. 'I have to admit whatever it was passed me by completely.'

He gave a short laugh. 'I can't tell you how pleased I am that you said that. For years my wife's behaviour was fair game for the press. Long lens cameras following her into hotels, pictures of her stumbling out with her shoes in her hand the following morning. Until she realised they were there and she was becoming famous for the wrong reasons. Back then I thought it was just a blip that we could weather, that eventually interest would die down and we would rebuild our marriage. That's what I wanted. I had microphones stuck in my face asking for a comment. She was followed into shops and restaurants. Even then, while it was going on, I couldn't believe anyone would care that much.'

'So what happened?'

'She left me for some hairy individual in a heavy metal band. She went off in their private jet to Los Angeles just after our second wedding anniversary and filed for divorce three weeks later. He had promised her a career in films, an exciting life where the house was decorated with gold discs and awards, not books and research papers about obscure illnesses.'

'And did she get the exciting life?'

He shrugged. 'I think so, until he took up with someone else and then she met an actor, and after that she married a basketball star, and when that relationship failed I think she went into running a wellness retreat. I haven't heard from her in years. I hope she found what she was looking for. I hope she's happy. It must have been difficult for her too.'

'And what about you?'

'For a while after she left, things got worse. The media wanted to know the most intrusive details of our marriage, which for years afterwards she was happy to give them. You know what they say – all publicity is good publicity. She did talk shows, in-depth interviews about life on the road with the band, glossy colour spreads of her new home in Hollywood or her wedding in Venice, relationship advice; she did it all. And meanwhile, back in London, every time she did something outrageous, I couldn't get out of my house without journalists asking me what I thought. As if my opinion mattered. Who was I dating. Was there any chance we would get back together again. I suppose there were fewer so-called celebrities around then, and that's why they were so fascinated. Then at one point they started going through my rubbish to find something interesting. I can't imagine what.

'About a year after all this blew up, I found myself on a panel show being quizzed about my sex life while another panellist, a woman I hardly knew, offered all sorts of inappropriate ways to cheer me up. And that was it for me. I couldn't take any more of it, and of course I had no time to actually practise medicine. So I gave in my notice and left. And I went back to Africa and then India, trying to get my life and my self-respect back. And it worked. No one knew who I was; they only cared that I could help them. And after all, that's what I had trained to do. And after that I did a lot of travelling, and yes, I was hiding from everything. I had a few short relationships which came to nothing, because of my inability to really trust anyone. And one of them went to the papers to tell them what I was like, how she was hoping we would get married. But then at last, I got to the time when no one cared whether my ex-wife was pregnant or not, if I was in a relationship with anyone new. There were new, younger, more interesting people to focus on, people who behaved far worse. And then I retired and bought a house near my sister and started renovating it.'

I sipped my drink, listening intently. No wonder he went to such lengths to avoid being seen after putting up with years of that.

I looked around, wondering for a moment how it would feel to know that there were camera lenses trained on me at that moment, snapping away as I scratched my nose or adjusted my bra strap.

'Oh, don't worry, I'm old news now, I'm sure of it,' he said, noticing my unease, 'but for a long time, those years left me with an inability to deal with the world again. And that took a very long time to get over.'

'I promise I won't go to the newspapers,' I said. '*Doctor Bill has drink with completely unimportant woman in Greece.* I don't think that would sell many papers.'

'Doctor Bill, even that was made up. Nobody in my life had ever called me Bill. They thought it would make me sound more approachable. It could have been worse; the other alternative was Doc Willie.'

I snorted with laughter into my drink and choked a bit, and after a moment he laughed too.

'Oh dear,' I said, 'that does sound bad.'

'I'm okay. Time moves on. Today's sensation is tomorrow's has-been.'

'You're not a has-been,' I said firmly, 'you're a very nice person.'

'I like to think so. And you're wrong, you're not completely unimportant. You've made me laugh more than anyone has for a very long time. And maybe you have helped me to see that a straightforward, simple life, which is what I want, is possible after all.'

We sipped our drinks in a companionable silence for a while. A few other people came in and ordered food and drinks, while outside the lights along the street flickered and shone out into the evening.

'Gosh, it's ten o'clock,' I said.

'Middle of the night,' he agreed.

'I'll remember this evening when I am back home, and it's raining and I am bringing logs in for the wood burner,' I said.

'I'll remember this evening too,' he said quietly.

We left the little café and headed for the hotel. Outside it was getting chilly as the warmth of the day cooled and I shivered in my thin cardigan.

'Here,' he said, and he took off his jacket and slung it around my shoulders. I'd seen that done in films, but never in real life, and I was faintly shocked by the gesture. But then I began to appreciate the warmth of it, and I snuggled my neck into the collar, breathing in the familiar lemony scent of his aftershave.

'Nearly back,' he said, and then he put one arm around my shoulders and rubbed the back of his jacket to warm me up. And I'm not ashamed to admit I felt like a teenager again. Just for a moment. And it was delicious.

Back in the deserted hotel reception, I shrugged off his jacket and handed it back to him.

'Thanks.'

'No problem.'

'Well, I'll see you tomorrow,' I said.

'See you tomorrow.'

And then just as I was turning towards the staircase, he took my hand, hesitated for a moment and then pulled me in towards him, put his warm hands on either side of my head and kissed me. Properly this time, not just a peck on the cheek.

I was stunned into silence. I hadn't been kissed like that for – well, I couldn't remember. It was certainly decades. Did people our age kiss like that? Yes, they did, and for a lovely few moments I stood in his arms and allowed the warmth of him, the scent of him and the strength of him seep into my cold body.

'Gosh,' I said.

'Good night,' he said with a smile that was almost shy and definitely uncertain. 'And thank you for everything.'

## 19

I went up to my room in a bit of a daze, my thoughts in a whirl. I went over our conversations, trying to remember what I had said, what he had said that evening. And all of it seemed quite ordinary. Apart from my meal choice and the incident with the fishbone and the toothpick. Remembering that made me flush with embarrassment again. And then we had sat and talked some more over our mojitos, until we had walked back and he had kissed me. Not that I had in-depth experience, but he was a great kisser too.

I watched more television those days than I did now, and occasionally I was lured into watching some terrible series or soap opera, where all the old people are stupid caricatures and the younger ones don't seem to have actual jobs but are cool and endlessly busy with vendettas, unwise romantic entanglements or ridiculous disasters. Nearly always there is an ongoing sexual tension between two unsuited people which can occasionally last through a whole series, a plane falling on the town and a Christmas special.

This is when the kissing starts and it's always unpleasant to watch as the hero plunges, mouth open like an excavator as though he is going to take a bite out of the heroine, and then there are closeups of tongues and a lot of tonsil hockey that no one wants to see.

It hadn't been like that at all. He was gentle and careful, with no slobbering or slurpy noises, which are always so off-putting. I was beyond delighted, and long-dormant emotions resurfaced in me that I thought had been utterly quashed until that moment.

I liked being kissed. Well, I liked being kissed by him. What else might he be good at, I wondered.

Tomorrow was going to be our last full day here, the last chance to get to know him better, to think about what I wanted, the last chance to – yes, actually do some painting. I could just imagine myself back at the art group in Lower Begley, and undoubtedly Cassandra would want us to display our work for the people who hadn't come with us.

Dennis would be able to pull out several things, and would explain where we had been, how the beautiful scenery had inspired him, how he had felt as he painted. Anita and Beryl would too, I expect. I knew they had been trying to capture the lovely light over the sea, the sense of the hot stones at the ancient excavations. I wasn't sure what Effie had achieved, but I had literally only one drawing to show them from this holiday: the sketch of Costas's foot.

I could almost imagine Cassandra's expression when she saw it. How could I explain to her that I might not have done much painting but I *had* enjoyed a buffeting ride on a ringo, developed a taste for Greek coffee and Metaxa, shared meals, and drinks in lovely cafés and restaurants? I'd relished the experience of being out in the wider world with friends who made me laugh and rethink my life and my future. And I had met Will. And he had kissed me.

He had been an added bonus, and who knew where the future might take us? It might be somewhere; it might be nowhere. What mattered was my newly emerging belief in myself. I could still make friends; I could travel and have new experiences without asking permission or approval or anyone's opinion. How marvellous.

\* \* \*

When I went down to breakfast the following morning, Beryl and Effie were already sitting down with their usual bowls of Greek yogurt and fresh fruit, Anita was patiently waiting for the toaster to popup and Jillian was handing out bits of paper to everyone. My three friends started up immediately, asking questions about the previous evening and how it had gone, but mercifully we were silenced by Jillian, who had something important to tell us.

'I like to finish these holidays with a little competition. Nothing to worry about so don't look like that, Susan. It's all in good fun, totally boney fido, and there will be a certificate for the winner, and the judge's decision is final. Here's what I would like you to do. Gaston is going to take us about twenty miles up the coast where there is a little town which is ideal for soaking up the emotion of Santorini. It has a delightful central square with cafés and shops where you can buy souvenirs if you want them. It's pedestrianised so no worries about traffic, and it shouldn't be as crowded as at the weekend or later in the year. Obviously your artwork is the best souvenir you could have, but then some of you may not have done *as much* as others.'

I was sure I could feel her eyes boring into the back of my neck at that point, so I concentrated on the coffee machine in front of me and fiddled about with the sugar sachets.

'I have suggested three categories,' Jillian continued. 'A

building you like, flowers or an object. We will be there for most of the day, and there are some lovely old buildings and places to sit. We will have a super, chilled day. So, the minibus will be arriving here at just after ten o'clock. Costas tells me Gregor was out at a quiz night yesterday so it's possible he might be a bit late, but we can be ready just the same, can't we? And yes, June, I know what you are going to ask me. There are public loos there, very nice ones.'

'Oh, good,' June said, with a smile, 'I always like to know.'

Gregor, looking a bit weary and pale from his quiz night, arrived just before ten thirty by which time Jillian was stamping about looking anything but chilled. She favoured Gregor with one of her best stares, which as usual he ignored and after stashing our bags in the boot and like all polite British travellers assuming our usual seats, we were off.

The little town was situated high in the rocky countryside; on one side the fabulous views over the sea, but further in some cute little cobbled streets bordered by the usual tourist shops and cafés. After a few minutes it opened up into a wide tree-lined square where there was some welcome shade from the morning sun. There were concrete benches and noticeboards with helpful information about bus times and taxi firms. The only vehicle was a lone police car parked at the end and two very handsome policemen leaning on the bonnet and eating ice cream. It all looked delightful. I wondered where they had got the ice cream. But then I noticed they had guns so I didn't think it was wise to ask.

Never mind. This was definitely the day when we would be inspired to paint something, we were all sure of it.

After a bit of indecision about where we were going to set up our group, we decided to gather in the shade of some of the trees and then of course the hunt was on for something to paint. There were so many things that caught my eye that might have been suitable. A tiny white church with a bell tower, a gorgeous cluster of flower tubs rich with colour and fragrance, and some dinky little shops with racks of postcards and sunhats outside.

'Greek windows can be so evocative,' Dennis said thoughtfully as he gazed at one, which actually was absolutely beautiful. Painted white with the typical blue shutters folded back against the walls, and a tumbling profusion of bougainvillea over the top. 'Who lives here I wonder,' he said, edging closer until he was resting his hands on the windowsill.

An annoyed-looking woman suddenly appeared inside and glared at him, which answered that question. Dennis gave a shout of shock and stumbled back, almost falling over a waste bin.

'The edges of those little buildings,' June said, 'are unlike anything you might see anywhere else. The shadows, the alleyways leading ever onwards into the town are gorgeous.'

'And that wonderful blue of the cupolas against the sky. Absolutely magical,' Susan agreed.

'I'm going to paint the church,' Beryl said, looking wistful. 'The carving on that old door is lovely. Who knows how many scenes of joy and despair it has witnessed? And the bell tower with that single bell. How evocative. I wonder how long it has been there? Ringing out across the town, sounding a warning of invading ships from Greece perhaps, or Venice, or calling the faithful to prayer for many centuries, I expect.'

Effie went over to look at a plaque.

'It's been doing that since 2004.' She sniffed. 'The original was built in 1920, fell down in the earthquake of 1956 and this one was restored with a grant from the European commission.'

'You always spoil everything,' Beryl said, annoyed.

'I'm just telling you what it says,' Effie said, wide-eyed.

'Well, I'm still going to paint it,' Beryl said, planting herself down on one of the concrete benches.

'Perhaps I shall too,' Effie said, 'and we'll see who does a better job of it.'

'You can't do that, this church is mine,' Beryl said crossly. 'Go and find your own. And by the way, Meg, we still want to hear all about last night so don't think you are going to get away with not telling us.'

I chuckled and wandered off to where Will was standing by a little stone wall overlooking the town. There were dozens of flat white roofs and terracotta tiles below us, like a jigsaw which could never be finished. But then I am hopeless at jigsaws, even easy ones for children. If there are more than a hundred pieces I'm stumped.

He turned as I approached.

'How are you today?' he said, smiling down at me from under the brim of his Panama hat.

I saw Anita nudge Effie with her elbow, and I could feel the others surreptitiously watching us. I resisted the childish temptation to turn and shout at them, *Actually, we had a good old snog last night, just if you were wondering. And it was really great too.*

'Excellent. Fine,' I replied, trying unsuccessfully to ignore my memories of how the previous evening had ended. I wondered what he was thinking, but thankfully I was not so unsophisticated as to ask.

'Have you decided what you are going to focus on? I quite like the look of this view, but I don't think I have nearly enough ability to paint it.'

'I don't know yet,' I said, damping down the little flutters of excitement. 'Jillian's going to be so annoyed with me if I don't produce something today. I like the look of that stone trough with the scarlet geraniums. I love those. I have some like that at home, but perhaps not so bright. And those irises are lovely too. Such a perfect purple. And the shading of the walls in the little alleyway we walked through was wonderful, but I don't think I would be able to paint fast enough to capture them, because the sun is moving round all the time. But...' I gave a helpless shrug.

'Coffee?' he said.

'Oooh, yes please!'

Sometimes I thought I was beyond help.

\* \* \*

We walked back a little way, down towards the shady alleyway I had mentioned, and took a seat under the shade of a big rectangular parasol.

Greek coffee. I'd never had any before this trip but now I felt I was getting a bit addicted to it. It was hot, strong and sweet with a delicious slightly smoky taste, and my jar of instant back home paled into insignificance in comparison. He ordered slices of cake too, rich with walnuts and orange syrup and topped with a dollop of cream. *Portokalopita*; maybe it contained the essence of this marvellous place, distilled down into warmth and sunshine and the feeling of possibility. Or perhaps it was because of those days of brightness, the brilliance of the sky above us reflected down those dazzling white walls. The murmur of people strolling past us, exclaiming with pleasure at the streets in front, the little square with its shady corners and picturesque views. The dusty dog curled up on a doorstep, asleep in the sunshine. What a life.

I didn't think I would ever think of the world in the same way again, knowing that there were so many wonderful places I could explore. New people to meet, new friends to make; it filled my mind with all sorts of possibilities. Perhaps I hadn't done much actual art this week, but I had painted a new future for myself in my mind, and surely that was just as valuable.

'I'm going to find Lower Begley a bit dull after this,' I said at last.

He stirred his coffee with the little spoon in the saucer. 'I know what you mean. I feel I've somehow woken up after a long, dark sleep.'

'That's exactly how I feel!' I said. 'Isn't it marvellous?'

'Yes,' he said, and he reached out and briefly took my hand under the table, 'it is.'

'You do realise the others are all watching us, don't you?'

He shrugged. 'Do you know, I don't care.'

'Good. Nor do I.'

We finished our coffee and debated for a while what to do next. In the square we could see the rest of our group apparently hard at work.

'We ought to do something,' I said, 'so we have something to remember this holiday by.'

'I already have something, I think,' he said, 'but yes. Otherwise, we have no chance of any certificate at all.'

'Beryl will win,' I said. 'She's better than the rest of us put together. I think I will paint that stone trough. Please don't come and sit by me or you will put me off.'

He laughed. 'Then I will go and sit next to Dennis and draw that ice cream stall. The one with all the waffle cones on the stand.'

'Oooh, ice-cream,' I said wistfully, and he laughed again.

'Go and do some work and I will buy you one.'

'It's a deal,' I said, and we smiled at each other as though we both somehow recognised something important in the other person. Something far more than a friend. It was a really gorgeous moment.

* * *

I went and sat down next to Anita, shifting slightly so that the tree shaded me from the sunlight.

'Well, someone's getting very chummy,' she said airily, apparently focusing on her painting.

'Just coffee and a chat,' I said.

'Of course it is. You are the talk of the group, did you know that? Dennis says he can't understand what it is you find to talk about. Or why, when there are so many other things you could be doing.'

I didn't reply. I just got my sketchbook out and rested it on my knees, took out a 2B pencil and started drawing the outline of the stone trough.

'And June said she thought you made a nice couple,' Anita added, 'and Effie said if she was ten years younger she would give you a run for your money, but she can't be bothered.'

'She probably would too,' I said.

'Apparently not. Beryl said Effie was talking nonsense because she was always far more attracted to short men who looked a bit dangerous. Not actual hired killers but the sort who might just be wanted by Interpol. And let's be honest, she would know.'

'And what does Susan have to say?'

'She didn't say anything. She's gone over there by the shop selling novelty t-shirts because there's a ginger cat asleep in the sale bin.'

I laughed. 'I think she would find a cat just about anywhere.'

'Probably. So what's going on?'

'We had a coffee and some orange cake, and a nice talk about how much we have enjoyed this week, even if we haven't done much work.'

'And? What about last night and the hot date?'

'It wasn't a hot date, and it was very enjoyable. And I think we like each other. He's had a few difficult years—'

'Why? What happened?'

'Just this and that.'

Anita tutted in exasperation. 'You're absolutely hopeless. You still haven't told us what happened last night and what the meal was like. And we all want to know but we didn't want to ask while he was around. When we get back I am going to tie you to a chair and torture you with – oh, I don't know – goat's cheese and pickled onions until you tell me.'

I giggled. 'I like pickled onions.'

'Did the meal go well?' Anita said impatiently. 'We were all up on the roof terrace drinking shots and playing I Have Never and waiting for you to come back. And then you didn't so we just went to bed grumbling.'

'It was fine, except my meal was much too spicy and that was my fault because I didn't have my reading glasses and I didn't understand what the waitress was asking me. And then we went down to a little wine bar at the end of the beach for a nightcap.'

'And?'

'And it was lovely.'

There was a pause then as Anita concentrated on her painting.

'Do you know Dennis was arrested once?'

'How do you know?'

'I told you; we were playing that drinking game, I Have Never, and he and Effie both had been.'

I looked up in astonishment. 'Arrested? What for?'

'Dennis for taking part in the 1964 Aldermaston marches – Ban the Bomb protests. He said he was put into the back of a Black

Maria in handcuffs. But his mother was a magistrate and she knew someone who knew someone and nothing came of it. And Effie was arrested for being drunk in charge of a horse. She was let off with a warning, which her parents thought was ridiculous as her father said he hardly ever went hunting sober. How the other half live, eh?'

'It sounds as though you had a fun evening,' I said, trying hard to capture the outline of the geraniums with my pencil.

'Not as much fun as yours. I think you're mean not spilling the beans. I told you we Old Ducks cast a web of magic over these occasions. We can't lose.'

I sighed. 'And on a scale of none to very unlikely, what are your predictions?'

Anita laughed. 'Oh, pretty good. We are all very interested to know what's going on.'

'Look, tomorrow we will be going back to the airport and flying home. I don't know what you think can be achieved in one week.'

Anita looked up. 'You'd be surprised. Has he asked for your phone number or your address?'

'No,' I said, slightly uncomfortable that indeed, he hadn't. And I wasn't going to make that sort of move. To offer them unprompted.

'There's time yet,' she said, nodding wisely.

'Don't be silly.'

I finished the rough outline of my painting and then tipped a bit of my drinking water into my trusty Play-Doh pot and started adding colour. A dusty grey-green for the leaves, brilliant scarlet tipped with flashes of darker crimson for the flower heads. Then a pale sandy wash of colour for the trough.

I tried to look with a critical eye and realised it wasn't really that polished at all, but I liked it. It was something I had created, and it wasn't as bad as some of the things I had produced since joining the group, so I was pleased with it.

I would take it home and I might even frame it and hang it up somewhere, and every time I looked at it, I would remember sitting here, under a Greek sun, with feelings of optimism and positivity. Two things which had been sadly lacking in my life for far too long.

## 20

We got back to the hotel just after five o'clock, and tired and slightly sunburned but happy, we piled off the minibus and into the cool of the reception area. I looked back as I reached the staircase to see Will outside on his phone, pacing back and forth as most men seem to do when they are on a call. He was looking rather serious and doing more listening than talking by the looks of things.

I went to my room, looking forward to seeing him later and wondering what was left in my limited wardrobe choices to wear for this last evening meal. Actually, I wasn't particularly hungry because true to his promise, Will had come to inspect my painting and then bought me a delicious pistachio ice cream as a reward. And it wasn't one of the usual and rather unsatisfactory ice creams I expected where the scoop was small and the cone had the taste and texture of stale paper. This one was three huge blobs of pale green deliciousness in a waffle cone with the edge dipped in chocolate. Perhaps I didn't need anything else to eat after all.

I had a quick shower and changed into my rose-printed

sundress, which was made of some sort of miraculous material which didn't seem to crease even though it had fallen off the hanger unnoticed and had been lying crumpled up on the floor of the wardrobe, so a win as far as I was concerned. And then I pulled on a white cotton cardigan I had forgotten about and some sandals and I was ready to go. Before I left the room, I refilled the saucer of water I had been leaving out for the kittens on the balcony, and while I was out there, a taxi pulled up. It was Hector, and seconds later I saw Will put his suitcase in the back and then he got in. I watched, puzzled, as the taxi pulled away. What on earth was going on?

* * *

If anyone would know it would be Jillian, and I found her downstairs in the courtyard, poring over some sheets of paper looking cross.

'Where's Will gone? I just saw him getting into a taxi.'

She looked up at me briefly, obviously annoyed at being distracted from her paperwork.

'To the airport. He said he needed to get an earlier flight.'

'Why?'

She pulled a face, grabbed a sheet of paper from the bundle and ripped it up.

'I've no idea. Perhaps he'd had enough. He was very brusque with me. And I was right in the middle of sorting out the group for next week. There are going to be fourteen of them. How I will keep them in order is anyone's guess. It's been hard enough with just eight of you, darting off in all directions.'

'So, he didn't say anything?' I said hopefully.

Jillian shuffled her papers into some sort of order and scrabbled around on the table looking for a paperclip.

'He just said thanks for everything; he was going to the airport. Perhaps you should have asked him? Honestly, I do what I can to foster a good group vibe, but sometimes it doesn't work. It's disappointing for me too, you know.'

'Yes, I'm sure it is,' I said.

Jillian was working herself up by then, obviously annoyed.

'Some groups just gel right from the start. I had a lovely group of twelve a few weeks ago. Everyone interacting and friendly. And sometimes it's not like that. Take this week for example. Only a small group and yet there's been no cohesion, do you see? People are here to paint, not just wander off enjoying themselves. I never seem to know where June and Susan are. Dennis is always badgering me asking for tips or to borrow my penknife to sharpen his pencils because he had his confiscated at the airport. And – well...'

She stopped before she could get on to me and the others, or me and Will if she had noticed.

'I see,' I said.

'But then, don't get me wrong, I have enjoyed getting to know you all,' she added hastily.

'Personally, I have found this week an incredible help, even if I haven't produced much art.'

Jillian had been rummaging in her briefcase and she looked up, puzzled.

'Have you? In what way?'

'It's given me a new perspective on my life. Time to think and see where I need to make changes. And to me that has been more valuable than any amount of sketching.'

Jillian gave me a puzzled stare.

'I just assumed you weren't getting much out of it. Or your friends. You just seemed to want to go off on your own all the time.'

'Everyone needs space sometimes,' I said. 'The time to plan and consider what to do next. None of us are in the first flush of youth, and we all have worries and problems. And being at home can mean there is no time to deal with them before someone else needs something or wants to chat. Trust me, it's made a lot of difference to me. If nothing else it has shown me how to have fun again. You often seem so stressed and worried, you should try it.'

'I have been feeling in need of a rest,' Jillian agreed, clutching her paperwork to her chest, 'but of course my life is great. Wonderful. Living here. The people and the climate. I know just about everyone and every street. It's all so lovely. What have I got to complain about?'

'Perhaps you need a holiday from your holiday,' I said, and she smiled, the lines of tension fading from her face for the first time.

'Maybe I do.'

'Well, I'll see you later,' I murmured and hurried away to find the others.

I was glad that perhaps she might take my advice, because with a dispassionate eye I could see her life might not be quite as idyllic as she made out. Effie had found out that her long-time partner had left the previous year and gone off to work on a cruise ship. I could see that Jillian was lonely. Maybe the feeling that she had control of this part of her life was more important to her than we had realised.

I thought about this for a few seconds and felt a bit guilty. And then I went back to thinking about Will and I was suddenly very disappointed. Apart from anything else, how rude of him, to leave like that. To spend that time with me, to take my hand, smile into my eyes and kiss me, to make me feel as though there was something between us that was different. And then just disappear without even saying goodbye.

But perhaps he was ill, maybe that was it? He needed to get back for an urgent medical appointment. Or perhaps his new kitchen had flooded or there had been some other domestic disaster with his house renovation.

I pulled myself up; I was doing what I had always done with Malcolm: make excuses for inexcusable behaviour. More fool me.

Still, I did want to understand what had happened, and like generations of women before me, I had started off by assuming it was my fault.

Perhaps despite everything he had come to the end of his flirting abilities. Perhaps he was bored by it all and didn't know how to get out of it? So instead of having a conversation he just did a runner.

For goodness' sake, what was the matter with people, that they thought it was okay to be so cowardly and discourteous? I hadn't behaved in an annoying, stalkerish way.

I imagined myself spilling the beans to the others; they were bound to ask. They had been so confident that the Old Duck magic always worked. Well, evidently not in this case.

\* \* \*

Will's absence at dinner was noticed, of course, and people wanted to know where he was on this last evening together, when Jillian was waxing unexpectedly lyrical about what a great group we had been, how she was sure some of us would return another year and how we would always be welcome. Which, in view of what she had said to me on the quiet, was a bit rich.

And then she said she was going to take a break when the summer season was over and visit Cassandra, and she hoped she would see some of us again when she did. And we all said we hoped so too, and she gave the first real smile since we had met her.

**\* \* \***

'There's a proper word for what Will did, isn't there?' Anita said later when we were sitting up on the roof terrace after dinner.

'Rude?' Beryl suggested.

'No – it's called ghosting,' Anita said.

'I've read about that. A couple get together and everything seems to be going fine and then out of the blue one of them simply disappears. I had a friend who had that,' Effie said. 'She met Lionel through their local bowls club and they had afternoon tea twice, and he was even talking about them pairing up for some tournament in the summer. In Torquay. Pauline got very excited. She was practically packing her case, and then nothing. He disappeared off the radar, never returned her calls. She was very upset.'

'So what happened?' I asked.

'She found out six months later he'd been run over. In the high street. He wasn't badly hurt, just a mild concussion and a bruised knee. But someone said they thought he had joined another team in Chichester. And apparently he had left his thermos in his locker at the bowls club, and some cheese sandwiches. By the time they opened it she said it looked like Day of the Triffids in there.'

'That's not quite the same thing,' Anita said reasonably. 'He might have had amnesia.'

'No, Pauline said he had a wife, *and* a lady friend in West Wittering.'

'Oh, it doesn't matter,' I said, 'let's talk about something else. I'm a bit hurt, but it'll pass.'

Beryl leaned over and patted my arm consolingly.

'Of course it will pass. It might pass like a kidney stone, which I've heard can be very unpleasant, but you'll be fine. I have to admit, I'm surprised though. Now then, I was thinking of ordering some drinks from Costas. What do you think?'

'Is that wise? We have to be out of our rooms by ten thirty tomorrow,' Anita said.

'As Scarlett O'Hara was so fond of saying, tomorrow is another day,' Effie said, waving to attract Costas's attention, 'and the plane doesn't leave until the afternoon.'

Costas had been peacefully sitting behind the bar reading his newspaper. He came over with a white cloth draped over one arm and a tray in his hand.

'Ladies?' he said with a broad smile.

'Costas! I hardly recognised you with your clothes on. Do you think we could have a bottle of white wine and four glasses?' Effie said sweetly.

He gave a little bow and ambled off back to the bar, where we could hear him crashing about for a few minutes.

'He's in a good mood for once,' I said.

'I expect he's hoping we will leave him a nice tip,' Beryl hissed. 'He was just the same last time I was here. Jillian too.'

'And how much are we expected to leave?' I asked.

Beryl shrugged. 'It's entirely up to you.'

'I've got a good tip for her,' Effie said. 'Bees Knees in the two thirty race at Doncaster.'

'I think she's lonely,' I said, 'and this place, organising groups like ours, is all she has. Which is a bit sad, isn't it?'

\* \* \*

I enjoyed our last evening together. We had a pleasant meal at the taverna down the street and while we were enjoying coffee and a last glass of Metaxa, Dennis stood up to say a few words, telling us how much he had enjoyed the week and thanking Jillian for organising everything and also commiserating like a teacher's pet, with her efforts to control us.

Then Jillian stood up, blushing and almost tearful, and thanked us all for being such a fun group and how much she would miss us. I don't think anyone really believed her, but it was a nice gesture.

'Now then,' she said, pulling out a folder from her capacious bag, 'down to business. This is, after all, the awards evening.'

There was a murmur of excitement then, and Dennis sat up very straight and tried to look modest.

'I'd like to thank my mother, my agent, all my fans and the whole team at Universal Studios,' Beryl murmured. Effie giggled and gave her a nudge.

'So, I have certificates of attendance for you all. And some of them have additional comments,' Jillian continued. 'The standard this week has been high, with a great many really accomplished pieces—'

'It won't be me then. I only drew Costas's foot and some flowers,' I murmured.

'Or me,' June hissed back, 'but I have nearly finished knitting Nigel's jumper.'

'—but without a doubt, the artist of the week – and this is only my opinion – is Dennis.'

Dennis stood up smiling broadly and went to accept his certificate with as much pride as he would have accepted an Oscar. He decided to give another speech in honour of the occasion.

'Well, I don't really know what to say,' he said, 'I'm not a great one for talking—'

'Could have fooled me,' Beryl murmured.

'—I didn't expect this at all. But I will say it's been a very enjoyable week, with some really splendid locations and vistas. A decent room in a very pleasant hotel; thank you, Nina and Costas. And the arrangements have been first class. Thanks to Gregor for driving us, and to everyone in this little town who have made us all feel so welcome. Apart from the man in the bakery who put onion in my sandwich when I quite clearly told him not to. And to the lovely restaurants and cafés who have kept us well fed and entertained. And also I mustn't forget—'

'I thought he didn't know what to say?' Effie said. 'He only needs to get onto the council workers, the prime minster of Greece and the Olympic movement and then he has all the bases covered.'

'—and so farewell, friends, it's been such fun. And getting this award is the icing on the cake. Or should I say on the *vasilopita*? Just my little joke. Sally will be thrilled when I get back and tell her all about it. I wouldn't be surprised if she frames this and hangs it up somewhere.'

'Bravo,' Beryl called from our end of the table, and she started clapping. 'Bravo, Dennis.'

We all joined in with the applause and Dennis went to sit down, looking very pleased and slightly embarrassed.

'So this really is the end,' Effie said. 'Still, there is always next year. Another trip, a different activity maybe?'

'Good idea,' Anita said. 'Anywhere warm, like this, suits me. Still, I'm looking forward to getting home and seeing Rick again, even if I do have to look at all his pictures of wet birds on a damp Scottish hillside. He'll be in such a great mood; I might even discuss the hot tub idea with him again.'

And me? How did I feel?

A mixture of emotions. Part of me was looking forward to getting back home, doing my laundry and sleeping in my own bed. The other part was slightly sad to leave this beautiful island where I had enjoyed myself far more than I had expected to, and also that things had ended like this, with Will leaving early without any sort of farewell or explanation. And why? That was the nagging question at the back of my mind. Oh well, I would just have to put it down to experience and forget about it. It had been fun and rather exciting, but all good things must come to an end, after all.

## 21

Our plane landed at Birmingham airport an hour late, and of course it was dark and raining.

'Flipping heck, talk about a come down,' Beryl said as we trudged through the corridors dragging our cabin bags behind us. As we went, we watched the bulk of our plane disappearing behind the rain-smeared windows, and then we were on to security and the scrum of baggage reclaim, and for a while it almost felt as though the days of sunshine and the fun we had enjoyed had all been a dream.

June and Susan were picked up by Nigel, who swept June up into his arms as though she had been away for months rather than days. It was very sweet to see and I hoped he would be pleased with the new sweater she had knitted for him.

Beryl had organised a minibus to take the five of us home to Lower Begley, and we piled in with our cases and bags, Dennis in the front seat fiddling with the heating and complaining about the vanilla air freshener, and the rest of us tired and rather cramped behind him. It was very different from our excursions with Gregor, and this too made us all rather subdued.

I leaned my forehead on the window and looked out at the speeding traffic, the lights from the motorway blurred by grime and the lashing rain. I wondered if all good holidays triggered such a response. Disappointment that they were over. Regret that life might be going to get back into a normal routine. And then I thought about Will again and wondered where he was and why he had left so abruptly.

I guessed he was home, in his latest renovation project near Bicester. That's what he had said. Was he the sort of man to wield a sledgehammer and knock walls down himself? Or did he have a team of builders doing it for him?

'Well, this is depressing,' Effie said as the traffic slowed and came to a complete halt after a few miles. 'And so predictable. It's like we never went away.'

'Roadworks,' the driver said gloomily, wiping the mist off the windscreen with the back of his hand, 'it never blooming ends on this stretch. No sooner have they finished one bit than they start on another.'

I closed my eyes and thought back to the dusty Greek roads I had left behind, the views over the sea and the scrubby landscape, and wished I was back there. I could almost remember how it had felt in the heat of a Greek afternoon as the sweat trickled down between my shoulder blades. No risk of that here.

And yet, I realised, it might have been a marvellous experience, but the probability was I would not go back there at all. After all, there were other beautiful places to find and explore. I would be like Captain Kirk and boldly go somewhere else. Warm French beaches. Cold, snowy landscapes. Walled medieval cities and shimmering lakes. Perhaps I actually would cross the Atlantic or go on a river cruise.

Maybe this really was the start of a new chapter in my life, when I stopped worrying about what other people would think and did things that I wanted to. In my own time. Other people did; why shouldn't I?

And Will? What about him?

I wanted to chalk it up to experience and forget about it. But I couldn't seem to forget those wonderful moments when we had stood together overlooking the craggy cliffs, the dark, silken sea, and the memory of him coming towards me, bringing me pistachio ice cream – had that really been only yesterday?

We had exchanged smiles and glances and laughter. He had sought me out. He had kissed me and made me feel things I hadn't felt for decades. Could I forget all that? It seemed as though I must.

\* \* \*

I got home just after nine o'clock, later than I had thought because of the travel delays, and Ivan was there sitting on the bottom of the stairs like a resentful loaf of bread. He favoured me with a rusty miaow, stretched and stalked off into the kitchen.

I sighed. It wasn't much of a welcome.

I dumped my bags and looked through the pile of post which Nicky had left on the worktop for me. There was a note too.

*Welcome back, hope you had a marvellous time. Ivan didn't like the new beef cat food with the gravy you bought for him at all. He threw up in your slippers. So I chucked them away. Sorry about that. He did like the remains of the Sunday lunch I brought him though. Did you know he likes duck breast? And he ate a roast potato too. Either that or he's hidden it under a chair somewhere. No mice brought in as far as I can tell, but I didn't look upstairs in case I found something. Hope you had a*

*good flight. Ring me tomorrow and tell me all about your*
*adventures. Nicky xx*

Adventures. Yes, me. I'd had some adventures. How amazing.
And all of a sudden I wanted to have some more.

It was crazy; I hadn't even opened my suitcase and already the
one thing I wanted to do was think about where to go on my next
journey. I'd sent off for a new passport before I made this trip, so
there were plenty of years left on it and lots of empty pages for
airport officials to stamp. Perhaps Beryl was right and it did
become a sort of addiction.

Anyway, that evening there was nothing interesting to do,
other than put the first load of washing on and open some of the
uninteresting letters that had arrived.

I made a cup of tea and sat down at the kitchen table. There
were bank statements, utility bills, a letter to tell me that the road
through Lower Begley would be closed for two days next month
for resurfacing. Well, that was about time; recently the road had
become more of an obstacle course with locals driving down the
middle to avoid the worst of the potholes.

There were uninteresting special offers from fast food places
that didn't deliver to where I lived, and even if they did I wouldn't
want them. Two glossy booklets from retirement villages, in
which I similarly had no interest. A couple of clothing cata-
logues, another selling horrible shoes for more mature ladies.
Okay, I might not be able to cope with stilettos any more, but
there was a limit. I slung all the stuff I didn't want into the recycling. I might be getting older but as of today, I would not go
quietly.

I drank my tea and mindlessly ate a few biscuits.

This time yesterday...

Tomorrow perhaps I would allow myself a lie-in to get over

the travelling, sort out my laundry and then I would phone Nicky.

I went to bed feeling thoroughly depressed.

\* \* \*

The following day I felt much better.

I had slept well, which was always a bonus. It was lovely to be back in my own comfortable bed and when I woke at half past eight, the rain had gone and in the distance I could see the clouds were blowing away over the Black Mountains. In the field behind my house there was a man on a tractor, busy doing something. I opened my window, enjoying the cool, green freshness, which was so different from the warm, slightly flinty air of Greece. Then I wondered how Anita was feeling.

What day was it anyway? I had to flick my phone on in the end to confirm that it was Sunday. I remembered last Sunday when I had been in Greece and there had been the sound of a church bell tolling somewhere in the town, and we had still been in the excited phase of getting to know everyone, exploring the little streets and enjoying experimenting with new foods and flavours.

I showered and dressed and went downstairs to find Ivan had left a dead mouse in the middle of the hall as a welcome home gift. Back to reality with a bump.

I got rid of that and wondered what to have for breakfast. Toast and marmalade and tea. I hoped whoever was now in my room at Hotel Costas would take a slice of breakfast ham up for the kittens on the balcony.

As I sat at the kitchen table, leafing through the rest of the post, my mobile rang.

'Anita! How are you this morning?'

'Fed up,' she said. 'I want someone to put out pastries and croissants for me. And I want to go down to the sea again and sit in one of those lovely cafés. Instead, I have my washing to do and Rick's as well. He seems to have brought back a lot of Scotland with him. Mud and bits of twig over all his clothes. Not to mention a bottle of whisky bought at huge expense from a distillery they visited, and some fudge, and he knows I don't like either of those things.'

'Ah, but you have that special present for him,' I said, laughing. 'Costas in all his glory.'

Anita giggled. 'He didn't know what to say when I showed him that. The nose still isn't right. He suggested we put it in the loo upstairs which isn't used very much unless we have visitors. What are you doing?'

'Laundry this morning, then general unpacking and sorting out.'

'Awful, isn't it? Rick says we should have a proper debrief this evening.'

'I say!'

'No, not that sort of debrief. Don't be rude. He means I tell him what I have been doing and he tells me about the garganeys and white-throated fossil pickers or whatever it is he has seen. I shall try to look interested. He said they had a marvellous time. He twisted his ankle in a rabbit hole while they were striding across the heather and had to drive miles out of their way to find a support bandage, Harry insisted on eating oysters and got food poisoning, and his friend Vince broke his glasses.'

'None of that sounds marvellous to me,' I said.

'That's exactly what I said. Anyway, men aren't like us. They seem to enjoy the strangest things. I don't suppose you've heard from Will? No extravagant bouquet of welcome home flowers left on the doorstep?'

'He doesn't know my address, remember?'

'Ah yes, I'd forgotten. Well, never mind, come over for a cup of tea this afternoon and we can rehash the glory days.'

'I'd love to. But now I'd better think about unpacking my case.'

Anita sighed. 'Me too.'

\* \* \*

Actually, it was nice to be home with all my familiar things around me and not having to go out every time I wanted some Greek coffee or a meal. I dragged my case onto my bed. It seemed heavier than I remembered and it still had the labels on the handles from the airline. I ripped them off rather sadly. If I was going to do more of this sort of thing, the first thing I would do was buy a new case, brightly coloured – pink or yellow – so I could spot it more easily on the baggage carousel and not have to peer hopefully at every identical black case that passed me.

I started to unpack, put the first load of laundry on and then sorted out all the little souvenirs and oddments I had picked up along the way.

Some sugar sachets, a couple of plastic cocktail sticks, a carrier bag with Greek writing on it which came from the shop where I had bought my new rose-patterned sundress, receipts from cafés and shops which I had carefully kept and now made no sense to me. A tiny wrapped bar of soap from the bathroom which I hadn't used. A fabric pouch with my charging cables and adaptors. There was even a little pile of grit in the bottom of the empty case, and there were my zebra-print shoes which would never be the same again. Silly little things which somehow held such memories.

Ivan followed me upstairs and sat on the bed, glowering at my suitcase, as though he was daring me to go away again.

'Don't worry, I'm back,' I said, 'and it doesn't look as though you have starved.'

The first load of dark laundry was done and I put in all the lighter things. And then I went out into the garden to hang everything on the line and see how things had fared in my absence. The grass needed mowing, but I was delighted to see it was far too wet to do it so that would have to wait until another day. I could hear Bonzo barking over the hedge. He sounded thrilled to be back from his stay in the kennels.

I went to have some elevenses: instant coffee and chocolate digestives. I would get some real coffee the next time I went out, and a small cafetiere. And some interesting biscuits.

The washing machine beeped to show it had finished and I went to unload it.

Ah.

Slight problem.

It seemed my new sundress, while reasonably priced, uncrushable and pretty, had bled colour all over everything, and now all my white towels, t-shirts and knickers were the same bright, mottled pink.

I held up one thing after another, cursing and wondering what to do.

Oh for goodness' sake. Realising it was far too late, I examined the care label. It said dry clean only. Like that was going to happen. Why would anyone spend ten quid drycleaning a dress which had cost about the same price?

The dress was still in one piece and uncrushable but also ruined. Unless I didn't mind wearing a garment that looked as though it had come out of a skip. I'd only worn it twice, so perhaps it hadn't been such a good purchase after all.

I went to look in the fridge. Nothing in there seemed at all exciting or tasty. I needed to go shopping and start buying some more interesting food.

I put my empty coffee mug in the dishwasher and gave a heavy sigh. Yes, it was nice to be back home again, but in a way it felt as though the colour had faded from my life, just as it had from my dress.

## 22

Following my trip to the supermarket, I made myself a rather exotic sandwich for lunch – cold chicken, hummus and roasted peppers – and then rang my daughter.

Nicky answered almost at once.

'So you're home safe,' she said. 'No problems or lost luggage?'

'A bit late but okay,' I said. 'So when are you coming over to see me? I've brought you a present.'

'Excellent! It's my day off tomorrow, so I'll pop over to see you for lunch, and then I can see my favourite boy too.'

'Do you mean Ivan? My word, you do surprise me,' I said.

Coincidentally, the cat in question was coming in, a small, suspicious-looking feather stuck on the top of one ear. He stopped halfway through the cat flap and glared at me.

'It looks like your favourite boy has been up to no good in the garden.'

'I've got some leftover minced beef for him,' Nicky said, 'he'll like that. And there are some little scraps of smoked salmon he can have too. I saved them from our starters at the pub last night. Do you think he would like them?'

'I think he would force it down out of politeness,' I said. 'He's back on the ordinary stuff now I'm home. It's no wonder he is sending me dirty looks if that's what you've been feeding him.'

Nicky laughed. 'Right, I'll see you tomorrow.'

\* \* \*

That afternoon I got to Anita's house just after three o'clock. I found her sitting in the garden with her laptop on her knee and a cup of tea at her elbow. Bonzo her dog was wrestling with some squeaky toy at her feet and at the end of their garden, Rick was doing something to the lawnmower which involved a toolbox and a cross expression.

'I'm just sorting out my photos,' she said, 'before I show them to Rick and he sees what we got up to. There seemed to be an awful lot of meals and glasses of Metaxa.'

'Marvellous, wasn't it?' I said with a sigh. 'I'm so glad I went. Do you know I was trying to think of excuses not to come along when you first mentioned it. I wouldn't have missed it for anything.'

Anita beamed. 'I knew I was right about you. You fitted right in. It's like I told you; the Old Ducks have a sort of magic. We have fun, we talk about everything, we don't take offence if someone disagrees and we don't particularly care what other people think. That's what I call liberation. And because of that we are very good at supervising new relationships. There is written evidence of that, probably in several scientific journals.'

I laughed. 'Not for me.'

She rolled her eyes. 'Not yet maybe, I think you might be surprised. A lot of women our age think life is slowly winding down. The Old Ducks don't think like that, not one bit, and it's very empowering. And by the way, I have put in a request to Juliette our president for you to join us. Don't tell me you feel the same about the future now as you did two weeks ago?'

'No, actually. I don't.'

She smiled. 'Right then, tea or coffee?'

'I don't mind.'

Anita held up a warning finger.

'Okay then, I'd like tea,' I said.

'Good choice. We must go to the painting group next week. There isn't a meeting this week because Cassandra is away. She will be wanting to know how we got on and what we achieved,' Anita said, passing me a mug of tea and a plastic box of biscuits.

'Not much actually,' I said, 'but I expect Dennis will arrive with a huge folder of things he did while he was there. And his certificate.'

'Teacher's pet,' Anita said, unwrapping a KitKat. 'I didn't have any comments on my certificate of attendance, did you?'

'Nothing,' I said, 'and I expect Cassandra will look hard at the rest of us. Not angry, just disappointed. I don't care; I had a great time. And I do have a drawing of Costas's foot of which I'm quite proud.'

'I think men probably have better feet than women because they don't spend years cramming them into fashionable shoes.'

'I wonder who is in our rooms now?' I said wistfully. 'In Hotel Costas. Looking out from the roof terrace, going down to the sea and trying out the cafés and restaurants. Lucky them.'

'Onwards and upwards. So, where next?' Anita asked, 'You said you wanted to plan your next trip.'

'Now I have unpacked and done all the washing, I'm going to see my sister in America and then I'll do some research. Perhaps a river cruise. Or Mallorca.'

'Oooh, I recommend that,' Anita said. 'My friends had a fabulous time there. A little place near Pollença. The pictures looked absolutely gorgeous, I'd love to go there. But then the old town of Rhodes was nice too.'

Rick came in through the kitchen door.

'Boots,' Anita shouted automatically, and he scuffed them off.

'Hello, Meg. Had fun? We had a marvellous time in Scotland. Pity about the rain. And the blackflies. And my ankle. And Harry having food poisoning. And Vince breaking his glasses. We had to mend them with a blister plaster. And the car having a puncture miles from anywhere. But the locals were really helpful. We'll go back, I'm sure. I like going back to places. I know where everything is and how it works. Unlike that blasted lawnmower, which still isn't working. I'll have to get someone round to fix it. Bashing it with a mole wrench doesn't seem to be working this time.'

Blister plasters. A mole wrench. Ridiculous things which reminded me of Will.

The image we had conjured up between us, of Mr Mole in his velvet waistcoat, living underground.

That was the first time we had chatted and smiled at each other. When we had connected. For a moment I felt rather sad to think I wouldn't see him again. He lived near Bicester. I could hardly just drive around there aimlessly wondering if I would see him, could I?

\* \* \*

Nicky came round the following morning to see me and hear all about the trip. I presented her with a rather lovely, blue-patterned tea towel and a giant bar of Greek chocolate, and she was delighted. And even more pleased when Ivan came and wound himself around her ankles while we sat out in the garden having lunch. She reached down to scratch his ears, and Ivan threw himself on the ground in ecstasy.

'That cat is a traitor,' I said, 'he never does that for me. All he has done since I got home is scowl at me and bring me a dead mouse.'

'But it's a sign of high favour when cats do that,' Nicky said. 'You should be proud. Now then, tell me all about this Doctor Bill person. Maureen was asking about him. She says she had such a crush on him back in the day. What's he like?'

'Really nice,' I said. 'Rather reserved at first. Almost shy. But when he realised we weren't going to take endless selfies with him or try to embarrass him, he loosened up a little. He knew all about the Minoans. And he was funny. And considerate. And kind.'

Nicky grinned. 'Sounds like someone else has a bit of a crush.'

I could feel my face getting rather hot. 'No, not at all, absolutely not.'

She laughed. 'It's okay, Mum. You're allowed to like him.'

I felt a bit panicky. Did I want to talk about him? I wasn't sure. 'Do you want some tea? Or a cold drink? I have some squash.'

Nicky narrowed her eyes. 'You're trying to change the subject, aren't you? What is it you're not telling me?'

'Nothing!'

'Nonsense. I can tell. You're hiding something. You did like him?'

'Well all right, I did,' I said, 'I liked him quite a bit actually.'

'So will you see him again?'

'I shouldn't think so,' I said, trying to sound light-hearted, 'he lives miles away, and anyway, we didn't exchange any details. So no.'

'Pity. I expect he still has a good bedside manner.'

'Nicky!'

'Don't be so stuffy. There's nothing wrong with it. So did you do a lot of painting and sketching?'

'Not as much as I thought I would,' I said, 'although I did do a nice drawing of Costas's foot.'

'Huh?'

'Oh, I must tell you all about that. It was hilarious.'

I filled her in on all the details of our life class session while over the hedge we could hear Bonzo barking accompanied by the sounds of Rick's lawnmower trundling up and down, so he must have managed to mend it.

Nicky looked at the photos on my phone with considerable interest, particularly the few with Will in them. She spent some time zooming in on the picture to get a good look at him and at last she looked up at me.

'That picture of him in the restaurant.'

'You'll have to narrow it down a bit. We went to a lot of restaurants.'

'The one where he is sitting across the table from you. And you were obviously there on your own, not with the group at all. That's a bit of a clue, isn't it?'

'Ah yes, that was...' I tried to remember. Was it three days ago or two when we had gone to the vineyard for dinner? It seemed like an age, another lifetime. 'We had dinner out together, that's all. A lovely evening in a fantastic location. It wasn't without incident.'

'I think he likes you. I can tell,' Nicky said.

'Oh, don't be daft. It was just one meal out. I expect it was the one that evening, where the waitress took our picture.'

Nicky grabbed my phone and found the picture again. And then she passed it over for me to look at.

'His expression. Don't you see it? The way he's looking at you. I wish Joe looked at me that way sometimes.'

I stared at my phone, and to see Will again, to see his expression and remember how I had felt – it took my breath away for a moment. The problem with the over-spiced meal, the fishbone, the toothpick, the way I had terrified the woman on the stairs – none of that mattered because after that we had gone down to the sea, not wanting the evening to end. And he had kissed me.

I gave a huge sigh, feeling rather sad and yet happy at the same time because we'd had that evening together and it had been so special. That feeling I'd had, that the metaphorical sands of my life were flowing again; that after all the years of feeling ordinary and unimportant, I did matter after all. And it wasn't just because of Will, although he was a bonus. It was because at last I was seeing myself, as an individual, not just as someone's wife or mother. Not simply a colleague or neighbour.

'He was rather lovely,' I admitted.

'I'd like to meet him,' Nicky said carefully, 'he looks – well – nice. Suitable.'

What on earth did that mean, I wondered. That my daughter approved of a man in my life because he was suitable. In what way? What was she implying? That perhaps he would look after me, be company for me in my old age? Maybe provide me with some sort of undefined security and support?

What she didn't see was what I saw. That Will was attractive, broad shouldered, intelligent, fun. Nicky would never consider the possibility that her aged mother – me – might have found this man sexy, find the touch of his hand on mine erotic. The scent of his aftershave stimulating, the sound of his voice thrilling. Nicky would never know how I had trembled like a girl when Will threw his jacket around my shoulders, and probably never understand how getting to know him had opened my eyes to so many possibilities.

But then he had left early. I could still remember how I felt when I saw him load his case into the back of Hector's taxi and being driven off to the airport to catch an earlier flight. He had gone without saying goodbye. And suddenly I felt the silly prickle of tears, which of course was ridiculous.

And after all, what would I be crying about? The childish disappointment at the end of a holiday? Or was it the feeling that although a door had opened in front of me, another behind me had closed?

'Finished?' I said brightly, starting to clear away the lunch things onto a tray.

'That was delicious. What was in that sandwich? You don't usually do things like that.'

'Lamb, rocket and tzatziki,' I said proudly. 'Greek food is lovely. I've decided I'm going to be a bit more adventurous. Now then, how are things going at the library? I was so glad to hear you have a bit of a reprieve.'

'Not bad actually. Joyce has revived the after-school reading club, and she's even printed out some certificates. Kids love those, don't they? And I am going to start up a mother and toddler reading circle three times a week. Now that there are all those new houses, there are loads of young families moving in. It's hard for some of the new mums to make friends sometimes.'

'It's not so easy for the old mums either,' I said, 'and women my age don't have toddler groups and the school gate meetings to find kindred spirits. And just because we are retired it doesn't mean we all want to knit or make cakes all the time. If you had met some of the women I was on holiday with, you'd know that. There were three of them, all in what they called The Old Ducks Club.'

'Actually, that sounds fun.'

'They were great. They had such a positive outlook. They were my age, maybe a bit older, but it didn't stop them. Do you know I went on a ringo? One of those inflatable doughnuts towed behind a boat.'

Nicky was genuinely shocked. 'Did you!'

'It was such a laugh. And we talked endlessly about everything. In fact, we were told off for not sticking with the group all the time, which I think was what the leader expected. It's given me a whole new feeling about life. Now that you and Joe are settled, I don't think I have to just think of myself as a support act any more. And I don't want you to keep thinking I need looking after and checking up on. And I know you do. There's a lot more life in me yet.'

'Wow, I thought you would just come home with a tan and some paintings,' Nicky said.

'I do have a tan, and I have a drawing of Costas's foot,' I said with a laugh, 'and I painted a trough of flowers. In a little town where life seemed so much easier. And of course, I know it wasn't paradise, but it's shown me that the possibilities are out there, even for me.'

'This doesn't sound like you at all,' Nicky said.

'Perhaps not, but women my age are still interested in life, in fashion, in seeing the world. If you can find a travel company where a single traveller like me isn't financially penalised for sole occupancy, please tell me.'

'That's an interesting thought, I hadn't realised that,' Nicky said.

'I'd love to go on a cruise, but if I go on my own I'd be stuck in a titchy little cabin with no window. Or have to pay nearly double the cost. And I know the companies have to make money, but you can't tell me every ship sails without some empty cabins. They could fill those with people like me at the last minute, surely?'

Nicky laughed. 'Sounds like you have a bee in your bonnet, Mum. This really isn't like you at all.'

'No, well, I've had time to think about things. And I've been looking on the internet too.'

'Okay. So where are you going next?'

'I haven't decided. But it will be somewhere. Maybe Washington to see Auntie Bridget.'

'And little Newt.' Nicky chuckled.

'He's not little any more, remember he's only two years younger than you and works in Wall Street.'

'By the way, while we are on the subject of things changing, I have some news. I didn't want to tell you until I saw you. I had an email from Dad last night. He's getting married,' Nicky blurted out. 'To Alison. Next month.'

I thought about this for a few seconds. 'Good for him.'

'You don't mind?'

I sat down on my chair again with a bump, astonished at the question.

'Of course I don't mind. Why on earth would I mind?'

'Oh, I don't know, I thought perhaps you might.'

'Well, I don't. Now then, shall we have coffee? I've bought a cafetiere and some proper coffee. I got quite a taste for it in Greece.'

After Nicky had gone, I poured myself a glass of wine and sat out in the garden again, enjoying the late afternoon sunshine.

Malcolm getting married again. Well, there was a turn up for the books.

Did I mind? No, I really didn't. The only thing that surprised me was that Alison had been as daft as I had, and she was in her late fifties and should have known better. He was one of those older men I had been thinking about. Set in their ways, laden down with emotional baggage. Good luck to her.

## 23

Without the painting group meeting that week, I lost a bit of focus.

I hadn't realised how much I had come to rely on it. To get me out of the house, to give me something to do which was entirely for me, and of course the company of other people who had become my friends.

I spent my time cleaning, rekindling my damaged relationship with Ivan, refilling the fridge, finishing off the ironing and catching up with the latest box set on television I had been watching before I went away.

How did that brave New York detective with the glossy perfect hair, designer suits and four-inch stilettos actually manage to chase after the criminals so fast, I wondered. And some of her male counterparts seemed to go to work in sharp suits and silk ties, which was odd considering they always ended up in disused warehouses or abandoned buildings full of rusty machinery. I wondered what the actual FBI or CIA thought of those programmes.

The weekend came round again, and I had the house straight,

the grass mowed and I was looking forward to the painting group on Tuesday.

Anita called for me and we walked down to the village hall together, our art materials in folders and bags. There was a cold breeze, and the verges were filled with cow parsley and wildflowers, which gave off a fresh green scent that was England in the spring.

'I'd give anything to be back in Santorini, wouldn't you?' Anita said, shivering in her wool jacket. 'Do you remember what it was like? Trying to go out with as few layers on rather than how many. Not having to think about it raining or taking an umbrella, or a warm coat.'

'I do,' I said wistfully, dodging a water-filled pothole at the edge of the lane, 'but it's nice to be home again. I'm beginning to like living here, even though it's taken me a while.'

'I'm so glad you moved in. The couple who lived at High Winds before you were always complaining about something. The state of the road or the late delivery of the post. And I don't think they ever really understood that having moved to a rural area, there would be farming going on around them. They told me they had moved from living in Hereford because of the noise. But when one buys a house called Cathedral View, surely one would expect to hear church bells?'

'I hope Beryl and Effie will be there today,' I said, 'I've missed them. In fact, I've been thinking of inviting them over for afternoon tea one day. You too of course.'

'They will say yes, I'm sure. They never refuse an invitation, and they are always up for a laugh. I intend to be more Beryl in future. I think it might be fun.'

'Me too,' I said, and we grinned at each other.

When we got to the village hall, we could see there were

already people inside, amongst them the unmistakeable figure of Dennis ordering everyone about.

'Come along, ladies, get those easels into a circle. Cassandra will be here soon, and we want to show her we are keen and expecting to start on time. Ah, jolly good, it's Anita and Maggie!'

'Meg,' I said.

'Absolutely. Now then, I suggest those of us who went on the painting holiday get our work out to show everyone. I'm sure everyone wants to see what we got up to. Well, some of us. Others didn't do much at all, did they?'

'Do you mean me, Dennis?' I said rather boldly, which was very unlike the old me. 'I was enjoying it as much as anyone. But you have to remember I was just the new girl. I think that's what you called me.'

'No need to feel like that,' he said, 'it was just a joke. I was saying to Sally only this morning, true creativity and the art of aquarelle is a great leveller. I would have liked to talk more about it but she was emptying the cat litter tray so I don't think she heard me.'

'What did he say?' Anita murmured.

'No idea,' I said.

'Dennis, you do talk in riddles sometimes,' said a loud voice from the doorway, and we turned to see Beryl and Effie laden down with bags and folders, trying to push past each other to get through the door first. 'If you mean watercolours, why not just say so? You're just like my cousin Patrick. He liked to use a lot of big words. He worked for the Foreign Office in the seventies; no wonder there was an oil crisis and a three-day week. Hello, everyone! We are back! The sailors are home from the sea and didn't we have fun?'

Gwen came out from the kitchen where she had been rearranging the mugs on a tray, and Maureen, Janet, Polly and Irene all clustered around us as though we were celebrities.

'How is your wall, Gwen?' I asked.

Gwen looked very annoyed. 'Don't talk to me about walls! Do you know John Patterson hasn't even started on the repointing yet. It was raining so much and he said the mortar wouldn't dry properly. Then he claimed to have man flu and his wife said he was feverish and had got through a whole bottle of Night Nurse that week. Which is marvellous stuff, but my friend Kathy saw him in the bakers on Thursday morning buying doughnuts so he can't have been all that bad, can he? He says he will start next week, so I could have come with you after all. I do feel cross about that.'

'I'm sorry to hear that, but I was delighted to go in your place. I've brought you a little snow globe of Santorini and a tea towel,' I said, handing it over.

Gwen flushed with pleasure. 'How lovely. I shall keep it for the best.'

'And where is Cassandra?' Dennis said loudly, looking at his watch. 'Honestly, why is she always late? Her sister wasn't like that. Jillian was always very prompt.'

'Calm down, it's only two minutes past ten,' Beryl said, 'and I've just seen her car pulling into the car park.'

Cassandra came into the hall a few moments later, carrying with her a big canvas bag.

'Ah, there you all are,' she said with a pleased smile, 'I have been hearing such good things about you from Jillian. She said it was one of the best groups she's ever had—'

'That's not what she said to me,' I murmured.

'Or me,' Beryl agreed, 'She said it was like herding kittens at a sheepdog trial.'

'—and she's hoping some of you will go back next year. I'm

sure the people who went will agree it's well worth going. And she's coming over to visit me in November so you will get a chance to meet her and hear all about it.'

We all nodded and smiled and said positive things about Hotel Costas and then we were encouraged to show the pieces of work we had done while we were there.

While people were milling around looking at the landscapes and pictures of Costas, Cassandra sidled up to me.

'I have a message for you,' she said out of the corner of her mouth. For a moment it almost seemed like I was in a spy thriller, and she was going to say something about the goose flying backwards across the moon.

She handed me a pink Post-it note with a dog doodled in the corner.

'Someone from your holiday group rang me. He had been researching art groups in the Begley area and eventually he found me on Facebook. He said to give you this.'

I unfolded the note and inside was a mobile phone number.

'Who was it?' I said, feeling quite faint for a moment.

Cassandra shrugged. 'I'm not sure, I was busy unloading the shopping and the ice cream was melting. And my husband was shouting from upstairs. He was being quite rude actually. I keep telling him where the spare toilet rolls are but he never listens. This person said you'd know who it was. Something about wrenches. Which seemed very odd to me. Ah yes, I've just remembered. Mr Mole. That was it. And if this is an undesirable, then feel free to chuck it away. If he rings again I will say I was mistaken and I don't know you.'

I looked at the number again. Mr Mole. It had to be Will. It couldn't be anyone else. I felt a slow smile spreading across my face and I immediately put the number into my phone so I wouldn't lose it.

Cassandra clapped her hands. 'Now then, everyone, let's settle and think about what we are going to do this morning. I have brought along a garden trug and some shears which might be fun to paint. Something rustic and simple.'

'Just like me.' Dennis chuckled. 'I'm rustic and simple.'

\* \* \*

I really couldn't concentrate after that and I made as good an effort as I could with Cassandra's trug, which ended up looking like a supermarket basket with some huge scissors balanced unconvincingly on the top.

Beryl came over to see what I had been doing and stared, unimpressed.

'Something tells me you are not exactly in the groove this morning,' she said, 'and I saw our esteemed tutor passing you a note earlier on. Which took me back to my days in boarding school, when the class bully would pass on a note saying no one likes you and you have stupid hair. Well obviously neither of those things are true in this case so perhaps you'd like to share?'

'Honestly, Beryl, you are so nosey,' I said, laughing.

'No, I'm incorrigible, and I have it on the best authority, from Henry Kissinger. And if anyone knew it would be him. So now, tell me what's going on.'

Anita came sidling up with Effie hot on her heels.

'What are we talking about?' Effie said. 'Have I missed anything?'

'For goodness' sake!' I said, trying not to laugh.

'Cassandra passed her a secret note, and I want to know what it was.'

'I want to know too,' Anita said, 'we all do, and there's no use just telling Beryl. It's part of the Old Ducks creed. Two people can keep a secret only if one of them is dead.'

I sighed. 'Cassandra had a phone call from someone looking for the Lower Begley painting group asking her to pass on a mobile number to me. Which is what she did. From a Mr Mole.'

'Mr Mole? Oh, I remember, that discussion we had about mole wrenches. Will, it has to be him,' Beryl said, her face brightening. 'We told you he wouldn't just disappear.'

'You told me he would pass like a kidney stone,' I said.

Gwen stopped collecting coffee mugs and gave us the benefit of her wisdom.

'Kidney stone? They can be nasty. My aunt had a kidney stone. She had a terrible time and then the hospital said they were going to use a Taser on her and she was terribly worried, because that's the thing the police use when there are riots, isn't it, but apparently it was a laser.'

Beryl flapped a hand at me.

'Nonsense, I'm sure I didn't say that. So what are you going to do?'

'She's going to ring him, obviously,' Effie said, 'and then they can arrange to meet up. What about that new wine bar near the reservoir? You know the place, years ago it used to be a water treatment plant and then it was turned into a conference centre and then a boutique hotel. Nice views over the water but someone told me they had terrible problems with the septic tank.'

'So hardly an ideal destination?' I said.

Anita nodded vigorously. 'Or you could try the place up by the castle? It used to be the Kings Head and then it was renovated and it's now the Dog and Bonnet. Will could be the Dog and you could wear... No, perhaps not. I remember the old landlord, Cyril somebody, who was the most miserable, bad-tempered man you could ever meet. He once threw out some customers who asked for clean cutlery. But I've heard it's very nice in there now. They do exotic, spicy nibbles.'

'Exotic. Spicy. *Nibbles*. Ideal, I bet both of them could do with that.' Beryl chuckled.

'Will you stop it! I'll be nervous enough as it is without you lot adding innuendo.'

'And you can find out why he left in such a marked manner,' Effie said, 'and then you can tell us.'

*  *  *

Anita and I walked home through the drizzle and after promising her that I would indeed ring Mr Mole, she left me to it.

First I made a sandwich, this time feta cheese and salad, and then I sorted out some laundry and cleared away the scattering of bird feathers which Ivan had left in the hall while I was out.

'So? Where is the rest of the bird, you horrible cat?' I asked him as he wedged himself through the cat flap. He ignored me and went to have a noisy drink of water.

'If you have taken it upstairs and left it under my bed, I will be very annoyed,' I said.

Ivan jumped up onto the draining board and swiftly knocked a teaspoon onto the floor.

'Will said he liked the sound of you,' I said, picking the cat up and depositing him on the floor, 'but then he doesn't know you.'

This of course reminded me of Will and the phone number and the expectations that I would ring him. Would I? At that moment I wasn't sure.

I put the Post-it note on the windowsill and weighted down one edge with the pepper mill. Then I went to get the ironing basket which was full of my clean holiday clothes. When I got back, Ivan was on the draining board again, patting at the Post-it note with one paw. And then he knocked the pepper mill over so that it fell into the sink, the lid flew off and all the peppercorns fell out.

'For heaven's sake, Ivan, what is the matter with you?' I shouted.

Ivan retreated to a safe distance on top of the fridge and watched me balefully. And then he jumped down and went back out through the cat flap, his back legs flailing.

I got on with the ironing, happily watching more of the glamorous detective scuttling around an abandoned warehouse in the Bronx, looking for criminals, and then I had another cup of tea and a biscuit. All the time, my eye was drawn back to the pink Post-it note on the windowsill.

I should ring Will. I had run out of reasons not to. I emptied the dishwasher and cleared some coffee rings off the worktop and wiped it down. Will had liked clearing things away too; he'd said so. I wondered what he was doing this morning.

My mobile buzzed, a text arriving. I saw with no great surprise that it was from Beryl.

BERYL

Rung him yet?

I didn't answer because at that moment, Ivan returned with yet another unlucky mouse in his jaws which he deposited proudly on the floor. It immediately scurried behind the fridge, much to Ivan's fury, and mine.

'How am I supposed to get at that?' I said.

I got down on the floor and peered hopefully underneath the fridge and Ivan did the same. We stared at each other for a moment and I laughed to think how ridiculous we must have looked.

It was doubtful I could move the fridge unless I emptied it, so I imagined I would have to bait a humane trap somewhere in the hopes the mouse would come out when the coast was clear.

'I have better things to do than sort out your unpleasant habits,' I said.

Ivan stalked off, offended, and then sprang onto the windowsill and knocked the Post-it note onto the floor.

And then he gave me a hard look, and if I hadn't known that Ivan was solely motivated by food or sleep, I would have sworn he was trying to provoke me.

'So you think I should ring him too?' I said, picking up the note.

Ivan gave a soundless meow.

'Oh, shut up,' I said.

I rang Will five minutes later.

## 24

'You got my message then?' he said.

I laughed. 'Well, yes or I wouldn't be ringing you.'

'Of course. What a daft thing to say. And did Jillian tell you why I left early?'

'No, and that was two weeks ago. She just said you had to go home.'

He sighed a bit. 'Oh dear. I am sorry. You must have thought I was very rude. That's why I started researching the art group to find you. I felt quite the sleuth. I knew you weren't far from Cheltenham and eventually I remembered the word Begley came into it, but I'd forgotten the English love of using the same name more than once. Begley on Wold, Begley Moor and Begley St James to name but three. And then I got on to Begley Mortimer and Begley by Ash. I spoke to a very odd man in Begley Norton who was very deaf and thought I was someone called Paul who wanted to buy his orchard. And I'm not sure we didn't agree a price. Anyway, here we are, so...'

I could tell he was nervous, which was very disarming, and it somehow made the conversation easier.

'Shall we meet up for a drink, and you can tell me all about it,' I said.

Gosh, I was being unusually bold.

'Love to,' he said. 'And then I can tell you all about my sister's appendicitis, my brother-in-law being in New Zealand on a fishing trip and my nephews needing to be looked after until one of them could get home. I say looked after; they are teenagers. What I really mean is I needed to supervise their revision because they are in the middle of A levels and not let them play video games all night or throw open the house to the general public for a party.'

'Ah,' I said, and I expect he could hear the relief in my voice, 'I see. Of course.'

'Silly, isn't it?' he said, and I could tell he was smiling. 'I didn't want there to be any confusion. After everything.'

'Great,' I said. The grin on my face was so wide I could hardly speak properly.

'And I have a present for you,' he said. 'It's taken me ages to finish.'

A present. That was exciting.

'It's not the painting of Costas?'

He laughed. 'I promise it isn't.'

'So what is it?'

'A surprise,' he said.

'It's not a mouse in a box?'

'Definitely not. Why, has Ivan been up to his old tricks?'

I was rather touched that he would remember my irascible cat.

'There's one under the fridge at the moment. I'm going to have to lure it out somehow.'

'Try peanut butter,' he said, 'or chocolate.'

'Not cheese?'

'Chocolate is better.'

*Why are we having such a ridiculous conversation?*

I realised I was hanging on to my phone so tightly that my knuckles were white. I took a deep breath and forced myself to relax.

'I'm more likely to eat the chocolate myself than waste it on a mouse,' I said, and he laughed.

There was a bit of a pause then and I wondered what to say to keep the conversation going. Which of course meant that we both spoke at once.

'Would you like...'

'I really think...'

And then there was a bit of, 'Sorry, what did you say? No, after you,' which made us both sound like a couple of teenagers. And it was very exciting.

'Look, I'd really like to see you again,' he said.

'When are you free?' There was the hint of a smile in his voice then, and it made me smile too.

'Any time but Tuesday mornings, when of course I go to the painting group. You could always come along to that if you felt like it?'

He laughed. 'No, I don't think I'm quite up to that just yet. What day is it today?'

'You're like me, I never quite know what day it is. Tuesday. I was at the painting group this morning.'

'What about tomorrow? Or Thursday? I have to be here for my builders on Friday I'm afraid, although I could move that if necessary.'

'I'll just consult my diary,' I said, chuckling.

'Oh dear,' he said, sounding genuinely worried, 'should I have given you more notice?'

'Don't be daft, I'm joking. Tomorrow would be perfect. Where and when?'

'I've been researching your area on Google and there's a place that sounds good. The Dog and Bonnet.'

I laughed out loud at that point, which I think confused him for a moment and then he joined in.

'That is a daft name, isn't it?'

'I'm told they do exotic spicy nibbles.' I giggled.

'Do they by Jove. That sounds just the thing, doesn't it? Would you like me to book a table? About six thirty tomorrow evening? Or is that too early?'

'No, that's perfect,' I said.

'Great. I'll see you then.'

'See you then.'

'Bye then. Have a good day.'

'You too, bye.'

'Great to talk to you,' he said, 'and looking forward to tomorrow.'

'Bye for now,' I said.

Both of us started laughing.

'Bye. Look this is ridiculous,' he said. 'Put the phone down. Although you don't do that any more, do you? It's just press a button.'

'Okay,' I said. And after a moment's dithering, I did.

I sat looking at my phone for a moment and felt a sudden swell of happiness rise in my chest. He had wanted to find me and he had. And we were going out tomorrow evening.

I made a fresh cup of tea and congratulated myself with two more chocolate digestives. And then I picked up my mobile again and rang Anita's number.

'Anita? It's me. You'll never guess what just happened.'

* * *

The following morning, Beryl, Effie and Anita came round to my house, ostensibly for coffee, but in fact to catch up on the gossip and advise me what to wear. It was such fun.

'You need to look as though you have made the effort but not tried too hard,' Effie said, 'so nothing glittery or low cut.'

'I don't have anything glittery or low cut,' I said.

By that point the three of them were sitting on the edge of my bed while I went through my wardrobe trying to find the right outfit.

'And nothing navy blue or grey or too short,' Beryl chimed in. 'You don't want to depress or frighten him.'

'This is like being a teenager again,' I said. 'I didn't expect things to be as complicated as they used to be.'

'Just wear something you're comfortable in, and some pretty shoes,' Anita said. 'What happened to those zebra-print ones you had?'

'Ruined, I'm afraid. They never did recover after my date with gravel, and then they got splashed with red wine. Oh dear, this is a problem all of a sudden.'

'Nonsense, a problem is when you don't have enough cheese in the fridge to make Welsh rarebit. Now this one,' Beryl said, pulling out a favourite pink linen dress of mine, 'and a denim jacket. That's very cool.'

'I haven't got one,' I said.

Effie stood up and pulled off the one she had been wearing.

'You can borrow this one,' she said, 'let me just take the tissues out of the pockets. And those pale blue trainers I can see in the back of the wardrobe. You will look like a rock chick.'

'More a rock hen at our age, I don't think there is such a thing as a rock duck.' Beryl said, 'but I get your drift. And you can borrow this for good luck.'

She unpinned a little enamel duck brooch from her jacket lapel and ceremoniously attached it to the denim jacket. 'That's until your official membership of the Old Ducks Club comes through. Now then, tell us again, what did he say?'

'I've told you,' I said.

'Well, tell us again,' Anita said, 'it's very exciting. I might even phone Juliette later and tell her.'

'Please don't,' I said, 'nothing has happened yet.'

'But it might,' Effie said.

I turned away to hide my smile. And I wondered if indeed it might.

* * *

I got to the crowded car park of the Dog and Bonnet ten minutes early and sat in my car, not wanting to go in early and have to look around for him. It was busy here this evening, with younger couples sitting outside in the garden enjoying the view over the river and the unusually warm evening. I shivered despite the warmth; I was just nervous I supposed.

After ten minutes I decided to be brave and got out of the car. The driver of the car opposite mine got out of his car at the same moment and we stared at each other and then both burst out laughing.

'It is you, I thought it was.' Will chuckled as he bent to kiss my cheek. 'I've been here for half an hour trying to pluck up the courage to go in.'

'So have I,' I admitted.

'We are here now,' he said, and we looked at each other for a moment and I had a terrible but wonderful flashback to the moment when he had kissed me properly, and I felt quite wobbly for a moment.

He was wearing a beautiful dark blue blazer, a blue and white striped shirt and dark jeans, and I could almost imagine what it would be like to slip my hands under his jacket around his waist and feel the warmth of his body through the thin cotton. I hoped I might have the opportunity later to do just that and equally I hoped he wasn't a mind reader.

'We should go in,' I said, my voice a bit croaky, 'but first of all, where's my present?'

He laughed and went back to his car, returning with a wine carrier.

'It took me a bit of time,' he said, 'but I hope you like it. I managed to get it home without breaking it, and then I... well, you'll see.'

I pulled out a familiar bottle of Assyrtiko wine, but this one had a hand-painted label stuck over the original. I peered at it in the fading afternoon light. It was absolutely lovely. Beautifully done, each little detail exquisite.

The new wine label had a scene of the sea, high rocky cliffs and a single seagull drifting in one corner and underneath in immaculate script were the words:

Chateau Meg.
Vin *not* Ordinaire
Good with salads, fillet steak and chocolate digestives.

I almost felt like crying. He had listened to me and more than that, he had remembered.

'Did you do this? It's beautiful, absolutely wonderful. I think that's the nicest present I've ever been given,' I said, trying desperately to stop my lower lip from wobbling with threatening tears. 'Thank you.'

He reached out and took my hand in his.

'I had fun doing it. And you deserve it,' he said, 'because you're not *ordinaire* at all, Meg. You're a wonderful, kind and funny woman. And I've missed you.'

'I've missed you,' I said, choking up a bit with the emotion of the moment.

'I hope you're hungry,' he said.

'Always, you know me.'

'Yes, I rather think I do,' he said, and he kissed me.

And the car park of the Dog and Bonnet this Wednesday evening was suddenly lit with a last burst of sunshine and was just as glorious and romantic as anything Santorini had to offer.

# 25

## ONE YEAR LATER

I'm in Mallorca, in a house overlooking the sea near Porto Pollença.

It's early morning and there is a lovely breeze coming in from the sea. And it's glorious.

Maybe July is the wrong time of year to come here because it will be hot later and the little streets will be crowded, but I love it. There are cafés and restaurants along the seafront just starting to open up. Waiters are unfurling the parasols to provide welcome shade and setting the tables with crisp white cloths. Later the tourist shops will open and visitors will flock towards them looking for souvenirs and bargains.

Pine trees line the walk along the edge of the Mediterranean, dipping their branches towards the water, and I sit on one of the chairs on my balcony looking out at the sea for ages, just breathing in the morning air and taking time to think. I like doing that. For such a long time I just ambled on from one day to the next, doing my best, keeping up with things and not really enjoying any of it. Not thinking at all.

But now, my life is different and I can see and appreciate the changes. Not that it was easy; sometimes it wasn't, and occasionally even now I feel a bit anxious about the choices I have made. But they are my choices and I have made them.

The sun moves around a little as I sit here, and I pull my sunhat a little lower. It's yellow and patterned with cartoon ducks because I am officially an Old Duck now, a member of a jaunty crew of women like me, and there are few things of which I am prouder.

In the house behind me, the others will be waking up, ready for another day when we will talk and exchange news and ideas and perhaps go to the local supermarkets to buy delicious food which we will cook this evening and eat on the patio behind the house.

I hear a familiar laugh and know that Juliette is awake. Perhaps she and Matthew will come out onto their balcony soon, to see the new day, and then she will be wanting coffee, and lots of it. And she will go downstairs and find I have already made some, and then Kim and Vince will appear, slightly bleary after our late night. He will talk about going to the nature reserve and Rick will want to go too, leaving Anita with us to do whatever we decide will be most fun. Or maybe we won't do much at all. Perhaps we will just talk and relax, and just doing that will be marvellous. I've realised that sometimes doing nothing can be fun too, in the right company.

We are planning a barbeque for this evening when the bird-watchers return. And someone will turn on the fairy lights around the garden and open a bottle of wine and maybe we will raise a glass to each other and I will smile knowing how I have come so far and learned so much over the last year. How to be comfortable within myself, how to cope, how to have fun.

I've managed to see so much more of the world than I ever thought I would over the last year.

I went to Washington to see my sister and then I had a week on my own in a tiny cottage in Brittany where the beams were low and blackened with age. I even took my car and drove on the wrong side of the road and didn't get lost at all. I went to local markets and bought fresh cheeses and croissants. I even explored some local *brocante* places in out-of-the-way places where the roads went through villages with unpronounceable names and bought a cute wooden egg rack with *Merci Mes Poules* stencilled on the side.

Then there was a weekend in Venice where we got lost in those ancient and confusing streets, and where the light sparkled and shone off the canals (which didn't smell at all) and the busy *vaporettos* buzzed under our window and the light on those unforgettable buildings turned the stones to gold.

Then we did something that had been on my bucket list for years: we spent Christmas in a place where the snow fell in astounding amounts. I remember we stood together on the raised deck and looked out over the soft, white folds of the hills and valleys, turned almost blue in the evening light, because it seemed, just for us, there really was 'Moonlight in Vermont'.

Nicky is looking after Ivan the Terrible this week while I am away, and he seems very content with the arrangement. She's busy though; all her ideas for the library meant that instead of closing, they had to take on another part time staff member and they have been given at least another eighteen months to stay open.

The mother and baby social group is well attended, as is the after-school reading group of which Joyce has taken full charge. There are plans for a second group to open soon. On top of that, Nicky took my idea about social groups for older mums and retirees and convinced the local council that there really was a need for something. The Old Ducks Book Group started up on

Wednesday mornings six months ago and has been very popular indeed. There is a Cake Club too, where people bring along their favourite cake each month, and there is a spirited discussion about the recipes and a certificate for the best-tasting one. There's even a special shelf in the library for recipe books written by local people. Who wouldn't like the sound of that? I've been along to see for myself, and it seems there are a lot of jaunty, older women with spirit and enthusiasm for life out there who want to join in. It's great to see.

Behind me, the door to my room opens, and I turn.

'Good morning, Mr Mole,' I say, and he smiles at me, one hand ruffling his hair.

He comes to stand behind my chair and puts his hands on my shoulders, dropping a kiss on the top of my head. He is wearing a white bathrobe after his morning shower, and I catch the drift of his aftershave. Still lemony and delicious.

'Good morning, Mrs Mole,' he says, 'and how are you today?'

'Happy,' I say, 'and hungry.'

'You're always hungry,' he says, and he comes to sit next to me. 'Churros and chocolate?'

'The bakery should be open,' I say. 'What about *ensaïmadas*?'

'You and your pastries.' He gestures to my coffee mug. 'Need a refill?'

I reach out and take his hand. 'In a minute.'

We sit there for a while, watching the little delivery trucks come and go. They unload trays of vegetables and fruit, boxes of fish covered in ice, huge cans of olive oil.

There is a man in a blue boiler suit brushing the street below us, whistling through his teeth at a scraggy dog, which follows him.

'I want to remember this,' I say at last, 'this moment, being here, being with you.'

He smiles. 'That's all very well but I need coffee, and I think I can hear Juliette is already downstairs, probably thinking the same thing.'

He takes my empty mug and returns a few minutes later with two full ones.

'Juliette and Matthew want to go on a boat trip later, up the coast to Cap de Formentor. She says she's done it before and it was excellent. And you can swim off the boat. I like the sound of that. The water here is so clear and such a wonderful colour. She said her friends Denny and Bruno are going to be here mid-morning; I'm looking forward to meeting them.'

I sip my coffee, hot and sweet, and then rest my head back and close my eyes.

Sunshine, blue skies, a few adventures and good friends.

'Yes,' I say, 'that sounds perfect.'

\* \* \*

## MORE FROM MADDIE PLEASE

Another book from Maddie Please, is available to order now here:

https://mybook.to/MaddiePleaseBackAd

# ACKNOWLEDGEMENTS

Thank you to the whole team at Boldwood Books for their invaluable support and encouragement but especially to Emily Ruston who always knows the right thing to say.

A special mention for my readers who are always so kind and take the trouble to leave reviews and send me messages. I love thinking that I might help to cheer someone's day. That's why I write the books I do.

Thank you as always to Jane who is always so supportive and reassuring.

Thank you to my family and other friends who keep me going when sometimes it's difficult.

Finally, the greatest thanks of all are for Brian, who made it all possible and who is loved and still missed every day.

# ABOUT THE AUTHOR

**Maddie Please** is the author of bestselling joyous tales of older women. She has had a career as a dentist and now lives in rural Herefordshire where she enjoys box sets, red wine and Christmas.

Download your exclusive bonus content from Maddie Please here:

Follow Maddie on social media here:

facebook.com/maddieplease

x.com/maddieplease1

instagram.com/maddieplease1

bookbub.com/authors/maddie-please

## ALSO BY MADDIE PLEASE

# Boldwood

Boldwood Books is an award-winning fiction publishing company seeking out the best stories from around the world.

**Find out more at www.boldwoodbooks.com**

Join our reader community for brilliant books, competitions and offers!

Follow us
@BoldwoodBooks
@TheBoldBookClub

Sign up to our weekly
deals newsletter

https://bit.ly/BoldwoodBNewsletter